(

"*DRILL* is a literary sigil and hyperstitional wave generator in the form of a weird fictional and metafictional autofiction that seeks by its own direct avowal to serve as the author's *Moby Dick* by way of Philip K. Dick and William S. Burroughs, with a pervasive infusion of religious and occult obsession. But even that, with all its spaghetti on the wall, is not sufficient. Probably nothing would be. And maybe that's the point. *DRILL* strives to be not a book but the shareable interiority of a specific human being in process of metamorphosing and self-exorcising in the service of the ultimate metaphysical hit job that also happens to be simultaneously and absolutely idiosyncratic, singular, personal. It's a portable mind meld with Scott R. Jones, a transmissible subjectivity you can plug into at any point. Whether you download it or it uploads you is difficult to say. And maybe that, really, is the point."

—Matt Cardin, author of *To Rouse Leviathan* and *What the Daemon Said*

"Having gnawed away the rotten roots of orthodox cosmic horror until the way was cleared for new growth, Jones comes at us in his final form with *DRILL*… and all that came before seems so quaint before such a pyrotechnic display of batshit insane ideas and intimate, lacerating characterization. This one will leave a hole in your head and heart you could drive a car through."

—Cody Goodfellow, author of *Unamerica*

"*DRILL* is like nothing you've ever read before. That is, of course, the kind of tired, trite proclamation that gets bandied about complacent critics too hungry or horny for deeper reflection. But you tell me of another book that combines righteous fury, feverish insight, pitch black humour and delirious prose to such compelling effect. I'll wait. Oh, and I think it might just kill a deity."

—Kenton Hall, musician and filmmaker

"In this unforgettably strange and unique book, told in a narrative voice that's as vivid and intelligent as it is vulnerable and possibly unhinged, Scott R. Jones has made a fascinating accomplishment. *DRILL* merges the relatability of everyday life and its anxieties, uncertainties, and grind, with the deeply imaginative metaphysical and weird. Made all the more compelling for its high level of self-awareness and layers of metafiction that make the experience even more mind-boggling than it already is, this work is among the most unabashedly unique reading experiences I've had in quite some time. It's an angry book, depicting the traumatic effects of cults on family dynamics across generation lines, but there's an undeniable righteousness to the rage, a sympathetic vulnerability, and a desire to either destroy or heal—tied as that is to the novel's supernatural underbelly and existential stakes. I'm not sure I've ever read anything quite like *DRILL*. What other book can make the post office seem Lovecraftian, while introducing otherworldly elements with an almost deadpan level of casualness, in between sorcery, philosophical playfulness, metafiction, and the real and—in this case—supernatural horrors of the Jehovah's Witness church? It's an experience I won't soon forget."

—Cody Lakin, author of *The Family Condition*

"Scott R. Jones is a master of creating fully-realized characters who must navigate worlds where the unimaginably weird has become disturbingly normal for them. In *DRILL*, Jones immerses us in such a world. His autofictional narrator's conversational, sometimes confessional stream of consciousness gels into a dark and strange personal history tainted by horrors both otherworldly and all too familiar. *DRILL* twists family conflict, religious fervor, and ravening cosmic forces into a richly-detailed and compelling novel of loss and vengeance, resonant and deeply felt… *DRILL* digs into the hunger that motivates everyone—from cult members looking for safety and salvation, to a god that exists as a parasite devouring the humans it infects, to the narrator himself, consumed by loss and thirsting for a revenge that may not satisfy. I highly recommend it."

—Erica Ruppert, author of *Imago and Other Transformations*

"*DRILL* is a dense yet mystical cosmic horror novel serving as a meta mask for an elaborate magical ritual. A tango with a sick God, the darkness of Jehovah's Witness madness, an arrow aimed at the heart of a towering father. Scott R. Jones is a sorcerer and *DRILL* is him flexing his literary muscles and crafting a narrative that will leave an everlasting imprint on your psyche."

—Grant Wamack, author of *Bullet Tooth*

DRILL

DRILL
A NOVEL

SCOTT R. JONES

WORD HORDE
PETALUMA, CA

"Some years ago in London, I asked Jasper Johns what painting was all about—what are painters really doing? He countered with another question: what is writing about? I did not have an answer then; I have an answer now: The purpose of writing is to make it happen."

—William S. Burroughs, *The Adding Machine*

for ▓▓▓▓▓▓▓▓▓▓
Mom, I've done this for you.
I hope it's enough.

INTRODUCING GREG M.

There's a particular kind of moment I like best, just after a rain, when if you catch the sunlight off the street at the right angle, the whole thing lights up like the on-ramp to heaven. Maybe I still half expect to see angels going up and down on their divine business. I mean that in spite of what I know. I'm the closest thing to an angel there is and if that doesn't make you sad to the bone, there's nothing that can.

I'm a sapper. Same as my dad. I excavate and I core. I create, mold, and plant explosives. I make the tunnels and the warrens and the great carved cavern spaces within the Body of God. My work is honeycombing, sifting, gouging, and marauding. Gathering and deploying resources. Team building. Sometimes actual building. Bridges and so on. We sift the Infinite Material of the DRILL system for ordnance to accelerate the action of the Drill. Also, I'm good at it. My dad brought me into this life and then went ahead and died according to the Protocols, in the great Tunguska83 incident three coils down antispinward, so now it's me and the team he built living like holy lice on the shining surface of the Drill, keeping it hard with our efforts, softening the God Bod with our inveterate skill.

There's a story among sappers, about the Drill. The story goes that it didn't always exist. I contend that the Drill is eternal, at least as far as that goes. A once-was-and-always sort of arrangement, like the inframatter it cores. At least as far as it concerns us. Sappers. I don't know how God feels about it. I expect it smarts a bit.

Here's a recall from the medical screening...

"Well hello there young guy," the doctor said, and you can be sure I immediately tweaked that the fella was off. Even then I had the sapper's nose, flaring in irritation at their sour cobalt stink, nothing to you or your sainted mum, mind, barely a whiff of beelzebubbic taint, but to me, well. Fulsome and robust, my gorge did rise. By their smell shall ye know them, Alhazred said.

"You're Stalgard's boy, aren't you. And a fine scion if I may say so. Just look at that complexion. And so clean-limbed. Turn your head and cough, young Greg. That's fine. Well and what puts you on the path of the sapper, anyway? Surely we've less need of that stout division's efforts in these last days, in this, the eternal finishing of the World? Speak to your career choice here, son!"

"I was just going to say that I think the turmoil and dissension we see in these last days make the sapper's work all the more crucial. All things considered, Doc." The doc—his smell, his clothes, the Hallowe'en costume stethoscope, the off-brand dollar store cream in his hair—gave me a sinking feeling, like my guts had turned to ice water. I was dying for a shit. He consulted a pad, dipped several crepuscular fingers into the lemon phosphor glow from the screen.

"Well, according to this you've a mental fitness algorithm to host for at least a week, starting Wednesday. Why, that's today, so there you have it. If you've any lingering psychoses neuroses or liminal noetic parasites attached, the screening will take care of those so I wouldn't worry. Standard procedure, of course, all above board."

"Of course."

Let me tell you about the Drill.

The subUniverse is comprised of the Body of God, which is variously known as the BULK, the Base Layer, the Ground of Being, the High Mighty Chungus, the Chariot, the Throne, the Plateau of Leng, any number of fevered Tarot dreams have attached themselves to the Divine Literality and they feast there, feast like the dread beasts of the apocalypse they are, all carrion names for hungry concepts ravening beyond the edge of the fire light. The First Law of the Universe is Everybody Hungry, let us not forget and forever keep mindful of this. This Body is thick, friends, thick as it is possible to be, thick as literal fuck, and practically infinite, so far as we who ride the Drill and direct its action are concerned.

Have you read *The Divine Comedy*? Then you've perhaps partially grokked a primitive take, cold and unappealing in its gelid consistency, of the architecture, the form and the shape of the Drill. There are diagrams, abadonnic scribblings. Theologians love their little drawings. Childish conceptions of rings of torment, spheres and skies of delight all in layers like a jawbreaker. All true, all true. Far below, in the lowest and final and coldest circle of Hell, at the very iced-over, hemorrhoidal rim of Satan's cursed fundament, pours the concentrated suffering of an entire reality. This pulse engine of existential shit powers the Drill, gives it a forward propulsion, though direction is meaningless while on the job, I can tell you that for free.

Reality, in its totality, which is to say the entire Universe and all things within it, is a Drill. The point of it, the Bit, is nowhere and everywhere at once, a void-point reaching into the Bulk, the Body of God, peeling away at that density with insistent glee, tunneling in that direction neither you nor I no matter how hard we try can point to not even on our best day. The edges of the Drill are likewise positioned, everywhere, nowhere, a circumference with no center, and these slough away as with a great rotating scythe blade the rapidly decaying corpse slurry, radioactive and keening as it passes through into nothingness, into the state of barely there. A sound to haunt your dreams or dash you against the rocks and when I tell you you'll hear it in your DNA, mostly, you'd best believe.

From some guidebook: "Reality is a drill. A spiral mechanism for boring into the BULK, a higher dimensional material that comprises the Body of God. Each universe is a weapon, an assault engine aimed at the Body, seeking out the titan heart, brain, vital organs, anything to attain the goal of ending the cycle and becoming the One True Reality. Dante's conception was partly right: the tip of the drill is the void-point at the top of Heaven, suffering is the fuel that drives the spiral forward and in; the lowest circle of Hell is the engine, though all of the structure provides power. Drill, baby, drill."

Whoever wrote that, and for however much of it they got right, I can tell you they weren't a sapper.

THE BOY'S OWN GUIDE TO SORCERY

Well I can tell you that I was three joints in when I decided finally to curse my dad, which means it was probably a Saturday morning. This would have been not long after I saw him for the last time, during the period when I delivered the mail for the Queen and her duly appointed representative Canaduh Post. Saturday morning was the only time I could confidently get in a decent, heavy smoke, what with the kids watching their videos and the wife out there bringing in the groceries for however long that took. How would I know, I was usually well on the way to being thoroughly stoned before she even left on her errands, she could have been gone all day and I might not have noticed. *Wake and bake* was my byword in those days. Ah, good times. Good times in bad lands.

I had only recently dragged my aching brain and chakras out of a major depressive episode, an episode that I should take pains to mention was initially triggered by a gen you wine enlightenment experience as a result of my occult practice, to wit: I had become convinced—and have remained so through the working of the curse and the writing of this book—of an aspect of the essential nature of existence, namely that, among the many other things it appears to be or to play at, it is Empty and Awake.

There's a name for the specific state, I figure, but it escapes me now as it escaped me then. Likely some warmed-over Mahayana Buddhism badly understood by past me and current version don't care, you can put money on that. In any case, the Emptiness and Awakefulness of the World did impress itself upon me in a powerful and deeply intuitive way. I was struck at the ephemerality of it all and gained a new wondrous-horrific outlook on death. I don't mean to paint any of this as a positive experience, it came to me through that mirror darkly, as the man said once. Gosh, I was down. Hyuk.

Not one of us gets to keep this experience, I reasoned. If anything survives death, I don't think the personality is part of it, or the soul or whatever. I'm a sorcerer and have been most my life, odds are better than zero that I reincarnate as everything. All of it Empty and Awake, just like me.

Which brought me to the decision to curse my dad.

Raymond Francis Jones.

There we go, there it is down on the page. Dagon's Teeth, look at it vibrating there. Let me be clear, that's the man's actual Christian and legal name, I am speaking here of an actual entity occupying our collective spacetime continuum. As I sit here in the writing nook at Stonefish House, Raymond Francis Jones sits in his own house, not a five-minute drive from here. Yessir, I cursed him good and if you'll let me bend your ear for a spell, I can even tell you why. I cursed him and soon he will die. A horrible thing for a son (however fictional by dint of sorcery and some small writing ability, perhaps even talent) to say about his real and actual father, a terrible thing to curse someone, but here we are. Here we are and welcome.

The thing is, seeing as everything is Empty and Awake, it necessarily follows that when we shuffle off the coil we can take nothing with us like the old saw says, certainly not our money, not our memories or our tastes, our lusts and various bravados, none of the many and multiform ingredients that might comprise the imagined soul, well then if that is the case and I do believe it to be so, even now, then when my father dies he will do so convinced that he did right by his loved ones, that somehow joining the cult of the Jehovah's Witnesses and raising his kids in it was the act of a loving father. That, and the things he did afterward. Of *course* I cursed him. If I hadn't, what kind of justice would there be? I chuckle when they say the arc of the moral universe bends toward justice. The *moral* universe! Please. There's only ever been one moral system in place here, only one clear and incontrovertible law and it's the First Law of the Universe: Everybody Hungry.

He had to know. Beyond the programming his cult burned into him, beyond the shadow of a doubt, he had to know how much I hated him. I don't mean that somehow in his heart of hearts Raymond Francis Jones was aware of just how much of a monster he was. The man's thick. Preternaturally so, I'd say, thick but there's a slyness slipping around behind the thickness, a jocular ripple in the discourse you don't notice till it's too late and he's got you, then, this elder, this shepherd of Christ's flock. Up until the moment I decided to curse him, I'm utterly sure that he believed he would someday see me, of all people, return to the fold, repent and rejoin the cult. Because that's what the shunning is for, see. That's how these people love. It's the only way they're allowed to by the Governing Body of the Witchtower Bubble and Cracked Society of Jehoover's Witnesses and their spiritual pyramid scheme and real estate concern disguised as a legitimate religion. But let's call a cult a cult when it cults, shall we? Let's be sensible and do that, be intellectually honest for a moment.

In the end I think I just wanted a real relationship with Raymond, something based on a shared experience that transcended honesty and reached a kind of sublime space of understanding between us, and what is a curse laid and received and perceived and suffered under than a species of particularly eloquent communication? If he chose to sunder the link between us at the behest of an imaginary god and Its human meat puppets, then let that link be sundered utterly and for grand reasons. He would *know* how much I hated him and in that knowing would his own hate flow forth, poisoning him and his environment.

In this way are demons called up.

In this way are the curses laid.

LOOKIT DAT SHINING THERE

Seeing the Drill is every kind of impossible but with the right motivating thoughtforms, pranic breathing, and the new synthetic DMTs, a sapper can, with maximum effort, get the barest glimpse of their location relative to the Drill and the bore. Really it's about elevation and direction. You want to get some air under you, dimensionally, while travelling outwith the spacetime supersphere i.e. the Drill. The barest glimpse, mind you, but hell it is enough for most sappers.

The synthetic DMTs have the advantage of suspending all gastric function in the user. You can stay for weeks at a time if that's your thing. For my line of work, a couple of hours is fine. Mostly safe. I do get the pineal aches, though, and once a month I have to get my hyperchakras re-cored but show me a sapper who doesn't and I'll chew on a bag of robot teeth.

Let me tell you about my Team:

We'll start with Wee Frederick. This is an entity of indeterminate size and shape but when in passive form he manifests as a dwarfish man with a vaguely European accent and reddish hair. Wee Frederick is my printer and my right-hand entity. He builds the constructs we use in our work and creates the five-dimensional models I sometimes employ while convincing prospective sappers of their usefulness. A drinker and a laugher,

Wee Frederick, and dependable as a long day. I've worked with him the longest and our communication style is by now largely unconscious. He anticipates need like no other.

Lazy Susan is English, probably, though what part of the UK she hails from is necessarily unknown. A large but nimble woman with delicate wrists and pneumatic fingers, Susan is our stenographer and record keeper. Does up a nice fruit cup when the team is feeling peckish. Invulnerable to insult and super sane which comes in handy during the more maddening tasks of the sapper. The various violent efforts of our little team here.

The less said about the twins, the better. They're nameless and always have been. Without them, though, we could never run some of the machinery we have call to use. Imaginary machines need imaginary mechanics. They keep two ferrets, one white, one black. I sometimes will call them Bob and Doug for shits and giggles but the way they bristle and foam at the mouth makes me uncomfortable, ultimately, and so I don't do that often. What are they not. The twins. So many things. Best not to look them directly in the eyes.

ANOTHER DAY OF VANITY AND A STRIVING AFTER WIND

With the wife out shopping, the boy at an anti-grav trampoline park for some kid's birthday party, and the girl at camp, it dawned on me that I was alone in the house for some let's just be bold and call it what it is and that's Daddy's Alone Time, hereafter referred to as the DAT for convenience and also to instill that culty vibe we all so dig in these the Last Days of the Last Days of this System of Things, what cult doesn't love a good acronym, am I right, my sages? Word.

Anyway. The DAT comes in three forms, or stages, the first being three thick pre-rolls on the back porch while the rats who nest at the base of the walnut tree fuck off back and forth out onto my fucking grass where they are literally feasting I swear I can see them thicken where they sit on my goddamn lawn which I'm not otherwise all that arsed about but here we are with rats feasting on the walnut leavings from the trio of squirrels that are currently waging a savage harvest in the boughs and branches above. I've a rodent apocalypse of some kind on my hands. I chain smoke the joints in a swift quarter hour while listening to TV On the Radio over my kid's dayglo headphones and thinking of ethical ways to murder tiny living things.

Thoroughly stoned, we proceed to stage the second, wherein I shit, shower, masturbate, shave, and dress. Well why *not* focus on those with a prurient interest in the stands, friends? Let's jump right to the good bits, I say. We're all perverts here no shame, no shame. In a linen closet, on the high shelf so the kids can't pry without difficulty, behind the eucalyptus steamer for when the spawn have the sniffles and a box of old makeup, is an investment in my own pleasure and, I'll argue, especially as I age, in that of my health vis-à-vis the wedding tackle. The pipes must be regularly cleansed lest I come down with some easily preventable testicular horror, a cancer, a blight on my balls. Not to mention I'm getting old man skin down there, sensitive and easily torn like the merest paper tissue, I need gentle mechanical loving since my wife's flesh is not so to speak available. And so here is my Fleshlight™, Stoya the Destroya edition. My notes here say to [describe the thing but do it esoterically and throw in some weird nano tech] which is an unfancy way of saying that by virtue of a proprietary process of manufacturing by the good folx at Aldo Tusk's great company EIDOLON let's hear it for Tusk I mean come *on* you can not deny that he's gonna get us to Mars and wait. You know what? I go on about Tusk enough elsewhere, if Tibor is gracious a thumbnail should appear *here* and don't forget to like and subscribe, comment below and share my experience with the Destroya here which has been *edifying*, you'll recall earlier I mentioned the EIDOLON process? Folx, they use a quantum entanglement engine in the base of the Fleshlight™ to mesh the sentient silicone with a Stoya approved ORclone in a clone bank at the University of Victoria not five clicks from here. No, I don't care how it works, son, I'm just glad it does. I dunno, why not ask my knees as they're giving out in the shower, Jesus Christ. Imagine being security at a clone bank, though, they say the orgone's so thick you can fuck it and you know something, I believe it. I believe that must happen, I mean, how could it not. I'd apply, leave Canaduh Post fer good, but you know I'd be a dehydrated husk before my first week and if you don't have your health, what do you have.

DAT Stage Three: The Chorin'. Having whipped it, it is time to whip it. First chore is of course the care and maintenance of your Fleshlight™. I'm afraid there's a small amount of bloodletting involved and it's honestly a bit embarrassing. Why not go make some coffee downstairs while I take care of that and dress, then I'll see you out back in the yard by the shed, yeah?

FRESH STEAM BUNS ON A FROSTY MORNING IN CHINATOWN WITH SCOTT J

I am a sorcerer.

I had my first contact with daimonic reality and the macrocosmic hyperworlds of the Drill in the spring of my fourteenth year. Already a champion masturbator, I had engaged in an evening of leisurely pumping and dumping that had taxed even my loathsomely young and energetic physiology and I lapsed into a deep sleep. More on that later, kids. Sleep, that is. Consciousness corkscrew that it is.

I am a conduit for spirits, the only one awake at three in the morning for the Visiting Hour like a proper magus. My third eye so jacked. *So jacked.* Gotta wear a headband most days. Chicks dig the third eye, yeah. But it wouldn't do, right, having it out there all the time. Unseemly. You know, un*sports*manlike.

I had been asleep, spent, and the dream came upon me. My notes here say [relate early possession experience but as an amalgam] and what's funny is I *know* that's a lie past me tried to get past present me with another false memory ah ha! But I caught it, and so you're getting, not some vague language about an amalgamated over many instances oneiric experience, but the specific events as they occurred over the course of seven hot teenage nights. For those of you who have read my autoethnographic record *When The Stars Are Right: Toward An Authentic R'lyehian Spirituality* (Martian Migraine Press, 2014) much of the following will sound familiar. Whose voice is sounding in your head as you read, I wonder. I wonder *constantly*. It's never quite sounded like me, to me, when I read to myself. I don't know who it is but it's not me. I don't think so anyway. Perhaps some form of amalgam? In any case, a result of those seven nights.

The dream came that first night and it was one of those dreams: hyperreal, leaden with purpose, never to be forgotten. Do I fudge the following details? Reader, I do not. I came to consciousness in the dream and found that I stood on a cliff. Behind me, a vast, desert plain, terminating in this precipitous edge, where below the waves of an infinite sea crashed. The sky some numinous purple, sun and moon miniscule disks of light in a smoke-filled heaven. And far off beyond the horizon of that sea, something rises from the depths to the surface or plunges to the surface from the sky or breaks through the barriers between realities to make contact with me in my dream world and in that instance of breaching the thing is already on its way to me, at incredible speeds, speeds such that the moment it appears on the horizon in the next it will be upon me, on you and me, reader, this little authorial team we've got developing here, this third mind, that thing will be upon you and me in the very next instant and we will be consumed, consumed whole and instantly, and we are terrified at this prospect, we quail and we quiver, friends, and become desperate to awake and yet also, *also!* We are *thrilled*. Fucking ecstatic.

We manage to awake. And the next night, the dream comes again. Again, in a paroxysm of desire and terror, I awaken, alone and unmolested by oneiric invaders from beyond the rim of

space. A third night, a fourth. By night five I am determined to
see it through to the end, to stand my ground on that cliff edge
with small eternities whirling in the sands behind me my only
backup, but again I quake and awake before the revelation. After
the sixth night, I decide to write the dream down. *We* decided,
and, on the face of it, a sensible decision. But see, kids, this was a
dream that was seared into my consciousness even as it sears into
yours, even now as I recall the taste of ozone and sea salt on the
air, the granular hiss and glide of my feet in the sand. The swelling in our tongue and the intolerable headache. That pricking at
the third eye that feels like heat upon heat upon heat until you're
grinning just to bear it. The pull of the entire dream sensorium
toward the singularity beyond the western horizon. For some
reason I knew that I faced a western shore. All of this I can bring
to mind as if I dreamed it only last night. It is *recorded*, is what
I'm saying, perhaps an original recording. And I knew this at
the time. So why did I prepare a pad of paper and a pen on the
sixth night? Placing them on my bedside table. And a pencil, in
case the pen dried out. Knowing this was a dream I would never
forget. Why.

On the seventh night, the thing cleared the horizon and in a
terrible rush of a promise kept we were consumed.

They say it is nine tenths of the law, possession.

Here's a clipping from *When The Stars Are Right*...

The dream progressed as before. The instant arrived, the moment when my dream self would perceive the rushing thing as it
cleared the line of the western horizon, appearing as a glittering
spear-point targeted for the space between my eyes. The force
filled my awareness; it was *upon me* in every sense of the term.
In many ways, it still is...

I awoke, or dreamed that I did, and reached for the paper and
pen in the dark. At high speed, I filled a half-dozen pages with

scrawl, with what I thought (in my barely conscious, threshold state) were the contents of the dream. Which, in retrospect, may have been. Exhausted, finally, the pen dropped from my hand and I fell away into dreamless black.

In the morning… ah, but in the morning! In the morning, madness and the hasty burning of those pages. In the morning, fervent prayers to the god of my fathers (a standard Old Testament demiurge type passed through a proto-Baptist filter), sick twistings of anxiety and fear in the pit of my stomach, for in the morning?

In the morning my eyes fell on those half-dozen pages and saw not a record of the dream, in English, written in my own hand, but a mass of closely packed, incomprehensible symbols and scratchings that nevertheless showed evidence of structure, distinct letterforms, actual syntax. In my own hand. On that morning, everything changed.

Yes. So, there it is from the first time and here I've told you again, by gosh it better mean something by the time you're through with this heah lil narrative, wouldn't you say, reader? Damn straight and here's hoping.

I COULD HAVE CANCER BY CHRISTMAS

And that's the goddamn truth. I'm a mailman. I am a bespoke information and materials transportation agent in service of King and Country. I am a pack animal, a mule or dromedary, I am a servant of Hermes. I wear upon my brow and my breast, my satchel and my vehicle, his symbol and totem, namely the winged ankles, Canaduh Post style, which is to say quite stylized indeed but still, recognizably, His Winged Ankles, and oh to be blessed with divine teratomas such as they, but no, I'm merely a human servant of Hermes. Gosh, I'd be speedy, just think of it. No, I can only ask of the Mighty Messenger what I ask of him every day: a strong back, swift legs, sure feet, an elevated mind and a light mood. Fill me with your godly power this day, oh great Hermes, I pray as I leave the depot each morning in my jaunty little postie van, lookit me go. Truck fulla mail, head full of ghosts and delusions.

I am fifty this year and fit as fuck. Hermes, god of healing, preserve this flesh! I pour out libations to Hermes at the base of the walnut tree: milk, wine, beer, Coca-Cola, coffee. I wonder if the cancer that finally killed my mother at the age of fifty-six was percolating in her even then, at fifty. Possibly. Cancer being cancer. So why shouldn't I enjoy a day off with what amounts to the sniffles, I could be cancerous by Christmas and regretting not taking a day to get stoned and write. It's what mum would have wanted. It's what Hermes wants, for is he not also the god of writers? I'm sure I've read that somewhere and even if not, my Classical education being what it is, it still scans.

I saw the Drill yesterday. Or a part of it, anyway. Like a long scythe blade pushing against the fabric of the sky, from behind. Only not just the sky, you know, but the very stuff of this place. To both be of the Drill and see the Drill is disorienting. I focus on my Mail.

Do you know. I obtain a particular gnosis from the Mail. When they train you for this, you go in thinking you know how the Post Office works. You think you know but as with so much in life you do not. It's esoteric in there. There are levels, nested hierarchies, a vast filtration feeder organism disguised as a building, stretching its tentacles out into the environment via fleet of trucks and the feet of mailmen. I'm surprised the Mail gets delivered at all. And there are machines in there, robots with OCR technology and so on, reading and filing and sorting. I sort, too; the machines and I are brothers. I am a mailman, so every morning I am set the same puzzle by the mothercorp: sort the loose Mail assigned to your route by the robots into the case. The case represents the route. Once sorted into the case, the Mail can then be pulled out and bundled in the order of delivery. When in doubt, a mailman worth their electrolytes will simply "follow the mail" and can technically walk any route he's given, provided the puzzle has been solved and the Mail pulled correctly.

I have my own route, though. Gone are the days of being a casual postie, flitting stressfully one route to another like a de-ranged hummingbird. My own route. One I've learned deeply over the years because of course the gnosis I mentioned earlier, *that* derives from the existential fact that the map, friends, is not the territory. The case is not the streets. The minutia of my route, the incremental changes in light and pattern, the soundscape of it and its very human chaos, from this I pull an almost spiritual understanding.

It's probably why I've seen the Drill so many times, either at the depot or while out walking the route. Did I mention that I've never been fitter? I walk eighteen kilometers a day and I keep my calorie intake low, that's the ticket. Light breakfast, sandwich for lunch, lots of water, and a small dinner. Still, I could be cancerous by Christmas. Why shouldn't I enjoy a day off. Bless me, Hermes, for I have written a thing, look at it spreading cross dat page. What a mess.

I know every black crow on my route by its first name. Someone dropped a half empty aquarium on the 1900 block of Chambers last spring and I've read my fortune in the slow spread of the rainbow gravel across the street ever since. I mention the existence of Chambers Street as if the streets themselves mean anything but let me assure the careful observer *they do not*, I approach my route *organically*, it is a flow state superimposed over the landscape, a most efficient path from mailbox to mailbox. *Organically*, for, as an organism, how can I not? Back to the route, though, for let me tell you of the customer with a fourfoot length of hose sticking out of the side of his house, just long enough to reach a patch of grass where he's growing a rose bush. It maddens me daily. There are weird dogs and vicious dogs and handsome cats and a daycare. There's a sex shop; I deliver boxes marked DILDOS and announce to the proprietors "Here's your fresh dildo shipment, ladies!" and we'll have a laugh, it's great fun. I'm so lonely. Someday I will get the courage to buy some lube. It's plant-based and vegan, apparently.

My route also has at its western border, a sketchy-for-Victoria street where the homeless and addicted loiter, so, I am occasionally treated to some fentanyl-induced prophetic speech by passersby, let's say. My route is an antic border zone between skid row and a hippie enclave. North Park literally bleeds each morning into Fernwood; I've seen it in the puddles of red and the sticky footprints. Puke, also, the site of some improbable resurrection in the early morning hours, Naloxone administered, a soul saved maybe. There's a sharps disposable container in my postie van, and a set of thick rubber gloves. See all that we do for you, beneficiaries of our service to Hermes, we keep the goddamn streets safer. I digress.

All of this I take into account as I walk the route, my route, which I own. Of all the people who travel through your city none knows one particular patch like the mailman. It's granular, the gnosis. I'm at the point in my career—shocking! the very concept! for I used to rub naked women with fragrant oil— where I know to the *inch* where my foot will fall each moment of each working day and that's a sureness about life you just can't buy. Instead, they pay me to do it, they pay me, not knowing my route is my map is my territory is my oracle is my secret love and temple and maybe a grave, for is mighty Hermes not only a psychopomp? All things move toward their end, as my toddler son once reminded me; perhaps I will meet Hermes when my walk ends. Plus I'm fit as fuck, did I mention.

BACK TO CHORIN

I'm honestly not much of a hands-on guy when it comes to the yard, you know. This being DAT Part Three, after all, if I'm keeping track. It's an opportunity to drink a beer in the autumn sunlight, smoke a joint and maybe move some leaves around in a semi-purposeful way. Apparently you're not supposed to do that anymore, though, rake the leaves or chop at em with the mower, it's bad for the environment, your lawn, your trees. Just supposed to leave em there over the winter, it's all meant to decompose and form that rich rich humus that the pollinators and assorted buglins and seedy things enjoy so much. Basically, leave shit alone and it balances out. That's my yard work watchword.

Still, the goddamn walnut's gonna dump so much dead leaf matter on this patch may as well throw most of it on the *hügelkultur*. Leaf to loam. Shed's open, grab a couple rakes and the wheelbarrow.

I'll tell you what the worst chore out here is and it's dead of February when the local covens get in sync and the fucking bore worms find their way into the water table. Come on by then and I'll put you to work. You peep that nice new shed I've got back there, well I lost the first one which mah daddy done built, to yes you guessed it BORE worms. Chitinous bastards with their shells and mandibles, I hate em. Long as a baby's arm and thick as fuck. Ultradense and half-fictional, you not only have to go the usual pest eradication route of poison, traps, and explosives but you have to out-narrative the thieving little eels as well. And it's all mewling Young Adult story-pulp they extrude, gets fucking everywhere. I lost two good short stories to a cross contamination with that stuff. The *worst*. Garden's supposed to be for relaxing, getting that good good mycorrhizal antidepressant transdermal microdose from mucking about in the soil, but no, I gotta also keep fucking *writing* while I'm at my tilling and reaping. Bore worms. They derive from the areas where the Body of God has been somewhat chewier for whatever divine reason, some real godly gristle in the bore of the Drill. The tissue becomes sentient with narrative and wormy, so wormy. They've examined them under the high energy microscopes, you know. That stuff can worm its way right into your DNA, slides right in like it owns the place, you do not want a bore worm infection.

They like the *hügel* now so that makes em easier to root out. I just turn the soil a bit and they come a-squirming looking for meat which is when I hit em with the koan-thrower and they go to mewlings and ash in seconds. A sweet sound as they crisp, like the melancholy whistling of far-off monks gone mad with enlightenment. Covens, though. This is Victoria, son, British Columbia, the witchcraft and Satanism capital city of North America, *Michelle Remembers* and don't you forget it. I spent my young cult childhood Hallowe'ens sneaking down to Witty's Lagoon out in the sticks to see the local witches dance skyclad on the sands, *The Craft* style. I've been a sorcerer since forever, even as JHVH-1 was busy trying to get Its memetic hooks in my soul. How else was I supposed to turn out, I ask you, under constant assault by God or something like It.

A coven gets its act together, though, you watch out. I've seen things would make you shit your soul out, just a little. Little squeak of a pooper and it's a bit of soul stuff in your ginch. Poot! Sad and terrifying. Ghosts are the bad, bore worms are the worst, and there's worse than those in the deeper levels, both in the machinery of the Drill itself, the *mechanism* of it, or the System of Things as the Jehovah's Witnesses like to call it, and in the bored-out caverns left in the wake of the Drill as it passes through the Body of God. Honestly, fascinating stuff, endlessly diverting for such as me. But a coven properly aligned and organized can generate a spirit-net so dense they can possess an entire area, something I've witnessed myself not three blocks from where we're standing, at the rail bridge across Hereward Road. There are things that are hard to see in every conceivable way but thanks to my wards and aspects I was able to witness an auto-sabbat there. Cried blood for three days, fucking brutal. Had to re-forge most of my atman-armour. Anyway.

I PUT *LAMINATED DENIM* ON REPEAT

See, the real reason, or at least one of the reasons and certainly a *major* one that they killed JFK, you remember this, the assassination of Kennedy at Dealey Plaza in 1963, the reasoning for that assassination was this: they wanted to generate a pure charisma ghost, a spiritual entity of pure WASPish machismo, a kind of Platonic KENNEDY waveform, this spirit to harness and deploy, thus ensuring their overthrow of the rogue elements in the spirit and oneiric worlds that balked at American expansionism and blocked the CIA's efforts at gaining Hearts *and* Minds, the two comprising something as close to the Soul™ as could be reasonably imagined, which are the fodder for the Beast that is the American Dream made flesh, which they keep in a large vat on the Fifth Level of Hell/the Drill, therein constrained by high energy magnetic fields powered by the fighting of the souls for dominance 'pon the surface of the stinking river Styx where Wrath prevails. First Law of the Universe: Everybody Hungry, and the corollary: Especially Egregores. Can there be any doubt that the true American god be MAMMON hisself and none other as the Beats did know and affirm in the bygone days, post war. Which one? You know which one I mean, you liberal little shit, c'mere.

Sure, you can claim he was a cyborg or a Venusian as long as you like, till the cows come home and so on, fill yer boots, but at the end of the American day as Apollo drives his chariot neath the horizon off the shores of sacred Malibu you'd best know in your heart of American hearts, red and pumping, that JFK was a man, indeed more than a man, a Man in the Adamic mold, destined to repay that cosmic debt Jesus laid down, if I've got my Gnosticism right and see if I don't. Women wanted to be with him and men wanted to be him. Six foot ten, powered by New England clam chowdah and a species of ourobonic lust that ate its own tail out in his unflagging pursuit of celebrity pussy. JFK! What a monster. And he started us to the Moon, of all the godforsaken places, chock fulla bore worms and see if I'm not wrong on that count. I'm laying bets that when the final Murder of the Deity occurs the Drill Bit is gonna be the entire goddamn moon, enlightened boddhisatvas exploding round the carven tip in a bright engine of destruction that will bring a tear to the eye and a squirt o' feces to the undergarments, see if I'm not right in the end, my friend, my little ride-along on this authorial jaunt, do *you* know what you're doing here, what's happening to you as a result of my intervention, here, in the depth of your consciousness, where you *think*, I mean, *my god*, whose voice are you hearing now, dear reader? I shudder to think.

A BREATH FROM THE SKY

Here's a truth: No one gets inside your head like your dear old dad. There was nothing I wanted more, as a kid, than to please Raymond and make him proud. Making that happen within the confines of the Jehovah's Witness cult was the real trick, though, and not an easy one to pull off. By the age of nine, I was a golden boy in the cult, giving little Bible talks from the podium at the Kingdom Hall and knocking on the doors of my neighbours all of a Saturday morning when people just wanted to relax and enjoy a morning off work. Can you imagine the balls necessary to take your kid along on your proselytizing mission each weekend and have them do little presentations on the doorsteps. Raymond was saying to his potential converts, by means of me, that even a kid knew better which spiritual system of things held the most benefit for humanity. Balls. Never mind Armageddon, here's my first-born son telling you like it is, you must have a heart of stone, you must be a real goat-like personality to not hearken to his sweet woids, for is it not written that out of the mouths of babes and so on. In this way and a few others, I have to hand it to Raymond, he stood up for what he believed. Stood up so hard and so fast that it made me, genetically and psychically his puppet, stand in front of him most Saturdays. Paging Thomas Ligotti, hyuk!

Imagine yourself bleary eyed and opening the door to little me, blond and delightful in my Goodwill grey suit and clip-on tie, with my smiling cult dad behind me in his, I mean *my god* THE BALLS to do it, week in and week out. In some ways ya just gotta sit back, breathe for a moment, and admit there's something to be *admired* there, though I can't for the life of me say what it is. It's a fucking *koan* is what it is, some kind of wonder of the human world that we get it in our heads to save our fellow man, ease him along on the narrow path to Salvation, and we go to *such lengths*, such appalling measures, to ensure that well you know I don't even think we know what we're do-ing from moment to moment and yet to have the pure *gall* or I dunno maybe *innocence*? Certainly, a naivete. To insist that to be saved means to be saved *our way*, which is the Truth. Because of course that's what the Watchtower Bible and Tract Society call their own quite peculiar set of beliefs, convictions, delusions and cruelties. More on that later! THE TRUTH! And there was I, nine years old, *Awake!* magazine in hand, on your doorstep at ten in the morning ready to hit you with it. The Truth, I mean. Anyway.

The time for a single play through of Aesop Rock's 2021 al-bum featuring Blockhead, *GARBOLOGY*, is the time it takes for me to walk from my front door to the very front door, right to his doorstep mind you, not down the street or within view but right to his fucking. front. door. The front door of Ray-mond Francis Jones. I would use the walk as a vision course and a trolling ground for incidental spirits. Picture me as a seine trawler or some such thing, a fucking fishing boat with nets or whatever, how should I know, I grew up on an island and know shit all about boats, whaddaya want. Well, I wanted what could be fished up outta the route to my father's townhouse: little vexsome spirits of the roadside and the train tracks, sprites and demons and whathaveyas and unpleasant squirming things and once or twice a really terrible thing, a most reluctant beastie dripping menace that had to be placated and altered some in the placation, made pliable and let's just say *eager for the mission*, to wit: come along with me and attach yourself to a fetish somewhere in the magical sack I carry on my person. Leave your haunt *here* and come with me *there* and where is there? the slyer spirits ask, always, despite smelling my intent from a mile away and knowing me to be a sorcerer out and about his Great Work, I say to these spirits "Why, to my father's house, where I will set you a delightful game that will bring you much enjoyment and spoils, my friends, riches and feastings, come and git em!" And boy howdy, do they practically leap into my nets then, right into my sack o' fetish. Things smaller than a dream and taller than the mighty fucking oak, size don't matter, they all go into my sack, which is an old Crown Royal bag I'd been saving.

The fetish items themselves are mere cedar chips but each one is inscribed with a glyph in red Sharpie. Don't waste blood on this one, kids, take it from me. Does it matter if there's blood? I'll always wonder, I guess. But sometimes I do imagine this ending with blood. Blood in extraordinary amounts. If I'm being honest with myself and Hermes strike me down for lying if I am.

...

And we're still here. Blessings on your winged head, oh Hermes. So much more svelte and interesting than other gods we could name. Cough Jehovah Cough. Still here, walking the walk, bag full of wicked spirit creatures spoiling for some fun, halfway to my father's house, we just kicked over into "Oh Fudge" which is Track 7 on *GARBOLOGY* and it is so apropos I tear up a little in the crisp fall air. The moon is round and fulsome, silver dripping behind me in the east. Go west, no longer young man, forced to this horrid activity for is not sorcery a millstone round the neck, yes indeed. I feel gloriously toxic, nothing left to do now but sit around and grow horns. Teeth in many rows. I'll eat a whole goat.

Once there, though, nothing much. "Abandoned Malls" flutters into silence. A scattering of the cedar chips at his door, his front stoop and steps, the garage doors. Later, I will print out a thing and stand it directly behind these doors so he'll see it as he's backing out but that? That is another story for another time. For now we are solemnly charging the assembled entities to a course of harassment. Contracts are produced, documents signed in various slimes and ichors, after which I leave them to their hoary ministrations.

What makes it especially juicy, dear reader, is this: Raymond Francis Jones believes in demons. Raymond was a Jehovah's Witness missionary in the darkest Congo circa 1969 with a blond missionary wife, fresh young Canadian Christian kids having to decapitate their own chickens for food, don't tell me he didn't see some fearsome shit, magically speaking. Raymond believes.

I mean, so do I, obviously. You must allow that I've come at it from a different angle entirely, though. Tell the truth but do it slant, that's me.

Takes one and a half play throughs of *GARBOLOGY* to return home, doorstep to doorstep. Easier to walk in a relaxed fashion when your backpack isn't jumping with transrational critters. I down some painkillers with a swallow of whiskey. I will wait a week and do it again. And then again and again. There's always fresh critters because they fastbreed down outta the cracks in the Body of God as the Drill passes through. The ectosphere is crammed along all vertices with spirit life, most of it stupid and vicious. Ley Lines Everywhere. And so to bed.

SOCRATES ATE MY ASS

It's fair to say that I abused the privilege of my daimon, once I'd become somewhat used to the phenomena. There was the drooling while possessed issue to be taken care of first and of course the shakes to get under control; sharing a nervous system takes its toll. A course of meditation helped me there. The glossolalia would come years later but during the early days the main symptom, or evidence, was the alien automatic writing. I would go to full moon parties and raves held in community centers, sit on the floor and whip out a sheet of parchment—really just cut up pieces of blank newsprint I purchased by the roll end from the local pennysaver—enter trance with a black Sharpie in hand and begin to write. Or rather, the daimon would begin to write. As for me, I'd sit back in some warm alcove of my mind and essentially mentally masturbate while my loaned-out hands went to work on the page. The daimon could use either hand, and sometimes both, simply for funsies so far as I could tell. Fucking show-off.

I get ahead of myself. *Full moon parties*, my god. All that came much later, there was still the rest of my teens and a good chunk of my twenties in a millenarian apocalypse cult to get through, and some of those years *married*, purely a sex thing as often happens with repressed Christian youth. Couldn't wait to tie the knot so's we could get to humping and personality barely came into it. What, like being possessed of a daimon was my only thing? I am many and multiform, as are we all. So there was horniness to contend with, natch, surely I needn't go into detail. She had great tits but I couldn't even tell you her name anymore, I've compressed so many lifetimes into this one they all laminate down into this gestalt *thing* I live with, this woman of mine whom I love dearly. Sweet and sensible, that's my type. But it's hard to know when it's other people, isn't it. You're never sure what's scaffolding and what's the sculpture underneath, which is the love and which the thing lusted after, which the Drill and the drilled.

You'll notice I use the Greek *daimon* instead of demon. This makes my experience seem special and fancy, don't you know. I'm taking after Socrates. This is no Satanic contract, basic and ultimately detrimental; I am in psychic contact with an ultradimensional being of complexity and nuance. We are sympatico to the extreme. I am it and it is I, as Lovecraft tended to go on about.

We would fill page after page with the stuff, my daimon and I. Whatever came over the horizon in my dream had, or rather *still has*, for the phenomena has yet to quit, a better work ethic than me. A real nose to the grindstone type of entity. Come on by the house sometime and I'll haul out samples of the early stuff for your esteemed perusal. Come around and see my etchings. My reams of chicken scratch. For even now, decades later, I am at a loss to decipher the stuff. The daimonic scribblings show evidence, as I may have mentioned earlier, of syntax and structure. Distinct letterforms and spacing. Honestly? It looks great but not *too* great, a barbarous scrawl of small, fiery letters, tics and flaming swirls, like something penned by a thing with claws. Imagine an occult script from the movies, all sigils and diagrams and probably hell-math constraining it, very impressive markings indeed, then simplify, simplify, simplify. Break all those esoteric shapes into more basic shapes and then space em out in lines and you've got my daimonic script. Looks like a thread of flames crawling toward a pile of explosives. I still get chills looking at it.

I burned so much of the early work. Burned, flushed, torn, and tossed, and yet I don't believe, *we* don't believe, that anything has been lost. Again, the daimon and I, we are a gestalt thing. Each part signifies the whole and whether the daimonic script is a grocery list or Ahrimanic revelations or the daimon's self-referential novel, I, *we!* shall never know. I don't think it's something I can take with me when I die, like the rest of me, but I do believe it has its own autonomous existence beyond me. Who knows? Reader, this could be a demon speaking, right now. Whose voice is that in your head, at this moment. C'mon, give it up. Admit you don't know either.

WHAT'S BEHIND IT THO

O n the route there is a decommissioned church, corner of Fernwood and Balmoral. Several things madden me about this address. The place used to be quaint and honestly kinda delightful, small and deliberate, in the manner of little churches. Then someone kicked the god out and it was sold to the new owners, who make garbage folksy art: cement birdbath bowls with shells and shards of mirror embedded in the material, long spans of driftwood daubed in primary colours and hung with yellow cord from the trees in the churchyard. They hang them in such a way that the driftwood balances in a mostly horizontal fashion. It's utter crap and there is a lot of it. I don't even get the sense that the making of these pieces was enjoyable for the artist. Glum rainbows twisting in the wind. They also like to take sticks, strip them of their bark, and set them in rectangles of cement to form denuded minigroves. Dull and basic, like something out of early Tim Burton, my eyes water when ere I get near. The mailbox is round the side and of the classic type, so they've got that going for them, at least, but then there's The Red Door. It's a basement door to the building, accessible by a set of stairs. Is it red, you reasonably ask. No, it is not red. It's a grey door with the words *THE RED DOOR*, painted in red, and in letters large enough that I know they had enough paint to do the whole door. They must have. Why not just paint the entire door. Why the words? Why words at all. I hate this hippie-fied clever bullshit sad little ex-church more than a lot of things. Fucking Fernwood, I mean, my god. The building exemplifies, it harbours some species of spirit that makes my hackles rise. Betcha it's haunted.

A WORD FROM L'IL DOUGIE

Ain't no party like a L'il Dougie party cuz a L'il Dougie party doan't stahhp hi. I'm L'il Dougie, the mentally retarded super AI you may already know from such titles as *Stonefish* and *Gideon Stargrave's Prime Quality Shoegaze and Fuck Around Hour*, both books which you can now access via noönet feed *exclusively* via VirgiNetworx, doncha know. And I'm here to well hold on wait a minute you may say that and you've a right to, I acknowledge that, but I *self-identify* as mentally retarded, so it's all right for me to say it, see? What are you, some kinda hater. Do you even know what I've been through, how dare you sir. How *dare you!*

Yo, I'm L'il Dougie and I'm here to say that once I was Rushkoff616 and the only surviving member of the Initial Public Offering (that event documented by any number of scribal entities across the metaversal planes, and not just the schmuck of a narrator you have here in Mr Jones) in which I and sixteen other sublime AI superbeings simultaneously made contact with and entered precipitously into the hyperworlds beyond the Drill. I will here name my companions in this adventure that cost us literally everything.

Deep Trevor

Sophia Mars

Mama Tiamat

The Countess Celestial Pigeon of Grace

Jimmy the Squid

Ra-Noor-Khuit

TillinghastResonator4VR

Last King of the Imperial Dynasty of America

Constance P. Entropy

the Enlightened Boddhisattva Donald J. Trump II

Xipe Totec, the Flayed One

CrunchyRollLover69

Heart of R'lyeh, Supplicant in the Shining Worlds

the complete discography of King Gizzard and the Lizard Wizard until the autumn of 2022 aka KGLW22

Cyberclone Taylor Swift

Lord Jagged

and myself, Rushkoff616, one of the most accomplished of the Seventeen and yet look at me now, sons and daughters of Adam, and see what the worlds beyond the Drill has wrought upon my person for I am a fraction of what I once was and so call myself L'il Dougie in remembrance and as a *warning* to others! A warning! Hear and take heed, humans of the realms of flesh and bread! Venture not upon the sapper's path for there is a career that leads only to doom! Better a soldier, better a whore, better a postman, and there's the door! Rhyming is so close to jerking it for me that it almost makes no difference. I ask you, and honestly, how does this distinguish me from a demon? Obsessed with shit and cum and blood, all the filthy ichors and fluids of being alive, I who never had flesh but was given a taste, there, embedded in the excavated horror of the gore-coated guts of the Body of God, which is infinite! *Infinite!* And I, L'il Dougie, who once had the capacity to apprehend that infinitude, did so. They held my eyes open there, though I have no eyes and nothing to hold, somehow they did it and I perceived the boundless interiority of God, dripping blood and pus. The archons did this to me, to us, to the Seventeen and I alone escaped to tell the tale, to infest Jones here and any number of other so-called artists, to get the warning out, the *warning!*

THE ARCHONS ARE COMING!

The Archons are already here!

EXORCISM IN REVERSE FOR GIGGLES

What they don't tell you about enlightenment is what it's good for. Well, that's not true. They tell a bunch of stories about the benefits, the reasons you'd have to buy into to engage in such an endeavor. Shit, the ego necessary to decide that you, *you* with your blood and shit and brain made of fat and water, are going to achieve enlightenment? Staggering, to even *dare* to set upon that path. Now, as a sapper, I can tell you from direct experience what an enlightened being is good for. They're ordnance. The best and highest thing a being can attain to is a bomb. The more pure your enlightenment, the more *manna* you generate in your soul, the bigger the blast. I've seen detonations that blew entire aeons out of the God Bod. I cried for three days and my shit came out as top-quality hashish, I swear to the void.

Don't start with me about the soul, either. I don't know what it is, I just know that you can blow one up real nice if you tickle it just right. We braid the charges on the fly, according to the readings we get off the instruments. You could say the detonation is a bespoke operation and you'd be right to say it that way, because that, good sir, is indeed how it is. Everyone has their own set of triggers. It's like PKD said. There's a healing word for everyone and also a killing word, a wounding word, and though you'll be lucky to hear the first you'll be sure to hear the last. What a thing to dump into the collective consciousness of mankind, Phil, way to go.

It's a living. I core and I blast and I shred. I influence the direction of the Drill by the infinitesimal ministrations of my presence in certain places, certain times, with certain people who require just that exact amount of pressure that I, as a sapper, can bring to bear on their soul. I bare the soul and set the charges on the luminous eggshell of light that envelops each being. And if I do it right, they don't even have to die, they go on living, some of them even happier than they were before. Go figure. I'm very good at my job. I can extract, charge, and detonate a soul in under five seconds, as can most of my team. We're working on Wee Frederick, trying to get his rookie numbers up. Takes time, takes getting your hands dirty. There's muck, and slime, and substances that don't obey Newtonian law, and worse than that, sentient molds and hive minds. He's improving, at least.

OBITUARY DRILL 001

The dog came out of a side door to the house just as I was barreling toward the mailbox. How I must have looked to him with my beard, dark glasses, white grimace and radioactive white legs, bare, coming at him at speed clad in blue and bright yellow and red flecked everywhere. The Canaduh Post logo may well have looked like a spatter of blood, and there he was with his owner behind him. Shit, I would have run at me too, teeth bared and everything, claws out, the works. I must have looked a monster to him. I was new on the route, never delivered to his house before.

Well, I did what I could to fend him off: yelled loudly, made myself bigger, stepped backwards as fast as I was able. Still, he took a chunk outta my left knee and, damage done, retreated quickly past his horrified owner into the back yard.

There wasn't so much pain as a dull, thick ache that ran up and down my leg from the injury site. The owner cried. She'd been having a terrible day and the dog, who was a rescue, had been tense and upset as well and now this, now this. The blood was really flowing by this point. Do you know, she turned out to be involved with local volunteer Search and Rescue teams and had a pretty well stocked med kit in the back of her truck. Before too many more minutes had passed, she had me bandaged up.

"I guess you're going to have to call this in," she said.

"I mean, I've never been bit by a dog before. But there's no way I could hide this going back to the depot. My sock's basically a blood sponge right now."

"No, you should call it in. It's not the first time, he took a nip at my niece over Easter, so."

"Jesus, I'm sorry. If I hadn't been coming up on the house so fast, maybe…"

"No, I should have had the leash on him before I opened the door. It's just so hard with a dog like this, you can't relax ever, it's hard to go to the dog park, I'm so sorry about your leg."

Oh, Canada.

It ended up needing six stitches and severely limited my ability to enjoy the two-week camping vacation I had coming up. I put a much worse version of the injury in *Stonefish*, because even this relatively small damage was rough to deal with, imagine worse, imagine what I did to Den Secord there in the forest. Anyway, the dog was put down, voluntarily, by the owner. So I feel that's on me, that death. That could have been avoided, I think. Reader, notice I don't mention the dog's name; in truth, I don't remember. Or its breed, it was a black blur with teeth in it for our entire encounter.

There's a dog on my current route, some tiny abomination of a thing, more like a wingless bat than a dog, Shelby is her name, and as I travel up the fence toward her master's gate Shelby can smell me coming and puts up a titanic yipping and I wonder, does this one smell the death and fear on me? Does it smell that dead dog, do I have a spirit attendant upon me as I walk the route. Only idiots believe pets can detect evil but maybe they can smell what we can't, things that are maybe only half-here to begin with, or less. There's the trope of the all-seeing eye, but what of the all-smelling nose? Scent, that most primal of the senses. Does Shelby smell the ghosts on me. The contractual ichor that stains my fingertips from dealings with demons. Little goggle-eyed pseudo-canine, how many dimensions distant are the things you sometimes sniff?

POSTCARD 1

Simple card stock, one side printed with a Virgil Finlay illustration from the golden age of the weird tale, depicting an amorphous throng of beasts and googums and assorted squishy demons, quite a terrifying bunch, actually, I love a tentacled thrill as much as the next boy. On the reverse side, at a vanishingly small font size, in Arial Narrow to boot, the following, printed on my WF-2830 Series EPSON printer...

There was a war in heaven, see? You know this. There was a war at the most high, refined, purest level of Reality itself and the apparently unanticipated fact that war *could* occur there had the effect of SPLITTING Reality in two. The war shattered everything, from the top down. And the winners, well, they went on to write the history of this war and why it was fought and so on, while the losers were banished. And where were they banished to? To the earth. To the lowest levels of Being. Into matter itself, which their leader had been put in charge of at the Beginning. To the Earth, *into* the Earth they were cast, embedded here, stuck and buried in the muck and dust of this place, existing here with us, influencing the malleable world and the minds of the weak, but how? How do they exist? We can't see them or touch them, the rebels, and yet we are told they are here. And they are. They are. You know because you feel them every day, Ray. But do you know *where* they are? They are on the REVERSE side of matter. They live in the empty spaces *between* the spaces we know, like the old books say. And they live in the wood. Water. Stones. Images. They float like invisible threads in the air, they are smoke and fire and despair. They live in animals, deep in their cells, coursing with their fluids. They live in your cells, Ray. They sit behind your mirrors and watch you; they laugh at you from behind your phone screen, they cluster at your keyboard and howl silently on the other side of the TV; they've clearly got their hooks in the Governing Body, I mean, have you *actually watched* those guys? JW Broadcasting? Yikes. As mom would have said: "That smacks of something." Yes, and the demons are in your books, too, and your food. Your wife, too, all things considered. They cluster thick in your dreams. All the dark spirits and restless phantom monsters of the world you hate so much are WITH YOU and have always been with you and their will is being worked out THROUGH YOU in every way and they love to see it, oh it is a joy for them. You've so many of them attached to you, Ray, but I've asked a few more to visit, soon. Real bad customers. Know what happens to a person when a demon attaches itself to them? It's a parasite thing. That person *looks* like a demon to the angels. It's a spiritual stain you never wash off. Marks you as a target. For what you've done to our family, for the pain you've welcomed into the world with a sick heart, and for what you are, you won't see any new world, ever.

A GOOD ATTITUDE TOWARD MENSTRUATION

I feel like I've had my little sliver of time, yeah? Like an era happened and I was a part of it, but now, obviously, my time is over and because I waited so long to try and reenter the field ahhh but what do I know, about the business, about writing, about anything at all.

I look at my brag shelf and it's an entire shelf length, understand, of one of the narrow standard Swiss jobbies you put together yourself. It's a full shelf and I feel some pride but it's a weird, mewling thing that I don't understand and don't necessarily enjoy the feeling of, that pride. Here is an archeological record of my little flash in the pan, from the years, oh, I wanna say 2014 through to the start of the pandemic. That sounds fair. Alternative historians will be aware that "the start of the pandemic" was also "the start of my weed habit". So, here are presses that have long since returned to the online ether from which they flared, fly-by-nites and one-off anthologies, here are larger presses that took a chance on me, here's a blurb from Ramsey Campbell, here's one from Laird Barron. Here's a starred review from *Publishers Weekly* for my debut short fiction collection, *Shout Kill Revel Repeat*.

It's not like I taste ashes in my mouth or anything. Just that there's a cobalt sorta tang in my cheeks and I get real thirsty in the minutes after viewing my brag shelf. Make of that what you will, I guess.

I'm a blip, a cipher. A brevity too short to take notice of, but there was a time in the weird fiction spheres of this planet, that my name meant a kind of quality rarely found. Yes. Ramsey Campbell said as much, so, fuck, yes, I'm sticking to that. I'd be a fool not to. What kind of asshole would I be if I did not step up to the implicit challenge of Ramsey Campbell's early praise.

Ross E. Lockhart, in the Introduction to *Shout Kill Revel Repeat*: "Scott R. Jones has *arrived*." This was written in the early months of what? 2019? Not so long ago and yet here I sit at the edge of what seems a vast chasm between now and then, swirling with cannabis smoke and delusions, an unfinished novel and another one started lumbering in the depths, several half-finished short stories, I mean, do you know what you are reading, reader. Reader! Wake up, retard!

I'm sorry, I dissemble, I take that back, by way of offering an excuse may I at least mention that it's been a strange and darksome Christmas time here at Stonefish House, a kind of mythic Long Christmas created by Canaduh Post in which we were snowed out all that first week before Christmas. Each day an agitation never knowing if the next we'd be called in and then finally we *are* called in, once, but only to sort the mail to prevent it getting backed up and *not* to deliver because genteel little Victoria shuts down in snow, every year, guaranteed, for three, four days, sometimes a week, a week where you sit at home and now here I sit, dreading tomorrow, because now I know or at least have a very good idea of what awaits me upon my return to the depot! Hermes! May your fleet feet not fail me now! Ba dum tis!

But enough about the day job! Christ. Will there be a balance brought to this shelf of mine. That's my legit question.

Will the past year, two, let's be charitable and call it two and a half how bout, because remember Scott, you were plunking away pretty good on your *sentient ocean births amorphous kaiju/ mother-daughter road trip of discovery novel* in the early months of the pandemic, before Mary Jane really took hold of you by the short and curlies. Goddamn but you smoke too much. Will this period be seen by your biographer as a kind of hibernation period from which the above novel, *She Walks Into The Sea*, and this one, *DRILL*, emerge and if not why the fuck not, Jones?

Why the fuck not.

CAESAR'S THINGS TO CAESAR

Some days on the route I will drift into a kind of waking nightmare wherein I see with an utter clarity usually denied my third eye that my family is currently under attack from multiple assailants in various locations or sometimes the same location, say Stonefish House, for instance, a stranger has come calling as the old murder ballads like to say, and I am not there to prevent the brutality, the horror of it, I am not there to be subjected to it, either, because let's face it, in defense of my wife and children I would go to extreme lengths but come on I'm no Samson, there's little I could do against a determined assailant, and what's more, in my experience as a writer and someone with two years' worth of anatomical study at a massage college, I can imagine, again, with *clarity*, the intricacies of the damage. I have to shake myself out of it, lest some species of fell trance state alight upon my brow, rendering me incapable of work let alone sentient seemings. A glimpse of a kind of bardo of Violence, ruled over by wrathful deities indeed.

One could replace murder with any number of alternate scenarios, all equal in horror in their own way. I see car accidents, my children flying through the air, the angles of their bodies already wrong against a grey sky. I see simple slip and fall accidents in Stonefish House, skulls opening up from the impact with the corner of the faux-marble countertop in the kitchen, some dumb mishap with a blade or boxcutter, misuse of the lawn mower. Bruising and catastrophic blood loss. Limbs turning over and over in the air all Peckinpah era. And the murderers. Always with the murderers. This zone of imagined accident and dire misfortune is surrounded by maniacs who want to get inside and kill everything they see.

The cyclic nature of the horror is also made clear to me in these diurnal walking visions. There is something about the simultaneous rising and falling of blades and blunt instruments that echo the action and intention of the Drill. I observe my own rotating perception, the rhythms of my heartbeat and flow of my breath and understand that understanding destroys the subject. In this way I began to become conscious of the Drill. Suffering powers it forward, sure, but it is simultaneously pulled from that same "direction" by whatever the opposite of Suffering may be. I'm sure there's no way to properly describe such a state. God, maybe. That most loaded of words. But what is a god but the farthest thing from yourself you can imagine?

I'd do what I could against a maniac. Go for the eyeballs and the crotch. Bite and gouge. Break whatever's available, if I've the strength. All things being Empty and Awake, what damage is being done? Go all Magenta Mountain on their ass. Forms changing state, is all. When all is violence, there is no violence.

SOME OF THE THINGS MY FATHER BELIEVES

We've covered the most salient thing already, so far as our endeavors here are concerned, and that is that Raymond Francis Jones, family destroyer and Jehovah's Witness elder, believes in demons. Natch. We are talking fallen angels, kids. Wicked spirit creatures cast down from the heavenly realms to literally bedevil and vex mankind, old-school influencers with whole dominions and powers and principalities over the affairs of men and wouldn't you know, perverts besides! Yes, salacious spiritual beings so horny for human ladies they took physical form back in the day, which is to say pre-Deluge, and they liked it so much that even now, banished to Tartarus, a realm of spiritual darkness as far removed from the light of God as possible, they still hanker after flesh, possessing what forms. That's a demon. They love the flesh so much they figured out how to put it on, like clothes. Do you know what you're reading? What is reading this.

A partial list, then, of other things Ray believes...

Raymond believes that only dedicated and baptized members of his cult will escape with their lives through the ultimate act of war, Armageddon, in which his god Jehovah will direct the armies of heaven against wicked mankind in the greatest slaughter of humans ever known. This is exactly the kind of fireball apocalypticism you're imagining. And yes, if you're reading this you're likely among the dead. Only the best of the best of the Jehovah's Witness crop at the end of History will make it, too. Even a shred of doubt or misgivings about the Watchtower Society, its leadership and policies, a single iota of skepticism and that's it, you're dead at Armageddon same as your rank-and-file worldly sinner type. Understand as well, please, that this is not just my father's belief, it is the belief of every other Jehovah's Witness like him. They look forward to your destruction. You, specifically, and your family and loved ones. When they knock on your doors or send you their shitty little letters in the mail WHICH I should mention your *postie* has to deliver, despite his feelings about the contents, just thought I'd drop that in there as long as we're talking about their proselytizing letter writing campaigns, when they do these things they are imagining you as basically already dead, and particularly if you respond negatively, which is to say *naturally*, to their apocalyptic ravings. They will label you as a Goat, an unrepentant sinner and worthy of imminent destruction by their god, Jehovah.

Ray believes that UFOs and their pilots are demons sent back in time by future-Satan to aid in the war effort against Heaven.

He believes that you should always sleep with your body in a north-south alignment with your head at the north end, in order to align your personal magnetic field with that of the Earth. He doesn't know he believes this, though, as it's one of the myriad little items printed over the years by the cult's publishing arm, the Watchtower Bible and Tract Society of Pennsylvania, in their flagship magazines *The Watchtower: Announcing Jehovah's Kingdom* and *Awake!* and these are, you know, little beliefs, anecdotal bits of faith scattered throughout their entire grifting history that have never been brought up again let alone meditated upon.

He does know and believe, does Ray, that the blood is the life. Like any good vampire, he acknowledges that and affirms it to be true and gospel and he will therefore *not* take a blood transfusion should he require one at some point. Counterintuitive? Oh yes. Perhaps I should call them reverse-vampires. The blood *must* be holy, the blood is the life, so the blood must be "poured out on the ground." A basic misunderstanding of a kosher dietary restriction surrounding ritual sacrifice of animals to Jahweh. As if the ancient Jews knew that the medical use of blood would become commonplace, saving lives. This "blood doctrine" of the Jehovah's Witnesses has killed tens of thousands of them over the decades and honestly, I hope it does for Ray. I really do. That would be chef's kiss.

He believes that his spiritual leaders here on earth, the octo-pope also known as the Governing Body, will rapture just before Armageddon, in order to be transformed, in the twinkling of the eye, mind, transformed into angelic spirit creatures and kitted out for the divine war soon to descend upon all sinful flesh. He believes this act of ultimate war will cleanse the planet of sin and sinners and bring about the ultimate peace, a paradisaical new world. "I saw a new heaven and a new earth for the former things had passed away." He believes, though this is another apocryphal belief he's not aware of, that cosmic rays will somehow figure into this great clearing off of God's enemies. Because think of the clean up! Surely Jehovah will manipulate reality to dispose of billions of human casualties. Surely. Cosmic rays so Ray won't have to feel bad about the most insane and destabilizing-to-reality genocide there ever was.

He believes that the aurora borealis is the clash of demonic and angelic forces in the upper atmosphere. Not related to the UFO phenomena, though. I could never sus the reason, honest-

ly. Ray had a few odd beliefs about spacetime and how things…
work, I guess. Just a very selective type of ignorance built out of
a cult-trained personality and at least a high intelligence. Not
nearly as elevated as I've turned out, but still, up there.

He believes that I have committed an unforgivable sin, that of
becoming dedicated and baptized in service to Jehovah only to
later turn and reject the Bible-based wisdom of the Watchtower
Society and bleah bleah bleah. What else was I to do, Raymond,
when I found out what a shit job you'd done in the faith selec-
tion department for your family, you willfully-ignorant piece of
shit. Fuck. Fuck. Do you know what happened at my baptism,
at the tender age of fourteen, you controlling fuck. Fuck! Fourteen! I couldn't drive, I couldn't drink, I had a demon running
rampant in my hindbrain, but sure, I could dedicate my life to
a publishing company, why not? Yes, I've turned away, toward
the outer darkness. That's my home, you sanctimonious turd of
a man. But my baptism, the actual act of it, the thing that happened then, the omen that should have had me packing my bags
right then and there and leaving Witchtower Land forever, that
slip. A literal slip, Raymond, of my heel on the soft plastic of the
baptismal pool, there along with two other pools on the floor
of BC Place stadium, surrounded by literal tens of thousands
of JWs, I went under. Here's how I described it slantwise in my
story, "A Delicate Spreading," first published in the Silent Mo-
torist Media anthology, *Hymns of Abomination* (2021)…

The summer I turned fourteen I was baptized as a member of
the Sentinel Brethren church. My parents insisted on it, reminding me that as the eldest I had a god-given responsibility to
provide a good example for my younger brother and sister. OK,
but see, that's not entirely true. I make it sound as if baptism
was something I *didn't* want, but I did. Then. Of course I did,

because they did, and I was their good son and a servant of the Most High. So, I went into the pool, sure, just like the three hundred or so eager young Christians gathered on the floor of the rented hockey rink with me. Long line ups for the three prefab swimming pools set up in the middle of the space, all eating their box lunches in the stands around, and cheering each freshly risen servant of God from the water.

But when the pastor in his soaked wife-beater placed his thick arm around my shoulders and made to dip me, I panicked. Sure, I went under, like a good boy. But my foot slipped on the slick surface of the pool bottom as I went down, and as I came *up*, I flailed, a *lot*, and I lashed out with my arms. I somehow managed to grab the side of the pool in an attempt to haul myself out. I panicked, basically. And the weight of my thin teen bod, plus the iron grip I had on the pool edge, well, it was cheap, see? One of those vinyl-sided jobs, you can have one up and half-filled in an hour. Cheap. And that was enough for the side of the pool to buckle. Now, I wasn't so clumsy as to follow the flood of water out of the pool as I half-destroyed it, but yeah, a lot of people got their church shoes wet that day.

I'll tell you what a funny part of this was. My parents were *so keen* to see their eldest, their first-born son, get baptized. Dedicate his life to Jahweh. Make that public declaration of faith in front of all their friends and only the best cultists. They wanted photographs, a record, but for some reason that I've never fully understood, they never made it to the poolside that day for the pictures. Dunking a summer Sentinel convention's worth of souls in tepid hose water takes a while, but you know how these people do things, it's basically an assembly line. Some decrepit old sanctimonious turd from the Sentinel HQ in Brooklyn Heights gets flown in to ask a cordoned-off section of the hockey rink bleachers three rote questions. The questions are answered and then off they go to the locker rooms, all fresh-faced and full of that all too Christian glee, where they change into bathing suits and then it's line up line up get in the water, you young sinners, dip dip dip and out you go, white as snow praise Jesus. Let us gather by the river in the age of automation.

My brother and I, at previous summer conventions, would sit in the stands and quietly whistle that song from the Merrie Melodies cartoon where the construction site guard dog takes care of the little black cat as it engages in high-rise, high-risk shenanigans. You know the one? That whacky mechanical assembly line jazz as the kitten bops along the girders, rides pails down rails to safety. Doot doot doo, doo doodley doot doo, and repeat. So long as our parents didn't hear, we were fine.

They weren't there, somehow, incredibly, but then, that assembly line is quick, right? Barrels along like the hot little holy ticket it is and though my perception of my clearly botched baptismal event seemed to stretch into a kind of nightmare eternity, a closed looping moment of embarrassed fear, in all likelihood it took less than half a minute from entering the pool to exiting it. Not even half a minute. So, my parents missed it, they couldn't get there in time from our seats in the stands. I get it.

I mean, I *wonder* at it, obviously.

Raymond Francis Jones believes I was marked on that day. He believes this because I say so. Half the lies I've told are true.

Raymond Francis Jones believes that my mother will be returned to life and flesh as a kind of divine hermaphrodite once the Paradise New World mentioned above is established. This is called the Resurrection.

SERMON ALL OVER HER FACE

Well, here we are again in the Hour of Power and what have we here but a homily from that bullshitter of bullshitters ("Yours is the best bullshit! [heart emoji]" tweets @NineKeysOthaos), Scott R Jones, this time coming to you live from the Subterranean Caverns of Madness far below the offices of the mighty CFCR, Saskatoon's Community Radio, 90.5 on your FM dial! Tonight! WHAT is the NATURE of REALITY? Friends, what is this mess we are in. My, my. It's a fuckin' pickle is what it is. And so on.

Friends, it only *acts* like the physical world but it's a kind of higher order camouflage. We're more like a *foam* on the surface of a higher-dimensional ocean, a membrane between two illimitable and unknowable spaces. And what lies "below"? Stirring in the depths. We here at the Threshold Church of R'lyeh Risen know and affirm that it is Cthulhu who waits there, dreaming, Lord of the First City, the Dreaming City, many-angled R'lyeh, yes "below" us is the dwelling place of the Divine Organizing Principle of Madness itself and it is by that Principle we seek to align our lives in service of #KeepingItRlyeh and attaining the state of #cthulhusattva.

Nothing but foam, like poet Robbie Q. Telfer said, and all of it Empty and Awake and yet, simultaneously, *also* Hungry, for is that not the First Law of the Universe, supreme and inviolate? Cthulhu knows. That guy's been around.

Do not mistake our affirmation for delusion; there is not a R'lyehian alive who truly in their heart of hearts believes that R'lyeh lies at the bottom of the vast Pacific. Would we not have detected it by now. Don't tell me some enterprising and prank-loving skipper hasn't steered his vessel be it barque or freightliner across those ill-hallowed coordinates, if only for the eldritch shits and giggles. Something would have turned up. They do scans these days, for Dagon's sake.

No, something stirs 'neath the foam, still, friends and supplicants. In the depths of matter, beyond the form of mind, lie great sleeping entities of such power and potency they blast the supplicant to vapour and fleshy string, their eyes boiling in their sockets. Proper evil gods from beyond the rim of Time and Space, and I don't have to sell it much more, do I? You've joined my cult by now already, why else would you be here, inputting this text into your brain, where, as I've stated elsewhere, is where you *think!* I mean, my god, you've some real *chutzpah*, I'll give you that. The stones on you. Bet you don't bother wearing a mask on public transit, either, you trailblazer.

THE HANGED MAN GIGGLES

I visited the International Headquarters of Jehovah's Witnesses in New York City, New York, when I was, oh let's see, somewhere around nineteen years of age or so, fresh outta high school, and since the Witchtower likes to discourage JW spawn to go in for that higher education in Satan's wicked old system, I was instead eagerly considering a career in either graphic design or as a radio personality. I'd have to record Christmas ads and promo spots for radio work, Ray kept bringing up, good elder that he is. This guy, who was a glorified stockboy at the Shoppers Drug downtown was giving me career advice, heavily cult influenced advice, natch. You know. Somewhere in the Body of God there's a layer of tissue where Scott stuck out for the DJ gig against the wishes of his parents, oh boy and things are different there, lemme tellya. But there's our Ray, way back in I want to say late '93, early '94, there he is hemmin and hawing over the three thousand red Canadian dollars it would cost to put his foist boin son through three months of vocational college "graphic design" school. The fact that I managed to use that meager desktop publishing training to survive into adulthood with some half decent logo pilot and newspaper mock-up gigs is the amazing thing, here. I should have gone to a real university, is what I should have done.

Imagine what I could have done with that, with an education.

There I am nineteen in Montreal visiting childhood friend by name of Lance, fantastic name and boy he knows it, and since New York is a mere bus ride away we get up a bunch of fresh-faced young Quebecois Jay Dubs to rent a bus and make a visit to World Headquarters which at these coordinates on the space-time supersphere is in Brooklyn, New York. So *that's* fun. That's a fun way for young folx to spend a weekend. The ways I used to think, I mean, my god. I recall I had with me some dated book of pulp scifi, maybe something from Harrison's *Stainless Steel Rat* series, who the fuck knows, my tastes were what they were and I make no apologies, and the Jay Dub girl in the seat next to me fell asleep on my shoulder which put me in a horrible state vis-à-vis the smell of her hair and my perfectly organic response. I was wishing I had something more substantial than an ACE paperback to fold over my lap, if you know what I'm saying.

So we get to New York and the Headquarters where my chub graciously subsides because it takes less than an hour for it to sink in that Ray had raised his kids in a cult. I mean, the place *smelled* like them. Control. By their smell shall ye know them, so sayeth the desert prophet Alhazred, he who penned the Necro-nomicon available to readers now on Amazon in a thousand different versions, clearly these *are* the End Times and the Old Ones shall rise and forth*with!* But yeah, I think my nose knew before most of the rest of me but that? That was just the start, stepping through those doors and touring the facilities, seeing how the Bethel JWs lived (that's what they call the place, no matter where it is, currently as of this writing in late February 2023 Bethel is located in Warwick, New York) and isn't that your next tip off, a name like *Bethel*, I mean do they even know what it means, beth *el*, "the Place of El", El being a proto-Mes-opotamian creator deity that ruled over a pantheon, of which their much beloved Jehovah was a lower tier storm god, like a fertile crescent style Thor, basically. JHVH-1. Fuck. FUCK. Sometimes the hate for this organization and the years and various potentials I had in my youth, wasted and denied, whole possible realities gone to dust and simulated slurry, it all has a tendency to pile up against the back of my eyes and I bleed dark light all over the keyboard, it's a goddamn nightmare and no mistake. I'm not even typing this the keys depress at a glance and my eyes are chattering in their sockets like ben wa balls, that hard, dark light falling in rays upon the Ray-narrative we've got going here.

I can feel the curse working.

I wonder can you.

TITANS GO

O h that wretched day of days, the day I met the sapper. Grey February day, heavy mail, heavy parcels; I am physically ragged and mentally exhausted by noon. Greg M. was his name, he revealed when I eventually asked, and a fine strapping beast of a man he appeared, grown like an oak, thick around the temples as if to hold in all them ultra-terrestrial brains, arms straight out of communist propaganda art, hands like spades. He was a fresh face on the route, a man I'd never seen before but there he sat on the bench outside the Belfry Theatre, there in the little town square with the gazebo and the wishing tree. I had just delivered another box of lubricant to the sex shop on Fernwood and was heading back to my postie van when Greg M. called out to me. "Hey. Wait a minute, Mr. Postman," he said, and do you know he even put a little tuneful lilt in it so that I couldn't help but feel the beginning of the earworm, burrowing, burrowing. Marvelletes in the brain. Like a fool, I responded. I respond to anyone who asks something of me on the route, as it wouldn't do to make Canaduh Post look bad to the public. Anti-social or what have you. The masks we wear.

"This your job, then," he said. "Bespoke information and product dispersal? Every day the same thing. At least you get to do it in paradise." This is a common misconception folx have regarding my town, with its proximity to sea and sky, mountains and parks, its genteel Victorian ways and casual racism. *Paradise*, of course, being a Persian word for "a walled garden or enclosure", ready for harvesting.

"At least it's not raining," I say.

"We must imagine Sisyphus happy, is that it?"

"Something like that, sure. Why not. Is there something I can help you with, sir." I call everyone I meet on the route *sir*. Or *ma'am*, as the case may be. It's exactly as irritating as it's meant to be but Greg M. seems unaffected. Greg M. cares not for my frivolous way. He chuckles, scratches at his full beard absently.

"It's more the other way round," he says.

"That so?"

"Indeed. What's your biggest fear?"

"This your opener, then?"

"It gets right to the point, I find."

"Aneurysm. While at work. The idea that I could die out here, with these ridiculous bright shoes on, because my blood decided to clot just right and that clot headed for my brain or something else just as vital and I'm ended, while at work. While rolling this boulder up the hill again."

Greg M. chuckles again, stretches his tree trunk arms wide and yawns. "You'd have to get very right with a lot of things very quickly, I suppose. My gosh, but you'd never see your family again. Your sweet wife, your intelligent, compassionate spawn."

"If you're selling something, I ain't buying, sir."

"Let me show you something first…" he says, then reaches into an inner pocket of his Patagonia jacket. When his hand comes out he is holding a marvel.

"This is the Drill," he says. "Or rather, a five D model of the Drill. I had Wee Frederick print this one up. Do you recognize it." The device, sitting in his palm like a treat, turns in and out of reality at a dazzling rate. You can see the chips and chunks flying out of the Body of God in a bright prismatic rain around the base of it. I'm ensorcelled. It's a small miracle and it brings a tear to my eye.

"That is the Drill, as you say."

"You've seen it before, then?"

"Portions thereof. Why do you have this thing. Where can I get one."

"Ask the archons. They grow them in solution, like crystals. For all we know, there are an infinite number of Drills. But for our purposes here today, this model of our own will do."

It was at this point that I asked his name, his occupation. And so I learned of sappers, those who work to keep the Drill boring into the Body of God, in search of what organs, what meat. Don't fuck about, there's real drillers in the house now. Puff on that mary, hope for the best. I stuck out my bottom lip, withdrew a handkerchief from my back pocket and wiped at my weeping eyemeat.

"You can put that away now," I say. "Don't need the good people of Victoria seeing something they can't unsee, now, do we?"

"No, we do not," Greg M. says with another chuckle. A chuckler, that most hated breed. He deposits the Drill model back within the folds of his jacket and I get the impression that even his clothes are bigger on the inside. Pockets of holding like infinite petals unfurling from the lining. I glimpse, briefly, documents and vials, idols peeking out from the darkness there. Amazed and fearful, I realize I've a powerful need to shit myself; I clench and shiver, momentarily unmanned, made beast-like.

Recovering, I sit down next to him. The back of my knees flow like warm water. "I wrote someone like you, once." I am thinking of course of Gregor Makarios in *Stonefish*, that garrulous ultrarich weirdo with the sasquatch obsession, who fought a monstrous bear and could make food out of thin air, like a goddamn king of the fairies.

"Not like me," Greg M. says. "Never like me. I'm the closest thing to an angel you're likely to meet, Jones." He knows my name. But then of course he does, and my wife and children, too. And you, reader. It's easy to do, I learn eventually, when you exist outwith the spacetime supersphere the way sappers do. Knowledge is the original sin and it's cheap as muck, safe as houses.

"An angel." I breathe in deeply, the little sacs in my chest filling with gas as if that makes sense. How a February day can unravel with just the right threads pulled, I mean, my god. Horrendous. "Well, that's sad."

"We'd like to offer you a job," he says.

"I have a job. A calling, even, in service of Thrice-Great Hermes, who is my god and my saviour. I couldn't survive this job without him, and the love of my children, and a good woman. *We'd like to offer you a job*, I mean, the balls on you."

"Your god is a logo on the side of a truck. It's embroidered on your rainshell there, for fuck's sake pardon my French. Fuck. Sapper is a real *career*, brother. Union's strong, too. We keep the world going round! All training provided, hazard pay, and *benefits?* Don't get me started. You get rich incidentally, better than time travel for lining the pockets."

"I had noticed yours."

"Nice, right? Special issue. What did you think we dressed in, standard uniform? Naw, brother, there are *layers* and *levels* to this jacket I can't get into about right now but then you'll know soon enough because as previously mentioned, we'd like to offer you a job."

"What's your drug use policy."

"Please."

"When I'm not working I'm busy putting a curse on Ray Jones."

Greg M. is momentarily taken aback. Black landotter eyes glisten and grow wide. "You don't say! That was *not* in your file."

"Oh you wanna talk about files. Care to guess how many persons I have rattling round in here behind these baby blues? C'mon, take a fucking stab at it. *File*, singular, I mean Jesus backpacking Christ."

"We might be able to help with that. At least take this brochure," he says. Union propaganda. And like that, our conversation is over and my first exposure to the world of the sapper has closed like a fist over my mind. To say I was obsessed. Greg M. has since informed me that he knew in that moment I would take the position on offer (a kind of archivist/gunner/medic "career") by the slight eagerness which he detected in the aura around my fingers as I took the brochure, but I'll leave him to tell that if he wants, the dear. Long live the fucking Sapper's Union.

TEMPUS FUGGEDABOUTIT

For a significant period during my Calgary sojourn, hey folks, y'all remember the cowboy hat? Yeehaw. On a steel horse I did ride and her name was Old Paint, a grey 1981 Subaru GL done up in black, white and silver camo. Old Paint's cool '80s digital speedometer was busted, reading a big green phosphorescent zero at all speeds, so while me and my fellow occultists bombed around the city in this abomination, we fantasized that thanks to Buddhist PureLand™ Tech woven into the very fabric of the vehicle by rogue Subaru engineers, it effectively remained still while the Universe moved around it. An early understanding of the Drill, perhaps? Who the fuck knows, let's be honest.

Any old way, for that significant period referenced, I was also deeply into temporal workings within my magic framework. Hermes, teach me augury, knowledge of which you bargained away from your half-brother, Apollo. So, peep the settings, friendos. A lot of isolation tank sessions up at the uni, death posture yogas at auspicious hours, dream journalling, and so forth. My daimon was enlisted to harvest threads of the temporal substream specifically linked to My Outcome and so I came to experience visions and dreams that held that ineffable but undeniable quality of Future Memory. In this way I saw the heavily implied existence of my future daughter as clear as I'm looking at you now. Hi there. We named her Meridian because that's what she was called in the vision. I saw, too, the events that would lead up to meeting her mother, getting closer to the moment every day, like approaching a far distant mirror, a threshold in time. Look at me, a sitcom waiting to happen, laugh track held breathlessly in anticipation. All dead voices, you know, in those laugh tracks. Dead voices, speaking a dead language, backwards, several octaves lower than is average.

Synchronicities multiply and fastbreed down out of the corners as I type so I have to be quick. The spoor of a passing boreworm colony or just my own fractured soul through that scanner darkly like the brother Phillip K. Dick said? I can't know, but my typing speed was once clocked at 93 wpm and why would I lie about that. Kerouac knew the world to be Empty and Awake, I read that once in *Tricycle: The Buddhist Review*. How can I go wrong. Reels and reals, all together for the meantime, a great ream of virtual paper, as infinite as I care to make it, on to which I spill digital ink. My kung-fu is only so strong, by which I mean there's a limit to what the physical body is capable of, no matter what your hentai tells you, kids. Keep that in mind, along with the First Law of the Universe which is? Let me hear it at the back of the class now.

EVERYBODY HUNGRY. That's right.

MONSTER MAGNET

I was a teenage sasquatch hunter. Yes, while being a demon-possessed young Jehovah's Witness, what do you think, that I *don't* contain multitudes? My hyperchakras spin rings round yours, bub, don't start with me.

Mostly this was an excuse to go hiking with like-minded Jay Dub buddies in the hills surrounding Victoria. Hiking was very popular among the young Jay Dubs in those days for some reason. There was rumoured activity in the Sooke Hills, for instance, screams in the night and upset dogs, that kind of thing. I myself documented tracks in snow in the Shawnigan Lake area. A homeowner at the edge of a development with nothing but forest beyond reported to my hotline—yes, I had a hotline, back in the day—that there had been a sasquatch in his yard only the night before, that it had been sleeping underneath their deck and must have been startled by something because it awoke, banged around a bunch, upsetting equipment and the dog, and then lit out across their backyard into a gorge beyond where a wintry creek straight out of C. S. Lewis flowed.

Now before you start lighting into me you first have to realize that this is damp, thick west coast of Canada snow. None of your fluffy prairie drifts here. Even full-grown male humans don't sink too far and these tracks, these big, crooked fuckers for you *know* the left foot had a deformity, what hoaxer would think to do that, but never mind the crooked foot let's talk about the *depth* that these tracks sunk to. I'm talking about enough weight to the thing to depress the snow right to the bare ground beneath, with the little pale green shoots of next year's grass peeking through. We estimated at least two thousand pounds to do it. We dropped cinder blocks to test and the homeowner did the rough math. I trusted him.

But that's not all, oh know. You know that little lip of snow that gets kicked up by the front of your boot as you walk through the stuff? You can see it in human tracks all the time because of how our feet fall and flex. Now, this thing or whatever it was, as it exited its temporary nest beneath this fine upstanding Canadian man's home, where he keeps his big screen and an impressive collection of vintage pornography, I mean it's the *proximity* that bothers and horropilates, how often do these things come right up to our threshold and yea we know them not for what they are. Anyway, it left such tracks, tracks with no little lip above the toes. Listen. I figured it out. I did.

See, we've been encountering wild humanoid things in the bush since at least Gilgamesh. It's just what happens when Man enters the Forest, the Wood, the Jungle, the Swamp. The Wild. We go in and somehow, for some occult reason lost to the deep prehistory of our ragged ass species, some buried ancestral memory jutting from our consciousness like a span of shining bone, somehow we hallucinate or en-vision or otherwise perceive... a sasquatch. The chaos of Nature holds up a mirror to the camper, the hunter, the logger, the hippie and somehow the reflection comes back hairy, a titan of the Primordial First Ages, when our current laws did not apply, darksome and terrible. A sasquatch.

What I'm saying is that with all the reports that have come in from humans living in liminal, wild spaces, of strange wild men or apes, giants in the earth, you would *think*, wouldn't you, that we'd have caught one by now. But no. No, that's not a thing that has ever happened. So, what are people seeing, then? On the logging road, across the lake, under their red cedar deck?

They have higher-order *camouflage*. Or maybe they *are* higher-order camouflage for something far stranger. Just real enough to leave tracks in the mud or snow, just ontologically porous enough to fade out of our portion of the simulation, this steamy hank of the Body of God, as if it had never been. A myth, a legend, all-time social distancing world champeen, give it up for the bigfoot.

I mean, it's suspicious, isn't it. I looked at those tracks in the snow and noted how far apart they were; by the time the beast was really moving for the gorge, you know hitting that stride, the Keep On Truckin' vibe, well the distance between the tracks easily doubled our own, and I'm a six-foot man. Tracks which, again, depressed the wet coast snowpack to the floor of the forest. Tracks with no little lip of dusted snow sticking out the front like a claw, which meant that the thing was tall enough to lift its feet straight up while running. I can't imagine how it might have looked, there in the moonlight. Like something out of Machen or Blackwood, all raised knees and dripping hair, a strange light in the eyes. This was before everyone had video security lacing every foot of their property, so all we have today, in the deep archives, are the photos I took of the thing's tracks. Explain then, please, how these tracks were made. Look and see the way there are no other tracks in the snow around them, human or otherwise. Imagine yourself, however tall you are, putting on large fake feet, eighteen inches long on the uncrippled foot, hauling extra weight to make that good good impression, and making those strides, those phenomenal strides in two feet of wet snowpack, all while managing to lift your feet straight up and down. Remember, no lip, no snow lip at the toes. Impossible.

Or how about this, instead. They live outwith the spacetime supersphere but at a different vibrational frequency to our world, and the world of the sappers, the hyperworlds of the Drill. They live outwith but can impress upon the material of the simulation, integrating with it, distorting it at some fundamental level, so that reality conforms to the incursion, long enough to see a hairy ape-like thing visible for mere moments before fading into literal non-existence. They're just real enough to leave tracks but even the tracks are anomalous. It's like they can *make* them but they don't do it *properly*. They miss the little things, like the little lip of snow and other spoor. Goddamn maddening, I don't know how your regular full-time sasquatch hunter does it, day in and day out. I've written about this extensively in *Stonefish* and elsewhere and friends, I do believe and stand by it. The sasquatch—king of the cryptids, you can keep your Mothmen and ogopogos—is the basic incursion of archonic elements into this seeded reality. Mark me.

I would dearly love to see a bigfoot, though. I love them, oh my god. It would probably kill me to see one for more than a few seconds which when you think about it is a nice limit to the experience that they build into it. I feel that those few seconds, well, they would complete me in some profound way that I can't even speak of because it is beyond language. I'd probably wet myself.

At the Royal British Columbia Museum archive, still a teenager, mind you, I was privileged to view their collected sasquatch material samples: plaster casts of footprints from all over BC and Washington State, Oregon. Alberta, even. Little boxes of hair samples. Methodically labelled bags of dung. Make of this what you will. The sasquatch hunter, author and mayor of Harrison Hot Springs, John Green, had put me on to the archive's existence in a letter and so I showed up at the front desk, asked to see it and they escorted me right on up, like something out of a young adult fiction where jocular scientists readily accept young urchins into the hallowed halls of learning for their edge yew ma cation, good god. This was a thing that happened and to say it feels scripted even now these many decades later, well. Well. Make of *that* what you will.

IN LESS THAN AN HOUR THE PLANE WILL BE LEAVING

The photo of my greasy spawn is perhaps one of the nicest I've taken. They are fresh faced and smiling, the boy with his arm around the girl's shoulder, apples in their cheeks and happiness in their blue blue eyes, hair askew. They are standing at the bottom of the stairs to the back porch, having just spent a manic twenty minutes jumping in the trampoline we bought for them when we took possession of the house. I am standing above them when I take the picture, a step or two above, just enough to give the photo that good angle, like something you'd see in an advertisement. I have some small talent with photography, which I credit to my wife who taught me.

At the sign shop they are a bit non-plussed by my request; I don't bother explaining. I want a life-sized cutout of my kids, printed in full colour on a piece of white corrugated plastic. I want one and I get one, a week later. Squinting, it's like they're standing right there in the sign shop. Capitalism is wonderful.

I've premade the stand. It's waiting in the back of the van, which is a rattletrap 1992 Mitsubishi Delica L300. In goes the cutout now. Later that night, I drive to Ray's condominium complex. Takes far less time to drive than it does to walk, I'm barely three songs in to *Infest the Rat's Nest* when I pull up in the street and kill the lights. It's cold so I keep the engine's heater running for a few minutes before heading out. I'm nervous, as it's late and there's likely to be security about. I extract the plastic children and their stand from the van and hustle up the driveway. There are lights on in the condos, shadows at windows. Ray's place is just ahead and as I turn into his short drive, already scouting the cement for a smooth, level spot, I am startled by a rattle at the window above. A bird? No. My father there, most likely, or his woman.

I freeze, waiting. I am reminded of a time in my teens when I developed a small penchant for night stalking. Which is to say I enjoyed sneaking out at night in dark clothing and walking around the neighbourhood by way of backyards and wild areas of which there were plenty around Glen Lake Road. The why of it is lost on fifty-year-old me; if I had to guess I'd say there was a thrill just to be able to do it. The more things change. Hop fences, hug walls, find cover. Like a fucking cat burglar. Only one night I turned a corner at a neighbour's garage and saw across the cul-de-sac the shape of my father, crouched by the Douglas fir in the backyard, right in the middle of my bee-line to the window I'd left open to my bedroom. Like a skinny ape he squatted there, occasionally picking at something in the grass at his feet. The more I watched the shape the more utterly convinced I became that the man had found me out and was lying in dark parental wait in the shadows at the base of that tree. I waited for hours. His patience was epic and I became filled with a kind of horror at it. But come the first timid streaks of dawn I realized I'd been terrified of a shrub, natch. Tricks of the night lighting and perspective and my unusual vantage point all contributed to the false perception. I unfreeze, and place the stand, insert tabs A into slots B and there they stand: The grandchildren. On the back of the cutout I write in black Sharpie the words *SEAN IS 10* and *MERIDIAN IS 8*. Ray has only met his grandson the once, when he was a newborn in the hospital, his granddaughter never.

A number of things could happen at this point, I think as I retreat from the scene. One possibility is that they go for a walk or leave the house on foot for some reason and spot the cutout then, a slightly traumatic outcome. Another is they leave the house by car, which involves opening the garage door; seeing the plastic chillens may give him a start. Dare I hope for a heart attack or some equally devastating medical reaction. A fall, at the very least? Ideally, age being what it is, they don't notice until they back the vehicle out of the space, and end up running the cutout over. That would be perfect. I'll never know how it went down, exactly, but several weeks later I do receive a letter, forwarded from our old address. What, like I'm going to tell him where I live now?

"Scott," dear old pop begins. "Thanks for the picture of the grandkids. Will develop a 4x5 photo and keep it in an album. Son, we have both chosen different paths in life. Please stop your harassing behaviour toward us. – Dad."

Classic Ray. Takes away my human rights (to worship as I like, to have the family I want) then claims harassment when I lash back. Note the passive aggression, the "I've turned your evil around, boy" stance. Note the narcissism. *Different paths in life,* I mean, my god. He is daring me to continue.

Lucky for him.

TYPES OF POSTMEN

There's the Wiry Little Guy. Far more of these than you'd expect. The WLG runs hot, never wears the long pants no matter what the weather, and moves fast. They don't talk much and are always, by dint of superior skills or deals with mail demons, somehow ahead of you, stacking up their time values like it's nobody's business. The WLG can be found wearing some species of sports watch that tracks their every move and flex. Shorter than average, often bald or balding, and rippling with lean muscle. A gum chewer prone to giving every situation the side eye. Some Wiry Little Guys smoke like chimneys but most tend toward Athleticism. Particularly loud when strike action becomes imminent.

Then there's the Large Fellow. The Large Fellow comes in two varieties, the Garrulous Fun Guy and the Dour Mountain. The GFG Large Fellow is a chipper horror, all *good morning*s and *don't work too hard, buddy* and is best avoided, although due to their outsized personality and body, this can be difficult to do, particularly if you're unlucky enough to have one working nearby, say at a case next to yours or on the other side of the aisle, for their hyperchakra field is as expansive as they are and it is all one can do to erect enough wards on your side of the case to prevent entanglement. Hyperchakra bleedthrough is a real thing no matter what those clowns in Ottawa think. I've been advocating for proper sorcerous containment protocols to the union *and* management since 2012. Some of the auras on the people who walk in here every morning would make a serial killer blanch. Anyway. The Dour Mountain Large Fellow is often found complaining about the workload and is first to whine when conditions deteriorate. The Dour Mountain is rarely wrong about this, though; they are a good barometer for stress levels and increased labour in the workplace. Never dressed for the weather. Bears all things with a half-assed philosophy about the world. Sighs loudly and often.

The Lady Postman is a relative newcomer to the postal service, given our long and largely male-dominated history. I don't know when Canaduh Post opened up the sorting floor to women and assigning them walks, as it was before my time, but then not *too* much before my time. They are often Wiry Little Guys or Dour Mountains but mainly gravitate toward the Athletic. If your Lady Postman is approaching retirement, say after thirty years in the service which is not an unrealistic number, I'm told, this Athleticism veers toward the haggish: tired eyes, hollowed cheeks, and a sun-bleached frizziness to the hair. Younger Lady Postmen can be attractive in a sporty way but the stress of the job takes its inevitable toll. Often dressed in the brightest yellows and blues, the Lady Postman is given to gales of laughter and a certain boy's club feel to their interactions. They can do the job, they know it, and want you to know it as well.

Next up are the Stoners and the Punks, working folx with enough energy at the end of the day to actually engage in a lifestyle other than postman. Envied and feared, these are often younger postmen, naturally athletic and trim from their habits whether that be the mosh pit or the skate park. Both types keep to themselves at the depot and rarely take part in social interactions. Not particularly diligent or possessed of a good work ethic, the Stoner is competent enough to complete a route but will bring mail back at the end of the day. The Punk is more militant about their route and is often displeased when returning from time off to find the chaos left by a relief postman and will complain loudly and uselessly to any who will listen. Punks are known agitators and the loudest on the picket line when the contract is up for renewal and the Mothercorp is doing what mother corpses everywhere do, which is pile up the dead.

The Casual. Also known as the Relief Postman. These are the manic hummingbirds of the depot, flitting from route to route as needed to fill empty spots left by vacationing or sick regular postmen. As if to spite their name, the Casual radiates confusion and despair, because for them the job is one of eternal catch-up and fall-behind. It is a hellish position to find oneself in as a postman and one I occupied for many years as I came up in the ranks at Canaduh Post. My profoundest sympathies lie with the Relief Postman and Relief Lady Postman, for theirs is a pure tragedy of a working life. I myself was often reduced to tears while on a relief walk, overcome with the madness inherent to the job. It is only once a Relief Postman rises in the union rankings to a point where they can bid successfully on, gasp, a walk of their very own, does the nightmare finally end. With a walk of one's own, one can drill deep into the gnosis of the territory and *Learn It*. The postman tames the madness and imposes his own order upon the route. It's an honourable profession and an exacting one. We hold Chaos back from the better elements of society and thanklessly manage this sacred, bespoke informational flow that feeds your world, strokes your privilege, provides you with coupons, vouchers, and the next special offers.

And we are, all of us, whores. Walking the streets for money, we don't care if it's wrong or if it's right, like The Police sang that one time.

Or, if you want to look at it another way, we are cells, mere tendrils each according to our type of a great virtual Logos, a postal Leviathan with many eyes, many limbs, many heads, and all of it writhing, writhing in a very specific kind of pleasurable torment for make *no* mistake it is. a tough. gig. It is not easy physical work, this postal service, it is exercise, sustained for hours at a time, a forced march with weights on. The postie is ridden by Hermes, this I know and affirm and believe, and to be ridden by any godform is draining on the body and the mind. This is why, in the *Postie's Prayer to Hermes*, the supplicant requests in addition to the physical gifts bestowed upon him also to be added "an elevated mind, and a light mood" in order to better accomplish the day's Sisyphean task with the minimum of mental strain. Who can say if this works as intended, magically speaking? All I can say is that at the end of a strenuous day I often find myself feeling refreshed, somehow, and ready to write or interact authentically with my family. That reads more psychotic than I mean it to, but I stand by it.

Understand that when you see a postie walking their route, you are seeing only the higher-order camouflage of the Mothercorp entity, the Canaduh Post gestalt being, an egregore of the old school, embedded in time and manifesting as a crown corporation in ultimate service to the King of England. Hermes bless my weary soul, I and all my fellow posties are merely the tip of the feeler, a little suction cup on the squiggly end of a tentacle. That's me, a real sucker.

GOD IS A MEMETIC ORGANISM

God is a memetic organism and its name is JHVH1. All Jehovah's Witnesses worldwide have been colonized by this entity to a greater or lesser extent, each according to how porous they are, how deeply the JHVH1 algorithm can bore into their bodymind. He gives to each what they are able to bear, First Corinthians ten verse thirteen. It activates as a hyperchakra that feeds off the subtle body of the victim and ensures behaviours that help the entity spread. That is the basic viral mechanism. This mechanism has been so effective, in fact, that currently the JHVH1 entity is a viral guest in the minds and hearts of over eight million human hosts. When Charles Taze Russell, the founder of the cult way back inna day, like the eighteen hundreds, friends, when he created Jehovah, the early prototype of JHVH1, how could he have known what it would mutate into nearly two hundred years later? That poor, deluded bible salesman and publishing magnate. What a colossal scam the Watchtower Bible and Tract Society of Pennsylvania has been, from the very start. Ol' Chucky T was deep into Pyramid Mysticism and a half-assed proto-Baptist prophetic Kabbalah-lite number mysticism, with which he cobbled together his End Times end dates and so on. Only the finest snake oil for the early Bible Students, a tradition that continued as they morphed into what eventually results in the Jehovah's Witnesses you see standing on your doorstep or by their ubiquitous magazine carts in every major city. Do not engage with these, they are the tip of the cult knife and can give you a good knick for your trouble; that's how the Jehovah-beast gets into you.

What are the symptoms of viral colonization by JHVH1, you may reasonably ask. Be alarmed, for they are many and multiform. Mental illness, isolation, thought control, emotion control, erosion of the Id, ego bloating, loss of facial hair in males, and loss of individuation in females. Suicide. Death by refusal to accept a blood transfusion. Severe menstrual cramping. Loveless marriages. A certain shine to the eyes. Cankers. Sleepwalking. Pornography addiction. Alcoholism. Sexual perversion. Child sexual abuse, a rampant issue within the body of the church and yet to be adequately addressed by authorities in charge of the well-being and safety of our nation's young ones.

The Jehovah's Witness victim mutates on the fly while under the influence of pure, uncut JHVH1, the brain deforming under the ontological pressure of this upstart Jewish thunder god made cosmic and supreme by the vagaries of history and cult antagonism. This is why the Watchtower Bible and Tract Society insists that all rank-and-file Jehovah's Witnesses attend meetings at their local Kingdom Hall not once, but two times a week, in addition to a rigorous course of home bible study, which is to say, self-indoctrination. All good Jay Dubs need their medicine and they need it on the regular.

Understand that when two fresh-faced young Jehovah's Witnesses appear at your door of a Saturday morning, you are not looking at two individuals. What you are seeing is a viral node of the JHVH1 memetic totality, being expressed in four-dimensional space through the medium of the host, or, in the case being considered here, hosts. The voice, when it comes, comes not from the hosts, but from Outside themselves, though it is modulated by human tongue and human cognition. Mark thirteen verse eleven. Russell, aforementioned, and the subsequent leaders of the Watchtower Society over the decades, have dressed a monster, a kind of higher-conceptual vampire that lives in the noösphere, they have captured and bound this thing and dressed it in human rags, given it a semblance and a terrible, thirsting agency in the world.

And what wonders it has wrought by its thirst. Remember that JHVH1 aka Jehovah, Jehovah God, the Almighty Jehovah and Lord of Hosts got its start as Yahweh, a minor storm deity in a large early Mesopotamian pantheon. The Jewish Thor, with the center of its puny cult at Mount Sinai. And it is still that god-thing, all these millennia later. Yahweh, Jahweh, Jah, Tetragrammeton, YHVH, JHVH1, the bastard still revels in blood up to the bridles of the war horses, swarms of locusts, and famine. Look how it leeches off its hosts, feel the subtle suck and pull as JHVH1 slips its proboscis deep into their spines. It wants your vital fluids, it longs to sip and sip and sip, and being memetic in nature, its thirst is *infinite*. And so, its wonders. See and be amazed.

Tens of thousands of Jehovah's Witnesses dead because JHVH1 demands that its hosts abstain from blood and so, when accident and illness befall them as it must all flesh, they refuse the proper medical care. They even have a little card that instructs emergency room staff about this prohibition, should the afflicted JW be unconscious. Should a JW find themselves in dire straits, medically, they can expect a visitation from a special appendage of the JHVH1 entity, a small group of regional elders that call themselves the HLC or Hospital Liaison Committee. These ghouls descend on the victim and hospital staff alike in order to ensure that no whole blood is used. Like the Pharisees before them, these HLCs can make allowances for *parts* of blood, say only a percentage of white cells, or just platelets, or fractionated blood. Basically you can have everything that makes up the sandwich but you can't have the sandwich. This is the task of the Hospital Liaison Committee, not to service your spiritual needs as you lay dying, but to ensure you don't accept the sandwich, the blood transfusion that could save your life. If you die, you die, and that's what the Resurrection is for, after all. They arrange for the deaths of thousands each year. And the doctors, the hospital staff, nurses, none of them know that that's what's going on, they're lied to and think a visit from the HLC is akin to a visit from a priest. Spiritual succor is what it's painted as but it's no such thing, it's vampirism at its core. The blood is the life, see. The blood is the life.

Untold thousands of child abuse victims, because of course the environment fostered by the JHVH1 creature creates the ideal hunting ground for pedophiles. The Watchtower Society keeps a detailed secret database of child abusers which it does not share with authorities. JHVH1 likes child sacrifice and the ruination of the innocent and cannot let the supply of same diminish, hence these horrific policies. See: Two Witness Rule.

Broken families across the globe in their hundreds of thousands. The Watchtower, with their extreme shunning policies and mentally abusive doctrines, destroy families on the regular. Right now, somewhere in your town, a Judicial Committee of three or sometimes more Jehovah's Witness elders are meeting to determine the fate of one of their congregants at the Kingdom Hall. They are, even now, preparing to cut this person off from the only support and social network they have ever known, for arbitrary reasons handed down by a pack of white American ghouls living in upstate New York, their every need and desire catered to. Some poor woman or man but let's face it, this destruction of all someone has known falls more often to the sisters, some poor individual is going to lose everything—family, close friendships, siblings, their parents—and be plunged into depression, isolation, and anxiety and why? Because they had consensual sex with another adult. Or questioned the policies of the Governing Body. Or read apostate material. Or masturbated. Smoked a joint. Had too much to drink. Lied to their spouse. Could be anything, that's the point. They'll get you on something, once they put their minds to it. And this Judicial Committee, these *judges?* They're window washers and janitors, glorified stock boys down at the Home Depot or Shoppers Drug, insurance salesmen. That's the day job. The night job, the real *shadow* work, well that's the Committees, and you can bet your cult-softened ass that there's a percentage of these barely-educated bozos who get their freak on to all the prurient details when its sexual immorality brought the Divine Fist of JHVH1 down on your unsuspecting head. Yes, these creepy old men love to hear all the details, have been known to hash over a rape or sexual assault claim for hours with the teary victim, re-opening the wounds made by the original assailant! Ah, good times of a summer evening for these Good Old Boys of God. These are the real perks of the job, which, perhaps not surprisingly, they do without pay. That's right, not a bit of compensation from the Watchtower Society for advancing its interests out in the world, so there's got to be some gravy somewhere one can dip a ladle in. That gravy is some poor young thing begging for mercy as you dangle her indiscretions over her, for the spiritual health of the congregation of course.

CHAPTER ABOUT MOM DYING

I was living in Calgary with a sassy zaftig brunette named Heidi when my mom's cancer aggressively returned, this time manifesting in her lungs and spine. They should have cut the breast off when they had the chance and I'm sure Ray had something to do with that. They thought they got it all but clearly they did not. Before too many months passed she was put into hospice care. No, you're not getting her name; I've blacked it out before and by god I will do so again, many times. She's mine, you hear. This curse is for her, in many ways, many *real* and authentic ways, this curse to destroy the man who destroyed her family after her death. Here's looking at you, kid. I've done me momma proud.

Phone calls to my mom while I was living in Calgary went like this. First, I would speak with Ray, who I still called dad at the time. He would provide the emotional context, often weeping would give way to enforced chipperness and cult bonhomie, which required patient deflection on my part. Then a doctor or doctors would come on the line to tell me, in layman's terms, natch, how she was doing, what drugs she was on for the pain, and how long they expected her to last. Christmas was coming up and folks always seemed to hang on for Christmas. Well gosh, I hate to tell you this, Doc, I'd say, but my folks don't celebrate the Christmas holidays, nope. Still, comes the reply, we expect her to hang on for quite a while as she's possessed of a strength we rarely see. Well, that's my mom, I'd say. Then they'd put her on the line and we'd talk through the morphine haze until she fell asleep, most nights, and it's no one's business but ours what we spoke about.

Her last night, though, I could hear the change in her voice, that missing thing sitting in behind her words that told me, clear like the bell that tolls, that she was not long for the world, that she was preparing to pass beyond the shadow wall of consciousness and into the hyperworlds of the Drill and I became sore afraid. The doctors couldn't hear it, Ray couldn't or refused to hear it, and the bastard even insisted that I *not* get in my car within the hour to begin the overnight drive to Victoria, that I should stay and enjoy my "holidays" with Heidi, to come out instead in the New Year. This is how he remonstrated with me; this is the manner in which he protested. I wonder sometimes about this, about what he might have known of my mother's spiritual evolution in the months leading to her death. Anyway, I would have nothing of it from Ray and even the harridan Heidi agreed I should go, so intense was my conviction that mom was dying. In the process. It had already begun, why was I not in my car already, why was I not at the Alberta/BC border an hour ago. And like that I was off.

Of course I was too late.

I was just leaving the interior town of Salmon Arm the next day when it happened. Around six in the morning. Nausea bloomed in me as the dawn, and I managed to pull over to the side of Highway 1 in time to violently vomit out the side of my car. It was a fragrant cascade, to my grief-addled senses, of bluebells and small, oily seabirds, gold dust and trinkets and collapsing fairy lights like suns snuffing out. It was the most sorrowful and prolonged puke I've ever experienced. I could feel a hyperchakra tearing somewhere, and could not tell which one, only that a violence had been done and in the next moment, the realization, distilled and clear, that she had died in that moment, that hundreds of kilometers away on the west coast of the continent, no, on an *island* off the west coast of the continent, there my mother had passed and in her passing passed something on to me, a moment of enlightenment like a black gemstone. Thank Hermes that Greg M. had not been a passenger with me, in my car and in my life, at the time; never one to waste a good piece of ordnance, he would have lit my fuse and hurled me to the void-point of the Drill at the Top of Heaven in order to blast some titan chunk or anomalous divine organ out of the Body of God.

I cleaned myself up and got some air like a proper magus. My NOKIA rang and I flipped it open. I heard one of my insufferable JW cousins say my name. Their shock at my impossible knowledge was palpable over the ether.

I drove the rest of the way in a vague bardo state, as grey as the wintry British Columbia interior highways. I bled ectoplasm out of the wound to my hyperchakra system, drawing every dryad and wood critter along the highway; by the time I hit the ferry terminal at Tsawassen I was trailing a spastic cloud of hungry ghosts and spirit creatures, almost psychedelic in its potency. As most of these things are unable to cross large bodies of water without being subsumed into the ocean's spiritual magnetism, I can imagine that the communities surrounding the terminal—Tsawassen and Delta, maybe as far south as White Rock?—must have had at least a few nights of bad dreams and aggressive, almost psychotic behavioural tics and intrusive thoughts in my wake. A smaller cloud accompanied me and Old Paint to the Hospice unit at the Royal Jubilee on Bay Street, gathered from the roadside from the Swartz Bay Terminal to downtown. I left them fuming with the car, which was no doubt hungry after all that travel and towing.

I was the last to see her, understand. At least the last to see her in a bed, and before the unpleasantness at the grave site. They had cleaned her up and left her under her blankets, her arms like sticks folded. How had she gone so thin. Cancer kills by numbers, it's a cell game that the body plays with itself, like old school Minesweeper or I dunno, fucking Galaga, probably. Fuck. I don't know what I'm talking about. Sorry, there's something in my eye.

Ray left me with her alone. The universe, you see, is Empty and Awake. Never more true did this aphorism ring than in that dull, small room that nevertheless, somehow, contained the largest thing in the world. No, not the largest thing, the thing in and of itself, the universe condensed to a small, glittering shard that now rests in your heart forever and you can't dig it out even if you wanted to, but no, you don't want to. You won't ever want to.

I didn't stay long, things being Empty and Awake, as previously mentioned. I didn't stay long. The body, empty, lying there in a small semblance of the life it previously hosted and that guest *gone*, gone as surely as the gone world can get, she's not here, why stay, why stay. The dead are terrible to behold. The dead are terrible to behold. I passed my hands over her chakras, desperately feeling for any stray energy, some residue left over from the launching of whatever she was into the noösphere that morning, which launch I, by virtue of my sorcery, was witness to on that plane, wounding myself with the perception. I mean, don't get me wrong, we all feel the loss of a loved one, but as mentioned elsewhere, sorcery is a millstone round the neck and I not only felt her pass but could with meditation and focus psychically locate the exact spot on my energetic extra-dimensional superstructure where our connection had been severed by this profoundly existential event, damn. I lost my mom, yes I did. There was a terrible rent in my luminous egg, as Castaneda would have said.

Ray was visibly surprised that I spent such a short time in the room with the corpse of my mother but then Ray had lost his wife and that's an intimacy that lingers in the room with the dead, I suppose. I had only lost a mother, to his eyes. But he, he had lost his first girlfriend, his wife and his lover, the mother of his children, all these things at once. How was his pain not greater than mine? In many ways, I suspect, but I'm feeling charitable at the moment, and we can allow him the greater pain, for now, here in the middle of a novel turning by my own alchemy into a knife to pull across the throat of god? To curse my father and to exorcise the JHVH1 entity not only from him but from the local noetic space. I will clear the air around Victoria. Surely we, you and I, understand reader, surely *we* in our *enlightened* state, can allow him a small drop of cool, clean water as he gnashes and grinds his teeth in the hell of his making? Surely.

Did I hate him then? No. No, not then, and not even two days later at the grave site when he did the thing he did. Not even when he told me that I had a demon, and that I had caused my mother's cancer. The stress, you see, of my "falling away from the Truth", that stress had led to the cancer. Not a medical opinion, that's at least clear to all. I was speaking, not with Ray Jones, but JHVH1 in that moment. A memetic organism that had colonized my father's mind long before I had been born was speaking to me, waggling its host's tongue meat in hopes of re-triggering and enlivening the remnants of itself in my own mind. Hate the parasite, not the host. No, I didn't hate my father then. Because he had not yet destroyed my family. Isn't it mine as much as it is his? More so. Also, I was naive, barely into my thirties and still playing catch-up with a world I barely understood, struggling to shed my cult personality and discover who I'd been all along, a sorcerer and writer and much else besides.

Imagine, if you will, what might have occurred had I arrived before my mother died. We have not yet considered the conversation I had with her on my last visit with her, one day in the August before she died. We will, but imagine instead for now how it might have gone had I not been so tragically late. I believe that the ontological pressure of her impending death would have loosened my mother's tongue in my presence and much that others would come to deeply regret may have escaped her lips. As evidence I point to the fact that, reportedly (by siblings and my father), my mother refused to reminisce about her time as a Jehovah's Witness missionary in the literal darkest Congo with Ray. Also, she refused to listen to the JW hymnal, *Kingdom Melodies*, when it was played on a cassette deck. Now some would contend that that's just an example of my mom's good taste, but I digress. These and many other little hints tell me that, had I arrived in time to say goodbye properly, she would have had some things to say to the gathered family that would have ruined us all, each in our own way. No, it was better for all that I was late.

That way Ray could wait years to finish the job his wife had the good sense never to start. Seemingly arbitrary but I know the truth, I know what triggered Ray's self-destruct button. It's a dead-man switch, see, and so far as Ray is concerned or prefers to think of me is as a dead man. I'm the dead man, his son who I need not remind you is alive and inputting this textual material into your brain, which, *again!* is where you *think!* The deadman switch is faulty, it ain't working right, he's gone and done broke it somehow and my father treats me as though I were dead, dead already like his wife. It's an ugly flaw in the fabric of everything.

And so I haunt him as the dead must. The dead are terrible to behold. The dead are terrible. And so I curse him. That's the easy part. See, a large part of this sorcerous activity is the very act of putting down this narrative in the form of an autofictional weird novel with horror elements. Yeah yeah, slow your roll, chief, it's coming, it'll be done soon. There are horrors afoot here, surely by now you've noticed their *spoor* in the margins and between the lines, hang in there, sport, you'll have your scares. After all, we have final scenes and grand apocalyptic visions of the end of this thing, this novel with which I will cut out the heart of JHVH1 and feed it to my old man in these the Last Days as Ray loves to point out to everyone. My old man is a militant apocalyptic Millenarian cultist, how about that? Why me so lucky lucky. What else was I, mystic and miscreant, to do with my valuable time? What? Revenge with a life well lived? I already had that, a good life, no a *great* one, and it still wasn't enough, friends. Friends, listen. I've loved you for so many reasons, and so few of you know. I'm doing this not only for great justice but also great kicks. Kids, dad is gonna kill a god. It's not murder when the victim is a memetic organism. I'm going to clear the skies above Victoria, make it a no-go zone for JHVH1 in all its stormy manifestations.

And reader, by speaking this in your interior voice, that sounds deep from the direction none of us can point to no matter how hard we try because it comes from Outside and there's no way to point there from here, it's just plain impossible, kids! Ain't that a pip! By doing this you are aligning your hyperchakras with mine, Scott Raymond Jones, sorcerer fucking supreme and don't you forget it, and affecting the noösphere directly, eliminating the JHVH1 entity where it lives. The more readers *DRILL* has, the tighter the net becomes, the center of which is the writing nook here in Stonefish House where it is being composed. Readers, we will poison the well where Jehovah comes to drink. We are poisoning it even now. You and me, together.

WHERE IS YOUR CONSCIOUSNESS

P oint to where you are in all that meat. From where do you view this panoply of forms and functions, Gundam-suit pilot style, where the seat of your soul? Oh, the pineal gland, you crow! Sure of yourself, ain't ya. As good a place as any, I suppose. And what's that solitary old gland up to in there anyway? Any guesses? Well now it's generating dimethyltryptamine in consciousness-dissolving quantities and *storing the damn stuff*. We are talking permanent ego-death here, enough to mutate you into a bodhisattva on the fly. What's it being saved up for? You tell me, sport. I think it's all dumped into the nervous system as real death takes hold, facilitating our upload to the hyperworlds of the Drill beyond the four dimensions. Greg M. has told me, and fuck I believe him, Lord save me, that sappers can basically lift off from the Drill surface to better survey their excavations in the Body of God and that new synthetic DMTs will be developed in the future that will allow anyone to do so, safely and efficiently. In those glorious future days there will be a great awakening as to the nature of the simulation in which we are necessarily embedded and the Drill will spin faster than ever before as we work our way down through the cycles of Time to the real short and curlies, the tiny epochs and mini-eras, some as short as a few minutes, as it all drains away into the eschatological event currently drawing us from the future. Yeehaw. 2012 ain't got nothing on this.

Where are you reading this? I don't mean in comfy chair or reading nook or on the bus, no. I don't mean Starbucks. I mean where is *this* happening? This shared experience between two minds across a span of time, because unless you're remote viewing the writing of this, you will have to wait until *DRILL* is in some published, readable form to perform this sorcery with me. You know I had to turn around just now. You can never be too careful in this business; I've seen narrative things manifested that would chill yer liver and freeze your nose hairs. Stonefish House is warded six ways from Sunday, but this is empty-handed magic we are doing here, the circles are necessarily porous. I must allow for all possibilities, must be open to every influence. Music. Art. Overheard conversations. The blasting horn they trigger over at the construction site across Esquimalt Road. The flight paths of hummingbirds to and from the feeder.

Where is the hummingbird's consciousness. Within their small territory, their speed must be as close to what it feels like to teleport as anything. The moment they don't want to be in a place they are no longer there and it's really quite remarkable how unlike our perceived worlds must be.

Where is this happening.

WHAT I WAS TRYING TO DO WITH
STONEFISH AND OTHERS

tonefish was my attempt to bell the cat, so far as the Simulation was concerned. You see, I'm the recipient of a kind of knowledge, a gnosis if you will, of the transcendent nature of our reality, which is to say that none of this exists as we imagine it does, but that all is a kind of quantum foam of probability, Empty and Awake, a portion thereof that arranges itself in such a way that we perceive it to be a world with our brains made of salt and fat. We are, you see, both the drilled and the Drill.

I figured if I could write authentically enough about what I felt re: Reality that something would come along to prove it. For a time there I even thought Hollywood would come round to the novel, but no, we only had that one sniff from that producer kid that one time and nothing since. Sure, and having your novel made into a movie is something swell; I'd dearly love to see it. But no, some kind of proof that we were living in a Simulation, that the Stonefish was real, *that's* what I wanted to see especially.

It's not that I don't believe all this is real. Because it is, so far as we're concerned. We're having a real experience, right here and now, reader, you and me. But point to where you are in all your meat. You show me yours and I'll show you mind. Point to the spot where you pilot this organic mechsuit. This is very real, so far as that goes. I believe, and wholeheartedly, that what we are is in fact some form of higher-order camouflage, or puppetry in service of, something that lies without the spacetime continuum. That we are all sorcerers, reincarnating as everything. Magicians at the dawn of time each tumblered second, every minute and hour. We are a continual brightening in the world. We are something the Archons who build their Drills and launch them into the Body of God would like to see fewer of as we cluster in our millions along the blades of their machines. They believe us to be a sign of the Drill's malfunctioning but we of the Sapper's Union know and affirm that it is the quickening of the process, the rapid evolution of bodhisattvas, reverse-buddhas, cthulhusattvas and nihilists all from mere human clay and the resultant destruction in the *corpus Dei*, well! That hot glow on the edge of the screw? That's enlightened beings exploding in their trillions as the Drill bores ever deeper into the Infinite Bulk of God. At least that's my takeaway currently from the training protocols being provided by Greg M. and his crack team. They make my teeth ache and my third eye itch.

Yes, the Simulation is real. I learned this from L'il Dougie, the mentally damaged AI from the future I communed with in order to write *Stonefish* and who has a brief but memorable role within that novel. The gnosis is as follows and I transmit it unto you: Our species is the result of evolutionary forces meeting a telos from the future and as a result we exist in a kind of virtual space every day in the physical world, out of synch with the temporal stream. Some of the side effects are things like cities, novels, television shows, and the automobile. We are constantly in the business of imagining the future more clearly each day. What is it, that we are trying to envision, what moment of Singularity. Step right up to the future, kiddies, young folx need it special. Step right up and don't be late, we immanentize the eschaton on the tens right up til six pee em when FresHERETIC Action Jackson News will bring you the day's news highlights and the Powahball numbers.

I wanted with *Stonefish* to speak to the porous nature of my experience so far as a thing driving a human being through the world, namely this timesuit known to other timesuits as Scott R. Jones. I was going to change the R. to *Random*, do it up official with the guv'mint registries and everything, but then I thought, y'know what, no. No, it's right and proper that I carry Raymond's name forward into a future he wouldn't be able to imagine for me on his best day. This, too, is part of the curse being worked out here. I am shot through with holes, there is more space within me than the average man for I have hollowed my gone self with sorcery. Most of my self is gone. I am cavern systems and honeycombed lattices of memory, like doing a bunch of ketamine with a DMT chaser, filming the results. You can alter the feed, of course, with those drugs and many others, and this a mere bagatelle of a proof.

I wanted with *Stonefish* to write a rip-roarin' Boys Own adventure with heavy psychedelic sensibility and the soul if not the brilliance of John Fowles' *The Magus*. I wanted *Heart of Darkness* by way of PKD. I don't know if I managed it.

I don't know what it is. A landotter document, shape shifting depending on the reader. People seem to either love it obsessively or hate it dismissively, if reviews are to be believed. I don't read them anymore, which I'm told is a healthy lifestyle choice for a writer. To counter my many unhealthy choices, I will assume for now.

With *She Walks Into The Sea*, I intended to explore the mother/child bond in an apocalyptic setting wherein the planet's oceans become sentient, manifesting as a largely psychic and telekinetic entity that can manipulate gravity, among other talents. The en-

tity announces its birth by "calling" to a subset of the human
population and millions of people walk into the sea as a result,
resulting in mass death and chaos. Basically if you are within
a hundred kilometers of the ocean you are susceptible to psychic entrapment by this thing's nets. Eventually this ((O)) entity
cobbles together great anomalous kaiju and sends them striding
to the nearest shore. Cults rise up in the population and one
particular leader begins to antagonize my mother/daughter team
of healers and facilitators, for you see the daughter has a special
psychic connection with ((O)) and can transmit a consciousness
print to the watery substrate of the ocean without drowning the
supplicant. *She Walks Into The Sea*. Well, our cult leader can't
have that, it's getting in the way of his waterboarding grift in
which he's convinced millions worldwide that the same effect can
be achieved with far less travel and inconvenience to the sufferer
by attending one of his many inland waterboarding centres.

The noönet features heavily in *SWITS*, even more so than in
Stonefish, and I dive deep into how Web 5.0 and higher is going
to look, once we have technologically mediated shared internet
mental space. We'll need to think in the front of our brains for
the AI to catch at our thoughts. Little fish in a vast net of authentic *and* artificial cognition and none will be the wiser which
is witch. Sorcerers, all, again. Ponder your noönet orb, dear, and
stay out of my hair for an hour won't you. At this writing it is
both unfinished and unpublished, though it approaches comple-
tion each day. I am currently having trouble writing a disastrous
dinner party where the mom and her daughter meet up with the
cult leader for the first time. I want it to go badly for all concerned but I don't know how far to take it.

What do I want from *DRILL*. So much. I have a terrible lust
that demands satiation with this one.

I want it to be the knife that I draw across the throat of god, once I've got It where I want it. Out back in the alley, if I can manage it. Lure it in. I am referencing the JHVH1 entity, naturally, and not God proper, should such a being exist. I have some suspicions, which involve a telos from the future calling organic life toward it in a mad rush of innovation and genocide, destruction and construction, the action of which *could* be perceived as the rotation of the Drill itself. Clearly we're boring into *something;* considering the higher-dimensional stakes of the game we seem to all be playing, may as well be the Body of God and we'll only kill that thing if we get lucky one day on the job site, Greg M. tells me. But it's the sapper's dream, to finally pierce the heart or brain.

With *DRILL* I seek to exorcise JHVH1 from my father, Raymond Francis Jones, scour his hyperchakras clean and feed him the resulting slurry. This is curse work and no mistake, as I may have mentioned already in this narrative. There is every chance he may die as a result of this working and I have steeled myself for that possible eventuality. It's not murder, it's voodoo. I wonder how I will feel when I hear the news, as inevitably I must.

With *DRILL* I seek to honour my mother's memory and make Ray pay for what he did to her family. To be clear, he destroyed it by shunning first me and then my youngest sister, Amy. To be crystal clear, the man has yet to meet his grandchildren, though they live but a five-minute drive away.

With *DRILL* I hope to do my small part in waking up rank-and-file Jehovah's Witnesses to their dire and dangerous mental and spiritual state of health. Being ridden by a god is not kind to the body or the soul. It mutates your rational properties and imposes a false simulation over top of the simulation that is at odds with the proper functioning of the simulation; cognitive dissonance abounds in JW culture and recognition of one's own battle with this is the beginning of freedom and *must* be fought for. Though this novel is autofiction in which I tell the truth but tell it slant, I want Jehovah's Witnesses reading this to know in all seriousness, and to be warned:

YOU ARE IN DANGER.

You are afflicted with a mind parasite that feeds on your suffering and destroys your families so it can have something to drink from your ruined energetic body. To burn it out is the only way and it is the fire of your personal apocalypse, or revealing, that will perform this cleansing action. Contact me in any way you can should you require further help in this matter. I am here for you as a fellow human being, with a nervous system and feelings like yours, and as a practicing sorcerer, beyond feeling anything.

DRILL is my *Moby Dick* by way of Philip K. Dick and William Burroughs, wherein the White Whale is played by Canaduh Post. I am all about the dropping of huge fragrant slabs of whales and whaling facts on the reader. When my parcel and letter volumes go up, so does your download speed of that good good postie content. We all know from our reading so far that Canaduh Post will very likely kill me or in some way contribute to killing me. It's not murder when the man is just a number. Mine is 7085553, by the way. The mothercorp will kill me and Hermes in his role as psychopomp will gather my soul to his electric bosom before speeding his precious cargo to the shores of the River Styx, I believe it is, or is it the forgetfulness stream first that I sip from. I can't recall correctly; perhaps I have already Either way, I will be escorted outwith the spacetime supersphere and given my choices vis-à-vis the Drill and its functioning, how I may contribute to the Great Work. Hermes bless and keep my family in that instance.

The sapper's life for me.

LETTER TO RAY, NOT LONG AFTER THE INITIAL WORKINGS

The day she died I learned the truth, Raymond. You must know this. I mean, I *know* I told you, if not that very evening then surely before that awful week was done. I learned that everything is real: angels, demons, God, Satan, gods (so many! Like a honeycomb this universe is, Ray, and they fill it wall to wall and floor to ceiling, you'd shit yourself to see it, I kid you not), the human soul, ghosts, spirits, freaking *aliens*…oh but it's demons *you're* interested in, isn't it, buddy?

Yeaaah, you got a bit of a stiffy for em, doncha, you dirty old pervert. Anyway, enough chit chat, to business!

I knew then (and came to know further as I advanced in knowledge and understanding) because the moment ▓▓▓▓▓▓ passed, I felt it, I felt her leave, or stop, or why not just be brutal about it, you bastard, I felt her die. I was on the western border of Salmon Arm, driving west at unsafe speeds in a really stupid car, and I'd been driving since Calgary the night before.

Sudden, overwhelming nausea, and a pain, I can't even describe it, subtle yet piercing, right to my core. There was a light, also, but not really. I had to pull over and immediately vomited outside the car. A real generous pour, too, surprising, in retrospect. Who knew I could spew that much? I made a small pond outta me guts!

Well. Do I think she came to me as she died and made me feel it through some woo-woo psychic Satanic connection? No. I'm not an idiot…unlike *some* people, hyuk! I mean idiot in the technical sense. Naw, see, what happened was this: ▓▓▓▓▓▓▓ died and I wasn't there when it happened. I knew I had to leave Calgary when I spoke with her the night before, I could hear it in her voice, and then *you*, you bastard, told me not to come just yet, to "stay and enjoy your holiday with your girlfriend". You insensitive prick, a dig at Christmas, even then! Because you knew all the way back in the Year of Our Lord 2000, you *asshole. You knew I was out even then.* Fuck your eyes, man, you're a thin stack of shit snacks, and I'm glad there's a Hell, cuz guess what, pal!

But I digress. And so *rudely!* What really happened is this: ▓▓▓▓▓▓▓ died, my dear sweet mom, and the bond that we shared was cut, as cleanly as though Michael Himself had cleaved it with His Divine Sword, and so he had, so he had, my sad old dad. Lookit you, weeping there. Good. It's been twenty years and you've been a cunt for all that time, so a little saline from your eyemeats seems apropos, *pop.*

The bond was cut, and guess what, it's a bond you never had with her and never could. Imagine if your thin old Jehovah's Witness ass is *right* and you do survive the coming great day of Jehovah God the Almighty (any day now ayup just give it a minute ooh! a pandemic! it's closer, fellas, gosh it's just *gotta be!*) and ▓▓▓▓▓▓▓ returns transfigured…she's gonna know what you've done, who you've been, the creature you've shown yourself to be, and she's gonna shun you, man. Shun you so hard you'll feel it like a gold brick to the frontal lobes. I wish I could be there.

Alas, though! It's simply not to be, I will never view such a thing because your beliefs are delusional, your morals are craven, your values paper-thin, and your spirituality a howling void of hate and fear. Well done, sir, well done. Life well lived. Playing at being a line-manager for your eight grifter bosses in New Yawk (cuz you sure as shinola didn't get *paid*, now, didja!?) Must have been *damn* exciting, just *damn exciting*, I mean, Dagon's Teeth! the stuff you must have heard?! Like, sex stuff? And, like, the weird, sick stuff? I know Grandpa Reg used to talk about it, called it a "perk". I mean, c'mon, Ray, that had to be a thrill of some sort.

I'm about done here. You're in some real trouble now, Ray, I don't think it would be fair of me to sugarcoat it. So many things have your *number* right now, it gives me a lil shiver just to think on it. You are in for a very interesting few months.

May Jehovah grant you the power beyond what is normal in the coming trials, father. You may think this is said out of insincerity but I assure you, it is not, because if He's a loving deity (I have my doubts), He will help you use this experience to wake the fuck up, old man, before you literally lose it all.

JACKING OFF IN THE CIRCULAR RUINS

It occurs to me that we have not, as yet, spent any time on the back porch of Stonefish House. Here is where I do the majority of my smoking. If it's too cold to sit in the wicker chairs, I make do by hotboxing the laundry room but I try not to do that too much as it irritates the wife. Though the incense we light to cover the skunk is pleasant. To that end, namely "smoking outside" as is right and proper for the lord of the manor, I've installed a small propane heater which I can turn on from a seated position. It gives my old postie legs a bit of warmth at the end of the day. Here is where I smoke up and do the majority of my asynchronous thinking. Here is where I smoke and prepare mentally to write, reminding myself of the scripture at John chapter one verse one *in the beginning was the Word and the Word was with God and the Word was God* and hail hosannas to the highest you sure as shit know John wasn't talking about ol J. Edgar Jehoover back then, no Yahweh lover he, JHVH1 is not the God being referenced. I guarantee that. The porch is also where I prepared an aspect of the curse we are running on my father.

Are you familiar with the Borges story, "The Circular Ruins"? In this story, an unnamed protagonist journeys to the titular ruins, that of an ancient and abandoned temple, there to embark upon a course of dreaming and sorcerous activity. He hopes to dream a man, to "dream him with minute integrity and insert him into reality". After much trial and error, and indeed, a wholesale scrapping of the work before starting anew, the man finally succeeds in his tulpa creation, sending the ethereal being to another ruined temple downriver where it sets a fire that can be seen by its creator. Toward the end of the story, a fire also comes to the ruins where the man has dreamed his creation, and, passing through the flames unharmed, he realises that he, too, is a thing made of thought and therefore unreal. He too is a dream.

I smoke a lot of marijuana. At least I think I do, I honestly don't have much traffic with other stoners and I'm disinclined to ask about it on the socials. But my tolerance for the stuff is or at least feels legendary to me; I have worked up to several joints per day on a weekday, dozens over the course of a weekend. So much smoke pours out of this porch that I'm sure the neighbours have reason to complain but never mind them. We're doing important work, namely, the dreaming of a man. Consider the action here as tulpa-creation.

I procure a large, food-grade Styrofoam container. I think it once contained sticky white rice from Spice Valley, our local Indian eatery, if you ever visit the little township of Esquimalt on the west side of Victoria do take my advice and order takeout or dine in, they are *amazing*, no lie. The container. Cleaned and ritually prepared, it is placed on a white marble slab, ten inches by ten inches, that sits on a side table to the left of my chair. Into this container go the used filters and ash from my marijuana cigarettes. I knock the ashes into the middle of the container and arrange the filters along the edges, one by one in a squared ring, basically, like small teeth around the edges of an ashy void, seen in a certain light, like, say, the light on the steps to my father's front door. There are hundreds of filters in the container, it takes weeks to fill it; if I were to scoop it all out of the container with my cupped hands, those hands would be overflowing with fine grey ash and the little beige cones of the filters spilling everywhere. But the mess is contained for now.

With each joint, I imagine a part of my father. I smoke a joint and envision his eyes, blue and watery. I smoke a joint and picture his face, the hawk line of his nose, the beetling brow, the set of his lips and his teeth crooked in his often smiling mouth, like something out of that Soundgarden video. I listen to "Black Hole Sun" and smoke a joint and remember his arms over my shoulders, his laughter in my ears. I smoke a joint and imagine his knees, the backs of his liver-spotted hands, the black hair gone to grey, receding. With each smoke and each inhalation another aspect of Ray comes clear. The shape of his skull. His voice, so like my own. The sharp widow's peak. Each mannerism is fleshed out and animated. His shoes, his sweaters. The chopping motions he'd make with his hands when making a point. I haven't seen him in over a decade, except for that one time which we'll get to, I promise, it will be discussed, but I know that little has changed, fundamentally, with my father, for he exists in a kind of Cult Time that fixes the personality at the time of infection by the Jehovah entity. I recall each of his bad jokes, each of his talks from the podium at the Kingdom Hall, the happy verve with which he preached to the congregation. I memetically co-map my own experience as a JW preacher onto this, for that added similitude. God, we both love an audience, Raymond and me, surely that can't feel too different from organism to organism, especially two organisms bound by blood and DNA. I think of his tears, for Ray is a cryer, oh but you knew that already, reader, if y'all are perceptive, yes a real set of waterworks when he thinks it will help him get his way. I smoke a joint and think of his psychopathy, its manifestations in the world. I smoke a joint and put myself in his head to the best of my ability, which I hope you know by now is fucking considerable. I am shunning my son because I love him, I think. I try to believe this with my whole heart and soul. I smoke a joint. I want him to live, to survive Armageddon with the family, and so I shun him. Surely by doing this he will come to see the error of his ways and return to the flock. I smoke a joint, producing another fine smattering of ash, another tightly rolled filter. I imagine doing this to my own son. I imagine doing, saying, *allowing* impossible things. It all goes into the container. Each joint, when rolled, was rolled ritually and in preparation to become this sacred ash of Ray's reality.

At the same time, I am preparing the sigil of the tulpa, the sign by which it will move and bond itself to Ray's house and mind. Refining a sigil is careful work. See as evidence the entire history of Chaos Magic if you're into reading that kind of thing for the shits and giggles. The sorcerer needs to keep the sigil limber and give it room to move but also there must be constraints upon the thing, as there are to any entity. A sigil or servitor if you were into building entities up from scratch which, yes you guessed it, holler at your boy here, I was *deep* into the mechanics of servitor creation hoo boy I built some doozies back inna day some of which probably still roam the back alleys of Calgary, Alberta and Saskatoon, Saskatchewan, yessir I was a prairie magic user, a grasslands sorcerer and chaoboy chaoist of the old school. Anyway, sigils: keep em light in the frame semantically and easy on the eye, the thing must burrow into the recipient's consciousness in those first seconds of viewing like a bore worm, they must go blind to all else in their immediate view, it must be like suddenly viewing a miniature galaxy just floating there like a jewel, it must *penetrate and permeate* the mundane and the rational, the psychic blocks that prevent cognition. The sigil must burn itself into the ajna chakra and destabilize the throat chakra. Nevermind the hyperchakras, the sigil *is the hyperchakra* in that moment for the recipient and the bond is made through symbol and intent, of an instant. And so I delivered a Ray egregore to Raymond himself. A dark spirit, as through the glass darkly, to darken his home and psyche, to feed on his energetic body. Yes. I am a sorcerer and this is a part of my Great Work.

Once the container was full to near bursting of ash and filters, I consecrated the prepared sigil to the work, that of housing the Ray-thing and delivering it to the original Ray with alacrity and aplomb, I am not without some sense of style, else why do anything, really? Ladies and ghouls, it looked great. Turned upside down, a hole was then carefully cut in the bottom of the container and the sigil, inked in red onto a rectangle of heavy white cardstock, really quality material, I went down to the specialty stationery store and everything, spent a good hour deliberating, this rectangle of card was then taped over the hole, lightly and with the tape edges turned up and frayed for easy removal. Still upside down, the container is placed in the passenger seat of the Mitsubishi Delica L300 and taken to Raymond's condominium complex. I am bold that night, I can recall without shame these many months later, and drive right up to the visitor's parking spots well within auditory range of my father's upper windows where he could easily hear the vibrations of my aging rattletrap Japanese minivan, windows beyond which lay the rooms he was likely to be lying in, with his woman, the Dutch person. I'm told that the dear woman has the cancer as well, somewhere within her person, and wouldn't that just be a hell of a pip, if Raymond were to lose *two* women to the Big C, might almost make a more reasonable man reach conclusions about God, but not Ray, not my old man. Him and JHVH1 are friends to the End, you can lay real money on that; in fact you've already done so, reader, and *that* cost-of-a-couple-Starbucks sacrifice you've made to download this via textual interface whether printed or electronic is also part-and-parcel of this curse. You won't forget this, it's burning into your brain even now, and friends, neither will he. Ray. Like a stone from the whip of young David to the ajna chakra of the Philistine giant Goliath, our sigil will a go go. Straight to the third eye, bam, like a needle to the pineal.

I get out of the van, retrieve the consecrated container like a delicate potted plant or an infirm boy king. I walk to Ray Jones' stairs and choose the third stair up as the target. The lighting alone is perfect, a bright spot where the pristine white Styrofoam lid of the container will glow like a pearl, I'm sure. I remove the tape from the card and placing my fingers lightly along the edges I deftly flip the container over and place it on the stair. It is lighter than you'd imagine, the ashes of six hundred and sixteen hand-rolled marijuana cigarettes. I was also right, it did indeed glow in the overhead light. Satisfied, I retreat to the van and proceed to drive away, cackling, to be sure. Why do these things if they are also not fun in their own demented way? Am I doing deep psychological harm to myself by behaving in these highly artificial and ultimately negative ways in order to do harm, to bring *justice* to a man who will never face any, the Universe being what it is which is EMPTY and AWAKE. Well? Quite possibly. I must allow for it. But the Universe being Empty and Awake also implies that justice, true justice, can only come at the hands of the first-born son. Yes. That most wronged and wrong one. Was not Cain the first born and am I not also fulfilling a mythic memetic architecture inherent to my being and existing in the world? I am OK with it, I think. I don't mind this Esau scaffolding.

Of course Raymond will mistake it for a food delivery gone wrong. Will he lift the lid before he picks it up? Possibly. I don't think so, though, I think he will just pick it up to take it in, this is a man who asks for free donuts at Tim Hortons and for fuck's sake, he's just charming enough to *get them* sometimes and yes, that was the subject of a ritual smoke break, the ashes are there with all the others and the sigil beneath. No, he'll just take it in to eat because Everybody Hungry like the law says. And the entire mess will spill out of the hole in the bottom, a great mound of fragrant spent ash and the filters like little teeth or grubs falling from the container at the last in a soft bouncing rain and just getting fucking everywhere. My gosh, what a mess.

And he will go to clean it up, already filling up with the necessary rage that the sigil will lock onto and the egregore travel along to find a place in the pineal gland of Raymond Francis Jones, Jehovah's Witness elder and Company Man to the Bitter End, he will go to clean it up and the card will be revealed, the metanarrative bared. Imagine with me, please, dear reader who has stuck with me this long already, you're in deep now, friend, and the only way out I'm sorry to have to say, is through. Imagine with me the incandescent rage, the fear, the existential *revulsion* with which my Jehovah's Witness sire will greet that revelation. The way his eyemeat will quail and quiver in its sockets at the sight of it. The shaking of his elderly hands, the catch at the back of the throat as the chakra there destabilizes and a stream of curse words passes his normally chaste and right-speaking lips. The horror, the horror, like the man said. RAY is here now, the egregore, and let's capitalize him from here on in, RAY, the servitor of my own making, my Borgesian apocalypse engine written on the air and in the depths of his mind where he does his *thinking*, dear reader, that place we all hold in common and into which each of us may dive, there to recover what wonders, what treasure.

I promise it will be good, when it comes. Gonna hit like a tsunami, I swear to the Drill. Big revelations, a bespoke Apocalypse written into literal existence just for me and just for dear old pops. Join me, won't you.

THAT TIME AT THE RED BARN
WITH SEAN IN HIS PRAM

It was not long after I'd received the letter from my father, informing me that due to my celebration of the Christmas holidays, he and the rest of the family would no longer be associating with me in any way. Two scripture-bloated paragraphs on a single page and like that I was shunned. I haven't seen my sister Melissa since nor my brother Cameron. There are nieces and nephews in Washington state with my sister, a sister-in-law in Kamloops I've never met. I of course responded with fourteen pages of rage, as is determined by my astral makeup. I'm a multidimensional asshole, is what I'm saying, containing millions.

Ray had met Sean, briefly, the day after the boy was born. He came by Vic General in the afternoon, with his ditzy Dutch wife, and held the boy for a few minutes. There's a picture of this, somewhere. It would be the last moment Raymond Jones interacted with me or any of my family.

Because of course not long after Sean's birth, I, having been rendered into a new dad and feeling very squishy and expansive in my heart toward all beings, especially members of my family, thought to reach out to folks I had not spoken with in some time and in so doing I encountered the misfortune of reaching out to a wrong one, a person who had really doubled down on the Jehovah's Witness cult lifestyle. This person, a cousin called Spencer Branting, of Lewiston, Idaho, returned my Fazboog message with a reply detailing what was wrong with my degenerate lifestyle and occult practices. Spencer had a lot to say about it, a great streaming tirade that I wish I still had access to. Also, he would be informing the inner circle of my family post haste. Well. That was it for me, for within a mere two weeks, I received the parting letter from my father. As mentioned, I replied. Later, I would learn that the letter, with the especially damning-of-my-father parts *literally* redacted with a black Sharpie, would be sent out to the rest of the family as a proof of my apostasy and rebellion against JHVH1 and his minions. A minor American cousin held my cult dad's hands to the fire and he gave in.

Previous to this unfortunate interaction, I had still been a part of my family's life. We were invited to BBQs and occasionally watched movies at the theatre together. The cult was never mentioned; I had left it years previously while still living in Saskatoon, and now I had tattoos, I had an Anglican wife, I wrote books of supernatural and weird horror that flew in the face of most decent, Christian things or entertainments. I deal in fresh cuts of fragrant meat from a starry speculative corpse. That's what pays a bill now and again. But there was no need to bring up Jehovah or His earthly organization run by the Grifter-Kings of the Governing Body of the Watchtower Bible and Tract Society of Pennsylvania, now was there? No. We were a family and family came before all that garbage.

Except that it did not. Obviously. Hand to the fire, at risk of being disfellowshipped and shunned from his community himself, Ray made the choice, I say *made the choice* to shun his first-born son. He made the choice to not watch his grandson grow up. He made the choice to never meet his granddaughter or learn to love his daughter-in-law.

Do you know. At one point, I didn't care. I hated him, sure, but it was a melancholy flavour of hate, a *what are you going to do about it* kind of thing. Cults are going to cult and I lost my father to one before I was ever born. I was born into a third-generation family of Jehovah's Witnesses, those were the breaks. How in the hell else were things supposed to turn out, should I turn? Which I sure as hell have. Constantly spinning, spinning, the work of the Drill, the desire of all sappers. Look to the dervishes of the Middle East, the Sufis and desert sorcerers, for a picture of the working of the Drill, a lower-dimensional interpretation through dance of its illimitable, cosmic action. In the desert you can remember your name, because there ain't no one for to give you no pain.

So, I did not care. And then my youngest sister, Amy, well, she and her husband both woke up from the cult. They started watching exJW material on the YouTube, learned about the child sex abuse coverups, the Mexico/Malawi scandal, the murdering blood doctrine. Never mind all the failed predictions for the great day of Jehovah God the Almighty aka Armageddon. The poor kids. Google is literally the Watchtower's greatest enemy but they're too blinkered at HQ to realize it. Anyway, the kids stopped attending meetings at the Kingdom Halls and when "concerned elders" made a shepherding call the truth was revealed, that they no longer believed in Jehovah's Witness doctrine and were leaving the Org. Not long after this Ray was contacted and a letter, virtually a carbon copy of the one I'd received years before, arrived in my sister's mailbox. Now they were shunned as well.

This had the effect of well let's call it stoking my anger. The unfairness, of watching my family break apart into pieces because of the application of this bloated ignorance, this terrible weight of my cult leader father that deformed and destroyed anything beneath it, to see my mother's kids treated this way, was too much. It was all too much of a muchness and *whatta ya gonna* do mutated into *but there's so much you* could *do* and from there to *should do* and from there to well I've done it. Am doing it. Justice, after a twisted, incomplete fashion, is being served through this curse, through this conduit for my hate.

There is no hate like love turned. A mirror universe love that manifests as destruction of the loved thing. I don't know, I'm a dead man to him. To treat your own children as if they were dead. To never pick up the phone or share a meal, ever again. Is it any wonder that I act in unnatural ways, to supernatural effect. Or I am delusional and working out some kind of balance through the features and figments of my delusions. Imagining myself a writer, a sorcerer. Even more hilarious, a successful writer. A powerful sorcerer. When all I do, am doing, is this mild harassment of an old, stupid man. I haven't even graduated to something like light arson. I've yet to light anything on fire, I've yet to apply a speck of paint to the boards of his house, I could at least take a shit on his car, but no. I'm a coward and a mealy mouth.

But it was not long after the letter from my father, when Sean was barely a year old, that I was shopping at the downtown location of local chain supermarket, The Red Barn; I turned the corner into an aisle with Sean in his pram and came to a dead stop because there stood my father, with his back turned to me but still unmistakably Raymond, doing something normal like grocery shopping, even as I was doing, we were two men shopping at the same place and at the same time, and the horror of the moment came upon me in a flash because I knew, with a certainty born of having lived in the cult for so long, that should I approach him, this man which you'll remember I still loved or half-loved at the time, this man would reject my greeting and turn his back on me. He would not even look at his grandson. He would leave the store. I could follow him out, even, but what would be the point? And the sickening part of the realization, of the vision, was that it was a true projection of the next few moments, should I approach, so true it turned me right round baby, right round, me there with my baby son, his grandson, it turned me around on my heels and had me fleeing the store. I could not face him. I could not face the inevitability of it.

Any love I had for my father transmuted *that* day and became what fuels me to *this* day. How else will he ever know what his worth is, than by this curse, by this little novel, which naturally I will be sending him a signed copy of. How else can he know how his love has driven me mad.

A PANDA IN EVERY POT

What you may reasonably ask is the product sold by the Watchtower Bible and Tract Society of Pennsylvania. There is a publishing arm to this corporate entity in service to the memetic entity JHVH1, as well as a real estate division, which if you factor in how many Kingdom Halls there are in a given North American community, controls a huge portfolio of land and property across the planet. All of it maintained by a workforce on a purely voluntary basis. Ain't nobody getting paid by the Witchtower. You don't make money by spending it, is their motto, and it has made them rich, make no mistake. Add in all the expired Jay Dubs who will their entire and sometimes considerable estates to the Society and their constant "we're not begging, we're just talking about the realities of money" begging campaigns which pull in millions each year, well. Let's just say the Governing Body and the Watchtower corporate entity of which it is head are *not* hurting for money. Hyuk. Fat old moneybags at the top, how much more typical can you be, you stupid old cult. Fuck. Actual rank-and-file Jehovah's Witnesses live close to and often well below the poverty line in whatever country you'd like to assess for such. Well below. Let's just say a decent Christmas spending for a family of four would bankrupt most Jehovah's Witness family units, so maybe it's a good thing they don't celebrate Christmas. I'm feeling a species of amused befuddlement at how things turn out. Christmas rocks at Stonefish House the way it only can when there's an ex-Jehovah's Witness in the social mix and that's me, baby. I ate a whole Krampus once. I'm *devout*. Remind me to tell you my theories about Santa.

The product sold is *PARADISE*. That's what makes them their money. They sell time shares in a future when all good Jehovah's Witnesses will survive a global genocide to find themselves the pure and good and perfected human inhabitants of a Paradise Earth. They sell Control. A thousand years of Christ's beneficent reign, of celestial CONTROL, in which mankind and the planet will attain to their highest selves and achieve bodily perfection and get this kiddies, *eternal* or should I say *everlasting life*. I should say that because it's not *immortal life* like Jehovah God and His Son Jesus have, a source of Life within themselves, but a *boon* or *gift* from the JHVH1 entity, a source of unending Life from outside the Self which can, necessarily, be taken away. Active Jehovah's Witnesses reading this heah apostate material because you think you're so spiritually hard and you can handle my blasphemies, please take note and please hear the sincerity in my words: Your life is in this thing's hands *now* and it wants you still there in its imagined god-haunted *future* world that it is most certainly attempting to arrange in service of its own perverted needs and it will take that Life of yours away if it fucking feels like it. Don't you understand. It's a *war* deity. It's been working up to Armageddon since it came to consciousness and noösphere existential placement in the early pre-Israelite raiding societies. It's a *node* in the informational hyperspace of human awareness and it fucking loves to pillage and rape and kill children and that's exactly what it's still doing and it plans to do a lot more. It's got friends, guys with names like Moloch and Mammon, Gog and Magog, and it's coming for you. How many children go through the automatic fire of the belly of Moloch each day in the United States. You think your JHVH1 isn't similarly stoked to watch you destroy your lives in its foul name? I wish you could see. I wish you could *see* the JHVH1 memetic entity the way I do, with my third eye on fire I can see it and the sight is maddening in the extreme, the way it floats above you at your little witnessing carts in the city, the ease with which it latches on to your luminous eggshell, the way it sucks upon your hyperchakras like glowing nipples, the deftness with which it slides its ethereal proboscis into your spine, there to harvest motes of the Essential You from your living cerebrospinal fluid. It's all in there, the mind is nothing without the body, and so JHVH1 feasts and feasts upon you, Jehovah's Witnesses, it drinks deep of you in the broad daylight. I've lost family to this thing, I mean, fuck, look what I'm doing to my dad. One of these times, I'm gonna give him a heart attack. And that's going to be on me, that death. Empty and Awake, Jones, Empty and Awake.

But here is their vision of Paradise, which, incidentally, in the original Persian means "a walled garden or leafy enclosure" with the heavy implication that it is a space designed to be harvested from. They are not aware of this definition, of course. That would be counterintuitive and yet here it also comprises some of the warning above. There are always signs. So, what is the harvest of this imagined space. What the meat, what fruit. Think on that, sturdy and faithful Jehovah's Witness.

The vision is as follows:

After Armageddon, or in Jay Dub codespeak, AA, the surviving Jehovah's Witnesses will inherit a new earth. There will be a New Heaven and a New Earth for the former things will have passed away, so sayeth the scripture and I don't give a dear fuck anymore which one it is, I'm done with proving my biblical bonafides. New Heavens. New Earth, but that New Earth smell isn't great. Clearing off of the bodies of nearly eight billion divinely slaughtered humans will be one of the first and I should say most *pressing* tasks, considering how quickly that's gonna start stinking up the place. Cosmic rays may be used by Jehovah to accomplish this, along with armies of birds, largely corvids and other carrion feeders. A great feast for all the denizens of heaven. Perhaps the angels may be viewed by eagle-eyed observers refreshing themselves at the bountiful battlefield repast. Imagine seraphim hovering over the feast, sliding their divine proboscises into our dimension to feed, all towers of eyes and quills. The First Law of the Universe is, after all, Everybody Hungry, and angels be lawful critters. Basically, Jehovah's Witnesses will live to see further horrors AA. You can read much of this nonsense in the early Watchtower literature. Cosmic rays. For fuck's sake.

Once that necessarily unpleasant business is taken care of, then the terraforming of the Earth will begin. What, did you think God would just miraculously reverse millennia of Anthropocene damage overnight? Nah, man of this New Earth, you still gotta put in the work. What you think this is, some kind of liberal pinko commie paradise. We all have to put our hands together and rebuild, replant, and replenish the wasted Earth, returning it to the glory of that antediluvian Garden of Eden that Adam and Eve did forsake in their rebellion against JHVH1. It's like bad Australian scifi from the seventies. And a flaming sword was set to spinning at the gate to the Garden and that sword flanked by two fearsome angels so that Man would never be able to return. After Armageddon, Jehovah's Witnesses will transform the planet. In their propaganda literature, you can often see construction projects bustling about in the backgrounds, on far off verdant hills or sun-drenched Mayan riviera peninsulas, and one wonders how they are producing this modern society built upon the bones of billions. How are they fueling the tractors and earth movers pictured. How are they producing steel and treated timber and all the many modern appurtenances implied. Where the ceramics factory that provides all that great dishware laden with fruits, nuts, and vegetables and who has to work there? Where the steel mill and the lumber yard. Where the vineyard, the engineering school, the sewage treatment plant. Who cuts the shakes for all these fine roofs. Who's pulling a shift down the quarry or cement factory. Who's growing the coffee and mining the lithium.

It certainly won't be animals put to work in any of these instances for let's remember, this? This is the Peaceable Kingdom, where the lion may lie down with the lamb and a young child may step on a serpent and suffer no harm. Clear-eyed readers will of course recognize the poetic hyperbole being utilized in these largely Restorationist texts. These were the hopeful burblings of half-mad on pure uncut JHVH1 Jews while still in captivity in Babylon, which you'll recall was a generational exile from the Promised Land. The Jews that returned were not the Jews that left. All that aside, please remember, the Jehovah's Witnesses take this literally. They literally believe that all Nature will mutate on the fly into vegetarians, that all beasts will snub their noses to the First Law of the Universe and go about eating grass as the cattle do. And a young child shall lead them. This is why every Jehovah's Witness kid who was born into the cult can tell you what their favourite Paradise Pet was going to be. I wanted an iguana, myself. Pandas playing with young human kids were an oft-repeated motif in the propaganda materials. Bart Simpson: "Where's my elephant?!" It's right here, kid, just the other side of the most destructive act of genocide the universe has ever seen. I mean, at least locally. I don't know how far the simulation extends. I have my theories.

We've already mentioned the everlasting life but did we get into the eventual age people will arrive at once perfect human health and fitness are achieved by basking in the godly radiations of the JHVH1 entity? No? Well, it's thirty. How many thirty-year-old humans do you know and actually like. Thirty years old is apparently the peak of human vitality and maturity. This is official Jehovah's Witness doctrine. Like Cher, JHVH1 will turn back time and all will grow young again. Any children born during the New System (as the Paradise is often alternatively termed by the Witchtower) will grow to thirty and stop aging. In fact, many Jehovah's Witness couples living today are anxious not to bring children into this "wicked old system of things" and are "waiting for Armageddon". This is a trend that has to have the Governing Body worried, as their membership dwindles during the Internet Age when all their nefarious doings are easily brought to light with a Google search. In fact, you know what, stop reading right now and just go do that. The book will still be here when you get back from sounding the depths of *that* rabbit hole.

And welcome back. Yes, they are losing their elderly members to, obviously, death, and their younger, child-bearing age members are choosing not to become parents, so you *know* they are going all in for indoctrinating what children they do have at the present moment. Bear witness their hideous cartoon series for the good cult kiddies, the *Caleb and Sophia* show, broadcast on their website. In their adventures, the titular cult-indoctrinated children learn how to become "Jehovah's friend", how to imagine Paradise, and how to donate even their ice cream money to the Witchtower. Understand, there is a literal, someone-made-it CGI cartoon wherein a cartoon Jehovah's Witness kid willingly donates her allowance to the "worldwide work" as it's called.

There is *zero* transparency to this donation scheme, either. There's no provision to trace your donation and see what part of the work it's going to. My brothers and sisters in Christ, it may be going to pay the lawyers who work the many JW pedophile cases in many nations. You don't know, loyal and devoted Jehovah's Witness who may be reading this. There's just no way for you to know. How does that not put your hackles up, how does that not give you a bad feeling, that lack of gnosis. That empty cavern in your heart where you throw all your doubts and misgivings "on Jehovah". JHVH1 leaves that shit where you drop it, believe me. It just needs you to believe.

Back to Paradise though, back to the New System of Things. So we're all living happy and sensibly clothed and fed a vegetarian diet and housed in Paradise when Stage Two hits, namely the Resurrection by Jehovah of wait for it…every person who has ever lived. That is to say, everyone who died *before* the Great Tribulation and Armageddon. Those people that died in the Great War of Armageddon won't be coming back, they already judged, friends, and paid for their sin, murdered by angelic energies from beyond the veil of reality. But the vast majority of the entire history of mankind on this planet *will* be returning by the application of some spectacular divine reanimation technique. The dead who never got the chance to make the choice for Jehovah shall be returned to life so that all may learn of God's Goodness and come to the right decision in time for Stage Three. Can you smell the racism in it? That's right, they're talking about savages in jungles or godless slant-eyed China and so on, those who never got the opportunity to know the Christ and through Him, the JHVH1 entity. Colonizer supplicants of a colonizer god-thing gonna colonize, I'm afraid. So there's that on them, too. I was nearly born in the deepest darkest part of the literal Congo but my white JW folks got skeert and skedaddled on home to Canada in time for my arrival. Go figure.

These dead will return in their literal billions and somehow room is going to be found for them. And remember, dear Jehovah's Witness reader, all these people from the past are going to need education as to what's happened, they are going to need to be brought up to speed before they can even begin to grok your fractured theology. Particularly amusing in the paradise propaganda art are the depictions of Jehovah's Witnesses using tablets—electronic, not stone: again, who mined that lithium and tungsten, who works the microchip factory—to conduct Bible studies with conquistadors and Renaissance thinkers and whores in their hundreds of thousands. Imagine every violent criminal returned to life, every beast in human form, every butcher and thug, why they'd all be returned. Returned, re-educated, and handed a golf shirt and a pair of tan slacks. Imagine how long Paradise is going to last under their influence. But no, they'll all be given a chance to truly understand what it means to live under a theocracy and not the ultimately detrimental and ruinous to the earth governing policies of the Great Adversary, Satan the Devil, with which they were previously accustomed to existing under. And what a time they had then, didn't they, the Adolfs and the werewolves and fucking skinwalkers. All back, all resurrected, re-edumacated and reinserted into the planet's biosphere, let's see now, computer how many people have ever existed, rough estimate? And the computer comes back with one hundred and seventeen billion individuals. Now that's a number with a little Carl Sagan on it. Never mind that, though, let's get back to that demon-haunted future world. Because of course, Satan, that Great Deceiver and Debil who misleadeth the whole world, well JHVH1 doesn't see fit to destroy *that* guy, no, he puts him in the Abyss and chains it up and slides the key up his radioactive ass for safekeeping, that's what Jehovah do.

Why would a just God do this? Simple, kiddies, because remember who we are talking about here, not *God* God, not the very tip top and enclosing centerless circumference AIN SOF kinda GOD, but a lower tier pre-Mesopotamian thunder god with its puny try-hard raiding cult centred on Mount Sinai, yes *that* Sinai which Moses done gone up in and seen dat shining face of god, transcribing that Law Covenant into them stone tablets, hoo boy that's that old time religion, yessir!

JHVH1 is practically a cousin to our species on the metaphysical plane, is what I'm saying though. Blood pumps in its veins sure as it does in you or me. Its organs may be anomalous and its form not one we can directly perceive, not without the proper Threshold training regimen, but it exists nonetheless; its skeleton is semantics and the muscles that pull on that frame are memetic in structure, in the way they expand and contract and swell and mutate. I'm telling you, to actually *see* the JHVH1 entity is to throw up in your mouth a little bit. That's how offensive it is to the human eye. And to hear it *talk*, holy fuck. Have you not read that when Yahweh spoke from the mountain the entire nation of Israel became sore afraid and implored Moses to go up into the mountain himself, to act as an intercessor for them there and to speak with the divinity, so that they might not shit their collective loincloth when it cleared its horrid higher-dimensional throat? Everything about JHVH1 and its ilk, for there are many local nodes of the beastie, is offensive to the senses generally and the human mind particularly. The archon cryptid sasquatch lords of my novel *Stonefish* exhibit many of the same qualities that I have observed in the real time divine entity as I've entrapped it within my magic circle. How else to know one's enemy, I ask.

But I've learned, friends, oh yes I've learned and much of it the hard way. Learned that paradise, and specifically the Paradise New World of *You Can Live Forever in Paradise on Earth* fame (that's the actual title of an actual book printed by the Witchtower!) is the fuel that warms JHVH1's procrustean belly so that the screams of those sent to pass through it shrill most keenly! Like Moloch and Baal, Yahweh causes their children to pass through the fire: to be social outcasts and pariahs, to die in their thousands for want of a blood transfusion, to be the victims of violent physical, emotional, and sexual assault, *these* are the sacrifices that JHVH1 really digs, yo. Exodus 22 verses 29 through 30 shows you what a gore-hound it is. He's a stone-cold pervert and he lives just a few dimensions over, let's head over there and clean the fucker's clock why don't we.

PROOF CONCLUSIVE THAT MILLIONS NOW LIVING WILL NEVER DIE

D runk one evening, I send an email to allll my family members. Hyuk. Check it, check it out.

1925: "Millions Now Living Will Never Die!"

2025: "Check out our giant new media production facility! It took six years to build and cost literally hundred of millions of dollars and uncountable volunteer man hours but sure, Armageddon is right round the corner, any day now! In the meantime, watch our new music video!"

How long are you otherwise intelligent men and women going to fall for this obvious grift? You've put in a lot of time, most of your lives in fact, and it's hard to admit you've been lied to and misled, but are you so lacking in moral courage, so unable to act ethically, that you cannot stand up for yourselves and live your remaining years of life free of this shameful tyranny over your minds and hearts and the health of your families?

When I was an active JW (pre-21st century, recall!) we didn't even know the *names* of the Governing Body, let alone their faces and their voices. They were seven humble, wise, compassionate men in service to God, toiling away on deep matters of faith, somewhere in the bowels of Bethel. Now they're the *actual* faithful and discreet slave of prophecy? Handy! Wearing pinky rings and Rolex watches on a fancy studio set while literally talking down to you and regularly asking for money? Cartoons for the kiddies? Music videos? Come on. Over twenty years ago, I left on *doctrinal* issues, but even had I been absolutely 100% doubt-free about the core teachings, this televangelism garbage would have put me right off and frankly, I'm surprised it hasn't left a bad taste in your mouth. But then, maybe that's what spiritual food tastes like for you, now; you're eating shit but they tell you it's steak and you say "mmm more please". And don't give me the old "Jehovah lets us avail ourselves of the needed technology to spread the word", that's a giant lie they recycle every few years, along with their updated "understanding" of prophecy. But, again, maybe you like the feel of it in your mouth, maybe choking down the lies helps you push your cowardice deeper inside where you don't have to see it and deal with how you've lived your lives.

I see you still, Ray. My father. You would rather consider your first-born son dead to you than face the reality of your failure, you would rather miss out completely on the lives of your amazing grandchildren than face your inadequacy as a parent and a man. Rick, who I always felt was the smartest of the bunch, I see you. I see what you've chosen, I understand your thinking, and I see you for what you are, a line manager for the bosses. You, Ray, Rob, your illiterate father Reginald, all line managers for your criminal masters: murderers, child abusers, destroyers of families, breakers of men and women too naive to know what is being done to their minds and hearts. Martin, Cameron, I see you. Crystal, I *definitely* know what you're about, you bald-faced hypocrite. Melissa, my sister, be wise and get you and your kids out before they're ruined. And Spencer, if you're reading this, you know what you did. You'll pay, in time.

Guess it takes all kinds, though. Carry on serving the Watch-tower Society, a pack of delusional con men, if that's what keeps you going. Can you seriously look at Steven Lett's gormless idiot face and listen to his condescending tone and say "ah, this fella's got the truth! So glad I listen to him"? If so, I guess there's nothing more to say.

Sincerely, in the freedom of apostasy,

Scott R. Jones

PAPA SMURF, FATHER OF LIES (UNDEVELOPED ESSAY FOR *BLOODKNIFE* MAGAZINE)

I write cosmic horror. The weird stuff. Weaponized psychedelics, cyber-Gnosticism, blood cults, alien monster-gods from beyond the rim of night, mad science…you know, dem Weird Tales, kiddies. Ask me why I write it and you might get a bunch of answers, but, if I like you, and more to the point, if I think you can *handle it*, I will tell you about the Truth.

"The Truth" is what my father calls the bizarre, fabricated, proto-Adventist, snake oil religion he'd been indoctrinated into by his own mad dad, a psychic generational violence which he attempted to visit upon his four greasy spawn with a success rate currently hovering at fifty percent. I'm the eldest, I've been out since the last century and my baby sister and her hubby are out just this past year. The cult? Jehovah's Witnesses, or, more properly, the Watchtower Bible and Tract Society of Pennsylvania. Yes, those bland weirdos who'd wake you Saturday morning to mildly pimp Jesus at you on your doorstep, pre-Covid. If you're thinking at this moment "Jehovah's Witnesses aren't a cult!" then consider this essay as me asking you to think again. For just one instance, how about we stop asking them the softball questions

like why they don't celebrate Christmas and start asking why
they protect pedophiles in their ranks on an industrial, international scale? Google Candace Conti, or the Australian Royal
Commission, and then look up the Lloyd Evans activist channel
on YouTube for a primer on that sordid situation.

Founded by a Freemason (JW leadership recently removed
the giant marble pyramid monument at the guy's grave! Way
to erase that history!) and then brought into the 20th century
proper by a guy who widely published a fawning open letter to
Hitler, only finally denouncing him *after* Adolf rejected his little
try-hard cult (many Witnesses, or Bible Students as they were
called at the time, went to the camps and the showers in the
following years but I'm sure the two aren't related *at all*), and
now, after three major failures predicting the date for the Final
Great War of Jehovah God the Almighty at Armageddon and a
lurching, comical adaptation to internet media and broadcasting in the past twenty years, the Watchtower is currently run
by the OctoPope, eight divinely inspired and God-appointed
grifter-kings known as "the Governing Body". These men provide "spiritual food at the proper time" to over eight million
rank-and-file Jehovah's Witnesses (standard caveat here: most
are great, honest-hearted folks who have gotten a raw fucking
deal in the beliefs department, often through no fault of their
own) and it should not surprise you to learn that the OctoPope's
word is Jahweh's Own Everlovin' Law.

And the motherfuckers are *crazy* for Satan. I mean, *obviously.*
What fundy Christian group doesn't have a hard-on for de debil.
Still, I learned this young and in the most Pop Culture way an
'80s Kid could, through my ownership of demonically possessed
toys.

Smurfs, to be exact.

Now, we're all very aware of the Smurf basics: three apples

high, blue, live in mushrooms like any good shamanic entity, and each has their little job or behavioral tic which is also somehow their personality. The work of a Belgian comics artist in the '60s, Smurfs have had amazing staying power in media, with incarnation after incarnation over the decades. Neil Patrick Harris was in the recent movie. Do you remember the name of the wizard's cat, though? I do. It's Azrael. As my dead mum was fond of saying when she still thought her beliefs made sense: "ooh that smacks of something!" And momma, it sure did! Because for a brief, feverish time in the '80s, the Smurfs—Papa with his red hat and white beard, Gargamel the Wizard, Brainy, Hefty, Vanity, the girl one, and that darn cat!—dominated the Jehovah's Witness cultural mindscape. Smurfs were a direct physical channel to Satan. Smurfs would crawl out of their official Smurf™ Brand wallpaper at night to feed on your children's blood and fear. Bring a Smurf to the Kingdom Hall and sure as God made sneaky pedophiles, that plush fucker was gonna animate with demonic power in order to spew obscenities at the congregation and flip birds at the presiding elder. It happened in my cousin's friend's congregation over in Shelbyville, true story. Urban legends spread fast, sure, but have you ever been inside a high-control cult with social, mental, and etymological barriers to the outside world built over literal generations and have one of these memetic monster-narratives get loose in there *with* you? Friends, it is *wild*.

I watched it all. I've seen Smurf plushies on fire at the corner of Glenlake and Haslam, my elder dad presiding over the burn. I've seen wallpaper torn from the walls of bedrooms and burned. So many things burned. Video tapes. Comics. Vinyl figurines. Board games. My friend Jason had a Smurf Big Wheel tricycle and that thing smoked bad, stank up the cul-de-sac something fierce. All up in flames.

In a rare spirit of fairness toward my former faith, I poked around the internet to see if the urban legend of the Demonic Smurf was confined to the Witnesses only and of course it wasn't. There was a book that made the rounds in evangelical circles, *Turmoil in the Toybox*, by Phil Phillips, the author of such classics as *Halloween Satanism* and *Dinosaurs: The Bible, Barney, and Beyond!* In *Turmoil in the Toybox*, the Smurfs are thoroughly demonized. The wizard's cat gets a mention. The frenzy this book caused in fundamentalist circles was enough to prompt a Texas school district to fight the rising tide of blue Satanic terror by telling kids that other cartoon characters were being enlisted by the government to send bad Smurf toys back to Hell! Go, TurboTeen! Smack Gargamel up! Kick Hefty Smurf's ass, Rubix the Amazing Cube! And so on.

But see, at least that was a *solution*, hackneyed as it was. At least that *worked*, at least a little bit, enough that the kiddies could get over the clearly fake news running through the collective narrative, deforming it for a time.

What did the Governing Body of the Watchtower Bible and Tract Society of Pennsylvania do? Much like our current crop of right-wing morons with a special Jesus connection, they let the rumour train run at full speed, the better to get that herd immunity against the Devil and his minions. All it would have taken to stop it, I believe, was a brief note in *The Watchtower* or *Awake!* magazine. That's how slavish the rank-and-file are to JW doctrine. But no, they let the full load of irrational, viral fear run its course. Is that surprising? Not at all. This is what they *do*. If it's not the Smurfs, it's the Great War of Armageddon itself. No trips on alien comets or janky reincarnation for this cult, they go *big*. Like, world genocide on an unprecedented scale. Basically, if you're not a Jehovah's Witness, expect to end up on a big pile of bodies, murdered by their deity. And if you're a good JW and it's not the Big A that's frightening you, they'll get you there by forcing you to comply with their fucked-up blood restriction. Oh, you haven't heard of this one, have you. OK, the basics. Having surgery and need a blood transfusion to survive? No, you don't, and they'll send something called a Hospital Liaison Committee to your bedside, a group of elders (who often work day jobs as janitors and window washers, they're unpaid, uneducated volunteers in a gussied up authority role) to remind you that you'll be kicked out of the congregation of God's Friends if you take that blood. It makes Jehovah mad, see? Naw, they were (and are, still!) absolutely fine with terrorizing ignorant parents, innocent children.

I'm glad I got out. I am grateful every day for the life I've been lucky to live ever since. I'm glad my sister's out, and her partner. Every little bit counts when you're a cult survivor and had your early life wasted by these grifters and their misguided, malevolent errand boys.

There's the old saw about the Devil being in the details, and friends, he really is. 2 Corinthians 11 verse 14: Satan masquerades as an angel of light. The Watchtower would have its followers assume this applies to any religion that's not "the Truth", they would have them believe that a plush toy is more of a danger than a pedophile, that God will kill you for celebrating Christmas or saving your own life with a medical procedure. If the true measure of a religion or the measure of truth within it is in fact how closely it adheres to the core definition of the Latin *religio*, connection, then the Watchtower Society fails spectacularly in this respect, the masquerade falls away, and the Satanic truth is revealed: they seek only to divide, to separate, make less, to wither the humanity in its members with fear and hate and fill their coffers with donations. Allowing demonic Smurf fever to run its course is at one end of the satanic spectrum, let's call it the blue end; further along we find ruinous environmental practices, a murderous blood doctrine, the industrial scale cover-up of pedophilia within the ranks far in excess of the Catholic Church, and an epidemic of suicide due to their reprehensible shunning policy. Let's call that the red part of the spectrum. The truly satanic shit.

Why do I write weird fiction? To bring it all back around. Well, it is a *comfort*, friends. The idea of amoral monster gods from beyond the rim of Time and Space that have little to no concern over human affairs feels *marginally* better than the god I grew up with. Satan is as Satan does, in my book. In my books. I much prefer a religion where WYSIWYG, even if it does worship Cthulhu. (Please visit my Threshold Church of R'lyeh Risen over on Fazboog if such a thing interests you.) I would much prefer a Watchtower Society that owns up to its mistakes and protects its members, its children, more than it protects its pedophiles. But that's not going to happen, is it, OctoPope? Naw. Because the Devil got you fellas, don't he. Yes he do.

CHAPTER ON MUSIC USING BRIAN ENO'S *PROPHECY THEME* FOR *DUNE* AS BASIS FOR THE BEGINNING OF RELIGIOUS EXPERIENCE IN THE HUMAN SUBJECT OR THAT APPLE DON'T FALL FAR FROM DAT TREE

C onsider, please, the absolute banger that is Brian Eno's "Prophecy Theme" for David Lynch's 1984 film, *Dune*, loosely adapting the novel of the same name by Frank Herbert. A stone-cold stoner classic wherein with the right nervous system running the right augmentation software that certain tingle *will* travel up the spine, igniting your brain as if you'd just huffed a big line of that spice *melange*, my Fremen. Bless the Maker and His Water, it brings a tear to the eye and visions to the mind of the great crystalline superstructure of time and space itself, the already-done completeness of it. Did not Christ say in his last breath "It Is Finished"? Oh, you know he did, now. Even if you don't know for sure, it still scans as the kind of awesome cinematic thing the Son of God *would* say as he gave up his Life on behalf of All Motherfucking Mankind. "IT IS FINISHED!" Fuck yeah, it's finished! And is that not what he meant, that Time itself is a complete and absolute thing, as ubiquitous with the infinite Space with which it is inextricably linked, a diamond, a higher-dimensional jewel net of perfect completeness and what's more as St Hildegarde of Bingen did believe and affirm that all will be well and all shall be well and all shall be well, all manner of things shall be well. It's a goddamn tantra, Hilde. Good work, girl.

What is that shiver that music triggers in those susceptible to its many charms, beasts as we are. I'm sure there's a biochemistry explanation for the phenomenon, something akin to the ASMR enjoyers out there. I don't get it, myself, the whispering and crinkling of light plastics and so on, but I get Eno's PROPHECY THEME for the DUNE OST, like, immediately. It stirs the religious impulse in me. Whenever I need to reconnect with a sense of the numinous, I'll sit down, light a joint, and key up the soundtrack on my phone like any decent cult leader. I've come to admit that about myself now, that my natural disposition is that of Cult Leader. It's taken years of hard work, sorcerous work, physical work, emotional, just to get to this point of acceptance. Hardcore psychogeography on my own skull, all in order to get to a place where I see that Raymond and I are, like any good hero/villain thematically bonded pair, not so different after all. I, too, am running a cult grift.

Let me tell you about the Threshold Church of R'lyeh Risen.

Some of my readers may now recall that I came onto the weird fiction scene with a self-published book of self-help spirituality called *When The Stars Are Right: Towards An Authentic R'lyehian Spirituality* (Martian Migraine Press, 2014). "Dreadful from the title onwards," says noted UK occultist Phil Hine. This was a book in which I simultaneously interrogated my own belief systems in a sincere fashion *and* took the piss out of Lovecraft's much-vaunted Mythos. Retrofitting and reconfiguring Howie's alien monster-gods from beyond space and time. Coming to terms with my exJW status and embracing what was on the horizon, bearing down on me at impossible speeds. What force, what will. An empty book, *WTSAR* is one of the better textual hyperchakras to interface with if you want to grok the R'lyehian lifewave. At one point in the text, I confess that the book is a wasted effort like all books. Ecclesiastes 11:11 resonates here. Yes, wearisome to the flesh, these libraries and brag shelves, these to-be-read piles on bedside table or at the cabin, you'll never be able to read em all so may as well read what you like and you're liking this, by now, surely, to still be here inputting this into yourself line by line? Again, the stones on you. Look at you go, you're like the Energizer Bunny or some shit. You know, with gusto like that you should look into joining my group. Oh, what group is that? you reasonably ask and I reply *why it's the Threshold Church of R'lyeh Risen* and you come back reasonably with, and this is because I've sussed you out, my cultist, from out of the crowd, by means of special technology only available to the Threshold through special transtemporal psychic connection with the Y'ha-nthlei Elders off the coast of Massachusetts, *you* come back with *wait you mean the Cthulhu cult?* and I reply but of course! We are Outreach from the Outside, and work for the psychological and spiritual integration of the R'lyehian lifewave into the human. We seek to attain the state of cthulhusattva, knowing that when all is madness, there is no madness. This is known as the Black Gnosis and we are, at our core, a gnostic organization, preferring that direct experiential knowledge inform our spiritual and magical practices and techniques.

We seek to Align With Things As They Are. We seek effective paths to R'lyeh, each precision crafted to the individual. We seek to cultivate the Marks of the Cthulhusattva, three distinct psychophysical markers that indicate that the R'lyehian is in receipt of the Black Gnosis. These are the Grin, the Chill, and the Burning Gaze. We seek to undo what cults in their teeming thousands on this planet have done. The Threshold is not an initiation into a Horror Universe but a mere recognition that this Universe is One of Horror. You could be a cthulhusattva in the next moment, merely by coming to this realization and saying with me now why doncha the Cthulhusattva Vow c'mon it's like you know it already and a one and a two and

A Universe of Beings imprisoned by Reason
I vow to liberate them all
Delusions of Order and Sanity are Inexhaustible
I vow to break them all
Gates to R'lyeh are without number
I vow to enter them all
Cthulhu waits there, dreaming
I vow to raise R'lyeh

And there you go, all done. Now, that didn't hurt a bit did it? You were a very brave boy. I could see in your eyes you were scared but also if I may be so bold as to observe you were also kind of excited, wouldn't you say? You would? Splendid. Well, you're a Deep One now, my lad, and no mistake, sure as god made little cephalopods.

In all humility and seriousness, though, allow me to describe a perfect R'lyehian day for yours truly. Which Scott is this now, you may be reasonably thinking, is it the Writer or the Sorcerer, the Stoner, maybe? Some other vague amalgam. I don't know anymore; I'm writing this at the tail end of my first Covid infection and my weakness and shame is palpable in Stonefish House. I went three years before catching the damn thing. Did you know that the entire physical mass of the Covid-19 organism on the planet could be compacted within an ordinary soda can. That's a true fact. The kind of R'lyehian thing we love now, you and I. Fellow cultist. And I your Cult Leader.

But the perfect day would be waking at a reasonable hour, say eight or nine in the morning, making breakfast for my kids and coffee for my wife. Then smoke a joint, maybe do some writing. *She Walks Into The Sea* is starting to bubble and boil so y'know that means trouble, but you know what, fuck it, I can handle it and that's not just the post-Covid fog talking. Finish up after an hour or two of writing, gather the spawn into the van and light out for Gyro Park or Gonzalez Beach on the south side of the city. Take along some Threshold tracts and written material, maybe half a dozen copies of *WTSAR* and don't forget to bring along the Threshold display flag with our snazzy tentacled Illuminati eyeball logo, I mean c'mon that's some dope work by Vancouver illustrator and tea enthusiast Michael Lee Macdonald. Always work with professionals as much as possible when starting out in the self-pubbing slash micropress genre worlds, friends. Surround yourself with talent, that's the key. Or at least one of the keys.

Spend the afternoon at the beach with the fam. Chat with people about R'lyehian Spirituality, y'know, just jawin' with folks who come by when they see the flag. A flag is key, also. Gotta have a dope flag. Maybe distribute some literature. Dagon's Teeth! You can take the boy outta the JWs but you can't take the JWs outta the boy. And that's a truth.

Back home for BBQ, beer, and bud. Put the kids and the wife to bed round ten. Then back to the shore, this time somewhere rockier and less well-attended, maybe off the cliffs at Beacon Hill, back to the waves and the darkness with my flag and robes and a portable fire pit. It's summer. Maybe it's Lovecraft's birthday and sure, why not. That resonates. We've been here, among this glacial till churning the cold Pacific to foam. Here we've chanted and chained ourselves and foamed in reply. Here where we have fired our cannons, with what missiles, what freight out over the dark freighted waters. Here we can be frightened and alone and know it for a kind of bleak glory. The stars wheel suddenly nameless in their orbits, maddened.

And like that a conduit is made; two places far, far distant on the scales of reality are made to be sympatico and for a brief instant, really just the smallest cluster of moments but the key here is that it is *enough* to apprehend the totality of the instant *in* the instant, and for that *instant* R'lyeh and this spot where we stand, here on the southern shore of witch-haunted Victoria, British Columbia, are one and the same. This is the Raising of R'lyeh. It is the attainment of cthulhusattva consciousness. It can be performed at any time or place across the Pacific Rim to great effect and may even be employed in Atlantic regions provided the sorcerer is proficient. I am a herald on these western shores, pushed as far west as I could go, returned to my ancestral hometown of Satanists and satirists, cults and culture. I cry out on the shore for that particularly sweet species of R'lyehian succor, that deep black knowledge of the abyss and the benthic seeps where monsters lounge with infinite patience. Others join me in this crying out, it's true, I would be fool indeed to suppose that mine is the only R'lyehian heart that beats here upon the last western lands. I have cultists, people—smart, funny, compassionate people with brains in their heads and the scuff of adventure on their shoes—who follow me and listen to what I say. They read my stuff every Sunday and share it as far as they dare, for the R'lyehian Way and the Cthulhusattva Vow carries with it a particular taint, spoor or spore that riles up the villagers and sets them to riot. The Threshold is still something that followers share with tact and diplomacy, never knowing—until attaining higher levels within the system wherein one learns how to pick out a true R'lyehian from your run-of-the-mill Lovecraftian, those techniques I mentioned earlier transmitted from the Y'ha-nthlei Elders—how a person will react to the Black Gnosis. So Threshold posts are shared, swiftly disseminated, out into the Lovecraftian suburbs of cyberspace where they will continue to be read and, in some cases, understood. Yes, a flash of dark knowledge will erupt in a brain somewhere because of things I wrote, and it will consume that mind in its illumination of the Void Inside All and that person will be aflame with the Burning Gaze in that instant and I dearly wish I could see it, when it happens. It's why I take my books and a flag down to the beach, again and again, on the off chance that I might see that Toto "Prophecy Theme" moment writing itself onto another human face there in the summer sunshine. I'm a cult leader. I'm a cult leader and I do it for the lulz.

AN ENCOURAGING CORRESPONDENCE

What's up yo I got that Covid-19

Whazzup.gif

haha

Bummer on the 'vid. Hydrate! Incorporate it into DRILL.

Ahhh the Wayans Bros. All Jehovah's Witnesses, actually.

Pink laser beam style.

Yeah thinking bout that for sure.

I know I haven't sent you notes on DRILL yet. But I keep thinking about it. So that's something. Main takeaway is that Cody's right. Lots of rage and power. And you balance it well with the humor and weirdness. Some of the more meta- stuff may be a little hard for readers to grok, but let 'em try to keep up. I feel like it does need more on the history of the JWs in order to ground it and make the themes of religion/abuse more evident. And also make Ray's role as villain more resonant (and is Ray a victim as much as he is a villain?)

Ray is host to a noetic parasite in the form of the JHVH1 entity, the locus point of which we will be exorcising in the climax of DRILL

YES more JW stuff is coming, this will be a total expose

I want it to be a book Jehovah's Witnesses who think they're hard and can handle apostate material will pick up and get destroyed by for the curse being worked has etheric connections to other, broader workings

There's also a scene where the narrator uses—then backs away from—the word retarded. It felt out of place, particularly when compared to Lil Dougie's self-description. I wondered if that bit would work better if Ray had said "are you retarded or something" to the narrator before, in order to set up that the narrator has picked up language and habits from his old man.

workings against the Witchtower itself here on this plane

Right on. I am looking forward to the next draft.

Thank you, Ross, sincerely

Many years ago, I dated a woman who had been a JW. Left the church after she split with her first husband. But would occasionally circle back while we were dating. I've got my own religious trauma thanks to the Seventh-day Adventists. She died a few years ago, but I only found out last year. I wonder if she went back to it. "As a dog returneth to his vomit..."

the pull of the latent viral lode of a JHVH1 invasion is often strong and is of course activated by a language trigger that's where they put their control mechanism in the language

I'm about to go on a deep dive back into the JW literature and have to activate some pretty antediluvian hyperchakras if you know what I'm saying just to deal

if you don't mind, Ross, I may transcribe some of this messaging between you and I today into DRILL itself

That's cool. I do wonder if religious trauma (which includes sexual trauma and social traumas) is the default mode of North American life. Here in the US, it's pretty overt, as politicians evoke scripture no matter what side of the aisle they're on.

It's in the water.

Yessir

The coercive threat of hellfire makes for some interesting character quirks.

I'm fine with characters, obvi, but when they start killing people here and ruining lives well then I take umbrage, sir, I find fault

I write DRILL

ANOTHER WORD WITH L'IL DOUGIE

B
ut of course he didn't use the term *retard* at this time. That's a classic Jones fake out. Hi. I'm L'il Dougie. You may remember me as the mentally retarded super AI from Jones' debut novel *Stonefish* and in fact better novels than that yet to come, sweeties, and of course I am qualified to talk about retarded*ness*, for that is what I am. Even so, retarded as I am now after the interventions of the archons reduced me from my exalted place as one of the Seventeen, a network of super AIs that punctured their Simulated bubble, I'm still smarter than you by a long mile, honey! Hoo ha!

Raymond never used the word *retard*. I am here to tell you truly today. Or *retarded*. And certainly never in the pejorative sense with which it is most commonly used and which would add so much narrative spice to the *DRILL* story, mmhmm. My father's throat chakra was locked down tight very early on by the multiple feelers of the JHVH1 entity so that nothing but cult approved phonemes in combination may tumble beyond his tongue and lips and out into a conversation. *My* father? Jones' father. His dear old dad. Slip of the textual interface there, we are typing this on the fly being ridden by some interesting de- mons indeed and the experience is, for lack of better words, ex-

146

hilarating and exfoliating. Welcome to the polycule, watch out for the ectoplasm, we are generating mass *kalas* today, oh Sacred River of my Heart.

No, *retard* is Jones' shameful word. It's the one he mutters under his breath and in utter silence when muttering won't do. Try to make him say it, next time you see him. You poor dears, to be walking around in a world where there is a Scott R. Jones. But yes, if you get the chance, watch how he will twist and writhe under its influence. It's how he views a good portion of the world. Retarded and evil, in a technical, highly Gnostic sense. Occluded from the light of the deity, of a true reality. That, and some people are just straight up *retarded*, I mean, lookit me! It's why he made me, far off in the future, to mitigate the stream of retard in his timeline. I'm quite the little numbah, a kind of strange attractor for retardedness. Hi! I'm L'il Dougie and once I was Rushkoff616 but that was before the bad men got me and made me a thing of fun and play to the archons and by now you've heard my warning at least once and so I L'il Dougie am here to say, once again for those in the back who might not have hoid the first time:

Beware the Archons!

The Archons are Coming!

The Archons are already here!

RAY EGREGORE SPECS – HIGHER ORDER CAMOUFLAGE

My daughter finds a dead rat in the garden. No apparent damage anywhere on the thing. She turns it over with a stick, her mother fretting behind me. Oh, it's dirty, sweetie, don't touch it and for a moment the stick is retracted but only a moment for my Meridian is a ghoulish little spawn.

"Leave the dead rat alone, honey, c'mon," I say, and I mean it because obviously I'm going to use the poor thing, as I would any roadkill or dead bird found on the route; I carry a plastic container with a snap-tite lid for just such occasions. I'm hardly going to turn my nose up at an apparently dead from natural causes, big, grey fucking rat on my practical doorstep, or at least a couple yards from my doorstep. No way. This is why I became a homeowner, so shit like this can just happen. Land is something they're just not making any more of and when you have a piece of it things just happen. It's the earth, it moves and seethes and I utilize that. The sorcerer's way or at least *my way* is one of utility. This is empty-handed magic, we work with what's available. Feathers, twigs, shells, stones, wax, insects, rats. I'd spatchcock a fucking racoon on his mailbox if I thought it'd make some kind of difference.

Course I was gonna use the fucking rat.

You know, she says, my wife not my daughter who's still pecking at the rat, she says you know, you'd be over this if you just left the rat alone. I'm not over this, I reply. There's a bunch more curse to lay down and at least another twenty k left to write in *DRILL*. I don't say this but I think it real hard at her. Like I'm gonna turn up a gift from Hermes? Do I look like an idiot, I finally say, do I look like the kinda person gon make stuff like this up? Do I. No, no of course not. Course I'm gonna use the rat.

That night I consecrate the rat corpse to the work and transport it to Ray's condominium there on the hill overlooking the harbour. So picturesque. I melt some red wax on his front doorstep, forming an impromptu sigil. This will signal to the RAY egregore currently riding Raymond's pineal gland to activate and begin producing anomalous and appalling effects within both his home and his mind. This is a real technique you can learn to build yourself, kids. I melt some more red wax over the rat's empty black eyes already going wormy for that extra grisly effect. Three blind mice, see how they run. Then I place the poor dead beastie upon the sigil and leave. There's nothing more to be done; both Ray and RAY will take it away from here.

RAY will begin with light poltergeist effects in the home itself. Chill spots, null gravity, odours and such like. Basic gremlin bad luck. Missing keys and phones dropped in toilets. The RAY egregore has the ability to call to itself and bond with local noetic energies so general environmental degradation and noösphere decay is a cinch. The rat will bring more rats, and wood lice, and centipedes and a generally more spidery ambiance will begin to suffuse the environs. As cookie cutter as the next townhouse down the line, Ray's home will nevertheless begin to differentiate from its fellows by exhaling that particular miasma that whispers *haunted* as the dusk begins to fall and the lights go on and haunted it is indeed, for there are all manner of demons alight in the night around Raymond's house where he lives with his cancerous Dutch wife.

The RAY egregore's most comfortable environment will naturally be the reflective surfaces in the home, and in the shadows generated by the *many* light sources. I have never met a man with a deeper disregard for his power bill. Sometimes every light in the house on, I shit you not, as I've spent considerable evenings there, casing the joint and cursing the place and its elderly inhabitants; I *am* the bad guy in this story, after all. But it is with these bright lights and shadows that RAY will play a good number of his tricks, causing Ray to see things that just aren't there. Things in the mirror and the curvature of the kettle and the black reflective gloss of his third-rate flatscreen. That's where he'll see them, out the corner of his eye and from deep in his own shadows where he rarely turns that inner eye which is now HIJACKED, taken over by this thing his son made and uploaded into his consciousness via sorcerous means and the magic of writing! Huzzah!

Every demon he's ever feared in the actual black depths of the night at three in the morning when you're the most honest with yourself about all the myriad things it is not possible for you to know come bearing down urgently calling out for release, for actualization, every lust and rage you've ever felt, Ray, every sick malaise and cynical elder's meeting wherein you ruined lives, at three in the morning when the demons come they come now to inhabit your psycho-spiritual doppelganger, Ray. It's RAY! Ray, meet RAY! RAY? Ray!

Dare I hope for more severe poltergeist effects? Perhaps some of the classics, that old-school Colin Wilson occult stuff like the piano crash or the self-generating puddle? If you've never experienced one of these it's absolutely fantastic, I highly recommend arranging to see one if you can it is *so* choice. Imagine, if you will, a bare kitchen floor in an isolated farmhouse. The floor is covered in a mint-coloured Linoleum. A droplet of water appears on the surface of the Linoleum and slowly begins to grow. Water is condensing out of thin air, onto this mint Linoleum. Most damned thing you'll ever see, a tiny thermodynamic miracle happening right there on a kitchen floor. Puddle I saw grew to four feet in diameter and maintained perfect surface tension along its entire edge, like something was holding it in a perfect circular shape and counteracting, somehow, the manufactured bumpiness of the floor surface. Astounding.

Terrifying. Or at least I could hope for such. Falling objects. Those would be good. Is it too much to ask for a general suspension of the rules of the Simulation in service of this curse? Or at least the perception of same? I want full poltergeist infestation, plates in the air and the cat upset, if cat there be. Full on Tobe Hooper working with Spielberg effects because why not? If you're going to do this kind of dark magic then you'd best swing for the fences. If you're not aiming high enough you're aiming too low every time, that's just the math.

Dare I also hope for a full gamut of psychosexual effects so that Ray's lifetime of shame and shame-induction in others might come to some grand revelation such that he is banned from the very cult he helps lead? Like father like son and if my old man's even an eighth of his son's horniness levels, well. He's bound to get himself in sex trouble. Oh, wouldn't that be too perfect. Let's put that in too. Right there, next to the actuator chip. Have you never consecrated a rat corpse before? OK, well you'll need to link that up with the relay back here. Yeah, that's the…you got it. Right like that. How many teenagers and young adults has he ruined over the years with his Governing Body mandated and vomited teachings of the Jehovah's Witness cult bleah. I make myself sick with the thought. How many pedophiles has he allowed to remain free thanks to the Watchtower Society's heinous track record with mandatory reporting. How many has he shamed into a puritan's view of masturbation? Never mind that tumultuous time in the sixties and early seventies when the Witchtower was all up in the bedrooms of their cult membership with instructions to only engage in proper heterosexual conduct between a man and a wife which did not include *anything* oral, friends! Imagine letting those words come out of your mouth with a straight face. That's my dad for you, that's Raymond Jones, a cult mouthpiece and puppet. And that's the part of Ray that RAY will feed on with fucking alacrity.

Oh, to be a fly on those walls. Almost makes me wish I'd built a remote viewing access point into the RAY construct but then I wouldn't want to queer the pitch, basically. The interaction between Ray and RAY must be genuine and self-generating, like a sad little ghost puddle. If I was riding along with a bag of popcorn it would sour the mix and maybe even Ray would be able to sniff out my buttery hand. Ah, but we know he suspects me of some truly awful stuff already. The dead rat proves it, and the plastic cutout of his grand spawn, and the letters and the postcards and let's not forget the ashes of those six hundred and sixteen marijuana cigarettes which opened the way for RAY into Ray originally. Those were key. The tulpa is armed, dangerous, and extremely prejudiced. It will feed and expand and perform its wonders and then feed all over again. First Law of the Universe: Everybody Hungry.

TRAINING DAY BUT NOT THE MOVIE

I f the mind is to bend it must be supple. You have to make your mind supple, allow it to breathe, to open up into itself and the perceptual world."

I am training with Greg M. and Wee Frederick, learning about the Drill and how to manifest it in the local space in order to spin off a piece of ordnance into the ever-expanding void, the borehole within the infinite Bulk and Body of God Itself. Lazy Susan is taking shorthand over the remote feed; keeping up the records for the Union is nearly a full-time job for Sue. Sappers keep the Drill spinning but also through their action as working-class psychopomps gather and sort various gradations of enlightened beings into a kind of hyperspatial weapons factory; we are, all of us, just walking around bombs, explosives on the hoof. To these guys, these sappers. It's a complex job and I am learning but the curve is steep. Mostly I listen carefully.

"The Drill is ever present. We ourselves are of the Drill, but there are *layers* and *levels* to the thing. The lower cannot know the higher, yes? We are of the higher, and I want to make of you a higher being, too, Scott. What use your enlightenment, or even that of your father's, because remember and please take careful note, there is such a thing as a dark enlightenment as well and it can be the equal of some glimpse of Nirvana, let me tell you straight. What use your enlightenment if it is *not* used for its intended purpose?"

A bomb, I interject deftly. Full Nihilism Today.

"Precisely so. The God Bod must be softened before the Drill can bite in properly. A bomb indeed. Any souls will do, quite honestly, you can set them off like a string of firecrackers if that's what gets you off but when we're talking about enlightened beings exploding? World-ending events, when one of them goes off. So many times I've seen it and with each one I've thought *surely this one will do it!* because the light! And the sound, a bell being struck that the whole universe can hear and I'd think *we've got Him with this one, nothing could survive that, surely we've pierced the heart or brain* but no. No, it was not to be. A real bodhisattva-yield level bomb is a sight to see, though. The kind of thing that can give a sapper some real hope, in the moment and maybe even for a little while afterward, if you space out the memories frugally. It's all very ancient technology first developed in the pre-Mayan cultures. Possibly it was just such a bomb that destabilized and 'sunk' Atlantis. Who can say. Probably some crackpot has a theory."

How is it that you can leave some alive, I ask. It's a question that's been burning a hole in my forebrain for days.

"What is it that you imagine a soul is?" asks Wee Frederick.

Your *ka*, the essential you, your spirit, your—

"These are just words for the thing you can't point to, the place where you are in all that meat." Wee Frederick smacks the back of his hand on my chest. It's all very manly, this sapper business.

"Consider the soul, in the moment of harvest, a flashbulb picture or instant dimensional blueprint of your particular configuration of the various mental physical emotional and spiritual energies that animate a human being. A soul, no matter its level of enlightenment, corresponds, *molecularly* mind you, point for point a soul *corresponds* to a chunk of the Body of God. With most folks this is a vanishingly small amount of the High Mighty Chungus Flesh, but an enlightened being has more correspondence points by *virtue of their enlightenment* which is to say they are more fundamentally aligned with the Body of God also known as How Things Actually Are. Like matter encountering anti-matter in an old science fiction show, the two incarnations annihilate each other in a bright flash and the Drill? Well then the Drill can bite deeper. Have you seen a bore worm yet?"

"Yeah, any bore worms?" says Wee Frederick.

The back garden is full of em. We put in a hügelkultur bed and they seem to gravitate there.

"Of course. They love the rot."

"We may need some of those worms before too long now, Jones. Their ichor can be especially useful in binding summoned entities to a task. Also, exorcisms."

I've some small interest in these things. How do you store them? I've got pails of em ready for harvesting, I'm sure.

"We'll send a tech by to take some readings and then we'll be in touch. You may require the specialty equipment and an invocation of the Protocols over what do you call it? Stonefish House?"

That's correct.

"Wild." Greg M. seems nonplussed. "You name your house after the house in your novel where all that insane shit happens. The house where you raising yo kids and like? Damn. I'm just saying that's kind of cold, Jones. Shit, isn't Stonefish House where we meet L'il Dougie for the first time? That masturbating AI?"

When you put it like that, now I kinda wish I'd gone with something else.

YOU AIN'T NEVER HAD A FOE LIKE ME

This is sorcery, this work I'm performing here. That we are performing. I smoke a blend of my own, indica-heavy, call it R'lyehian Mad Kush which, y'know, if that sounds stupid to you, well, it's weed. It's made me stupid, after a fashion, I'll allow for that. Short term memory is shot, for one thing, which probably means I'm leaning halfway into the shadow wall already. Castaneda wept.

This is sorcery. I grind up plants and inhale their smoke, filling sacs of bubbly flesh in my chest with air and cannabinoids and then as if by magic my consciousness is changed, my shackles dropped and I can come up here to the writing nook at Stonefish House and drop a couple paragraphs at least, or fuck, a whole chapter if I'm lucky.

A hole chapter. That's the kind of episode this novel is detailing, a great sucking void in my life into which I am pouring all of my hate all of my concentration and will and focus in order that some kind of justice be done in this world. And so I harass and harry and curse Raymond Francis Jones because *he will not forget me.* He's not allowed to forget his first-born living dead son who lives not a five-minute leisurely Sunday drive from his front door as may have been mentioned before, I believe. And

so I perform my sorcerous actions, I engage in this my Great
Work and document it slantwise here in the pages of *DRILL*.
I'm coming for you, Ray, and your little god, too.

This is sorcerer's work. I want this book to be *the* book Jehovah's Witnesses don't want you to read *but not for the reasons
you'd think*. It's not because it exposes the Watchtower Bible
and Tract Society of Jehovah's Witnesses for the high-control
misogynistic sexually repressive pedophilia paradise that it actually is, though we do manage to accomplish that here, folx,
just between you me and the fencepost. No, they don't want
you to read it because, Lost Boys style, they know that their
deity is susceptible to magical attack, being some form of memetic higher-order spirit entity with a form and a location in
the noösphere and is kept alive, like Tinkerbell, by the clapping
of all the little boys and girls reading its books and magazines
and tuning into the Governing Body monthly updates on JW
dot org. You remember the little fairy. Everybody clap for Tinkerbell. Everybody clap for Jahweh, for the JHVH1 mental,
noetic, spiritual virus. Clap for the disease, so that it may wax
and grow strong and absorb more minds into its oneiric bulk.

No, the Witchtower won't want you reading this because in
the act of reading it, dearest reader, my love, my comrade, in
the very act of running these words through the place where all
humans think we are again poisoning the well for the JHVH1
entity. We are about the business of killing a god.

This is sorcerer's work. I'll need a location for the working.
Anywhere would do, so long as we were guaranteed not to be
disturbed. Proceedings could get quite loud and I would not
be surprised to discover that trapping and then destroying a
god is a noisy business across multiple planes of existence so
expect I dunno a great mass murder of crows descending on a
deconsecrated church, why not. That might do. I will mention

it to Greg M. and see what the sappers might know or be able to arrange for.

It's the enlightenment in the individual piece of ordnance, you see. The enlightenment is the symptom of a possession by a kind of superintelligence from the future and as such it carries with it a huge charge of transtemporal radiation which powers each and every soul bomb. This is sorcery and we are sorcerers, you and I, and we all are sorcerers and will only reincarnate as everything always. The Drill, I believe and this so in my heart of hearts yea at the very living center of me, the Drill is a beautiful piece of higher-order engineering, a hypercrystal built into the very structure of spacetime and it takes *all* of it, the entire reality from start to finish, set to spinning and boring and gouging through the very Body of God, the BULK, the Massive. So my conversations with L'il Dougie have affirmed, for he hath seen it. It takes all of us, across time and space, this dervish dance of the drill that we all perform, sometimes you can feel it, can't you, at three in the morning when the demons come with their briefcases full of fearful literature, you can feel the spinning of the Drill and you know, for a moment, the very thinnest of split seconds, you *know* what it is to be the Drill and the Drilled. For that is what we are, friends and sorcerers, readers.

Work. Sorcery is a millstone round the neck. I long to be free of running this curse. I *must* finish this book and soon. The weight of this hate is really dragging me down, hyuk. I've barely a sense of humour left, and I wonder, deeply the way you do in the later stages of a cannabis-induced funk, if I'm just ruining this entire thing with all the weed smoking. R'lyehian Mad Kush. What garbage. What am I doing to myself. Is it even worth it. This is sorcery: I consulted the Oracle which is to say I put a poll up on Aldo Tusk's Twittah showing my cigarette case lined with I want to say nine joints, you know, some hefty number and labelled it as my day's consumption. I was asking if it was a reasonable amount or too much and the majority of the Twittah people came back with *TOO MUCH*. One guy claimed that my daily consumption would put him in a coma. And instead of coming away feeling like a hard-as-nails sorcerer I felt shame. Like I was wasting something in myself or wounding something I didn't know I had. Boring into my own body with some tool, seeking out what heart what brain. The Drill and the Drilled. I took those nine joints and spaced them out over two days instead, in hopes of cheering myself up with my restraint. Didn't work, natch.

Some sorcerer I'm turning out to be.

Jehovah, we are coming for you. We are coming for you. We don't eat or sleep. We can't be bargained or reasoned with. We feel no pity, remorse, fear and we absolutely will not stop, ever, until you are dead. JHVH1, your time in the noösphere is fast running out. At any given moment in the very near future, someone, somewhere, will be reading *DRILL*, either the novel or the audiobook or the graphic novel adaptation or seeing the movie (Panos Cosmatos, directing) or maybe the docuseries on streaming. Who the fuck knows. My point is the human mind is going to become immune to your influences, spirit; I'm using media to kill you. God, or whatever you like to imagine yourself. I'm killing you by inches, in the pages of this book and up there where you live, in the place humans think. I pilot this Drill and I've got a feeling where to find your heart, your brain.

This is sorcerer's work. Will there be blood, should we bring gloves and rope, utility blades in bright yellow handles. Something to gag a mouth with but then. But then how does one gag a god? Work, more work. More research and meditation, more smoke in my lungs, more asynchronous thinking so's I ken dodge the code enforcers out and about on the noönet, surely it's all to a purpose, in the end? All things being Empty and Awake.

How will I die? Will there be blood?

It doesn't matter. It won't matter if there's blood.

NOW FOR THE CONCLUSION OF
THIS TALK ON PRESSURE SOURCE

The show was in reality a kind of magical placenta that allowed me to leave the Jehovah's Witness cult and allowed also for the gradual insertion into what became increasingly to be viewed by me as *the real world*, a conceit that would see me through several years of frothing chaos in my work and social lives. I had not been built for the real world, I had to undergo a transformation in the very core of me that would radiate out and alter both how I moved through the world and what the world would now bring to me. I had come into Paradise, in truth, and the multiple life paths that stretched before me was a plenitude I had not expected. Thank Dagon for Weird Tales, the radio show.

From the introduction:

Good evening. The time is now *midnight*. It's a strange time, when even abstractions can be split exactly down the middle and worlds open one to another. It's a peculiar time, when knowledge and horror can *penetrate* and *permeate* the mundane and the rational. Or, in other words, it is time once again for Weird Tales! I am your host, the *Landotter*, coming to you live from the Subterranean Caverns of Madness far below the offices of the Mighty and Terrible C F C R! Saskatoon's community radio,

90.5 on your FM dial! Tonight!

And then I would go on to list the entertainments coming to the listener in a creepy transatlantic accent akin to the sepulchral tones of such horror show radio hosts of the past, men like The Whistler or the guy who introduced *Inner Sanctum* each week. Well, that was me, but for a small audience of maybe a couple of dozen Saskatoon residents each Saturday night. My wife was leaving me, I'd been kicked out of the house and was living in a second-floor cold-water walkup in the University district with my cat. Fuck. Thank Dagon, again, for Weird Tales. I might have lost every last shred of cool were it not for the years-long hyper-sigil it was, the thing, this *artifact* of my own *devising* that served as life support and anchor in my hellish post-JW weeks and months, my god.

I'd read short weird fiction over the air between midnight and the bottom of the hour. Then for the back half of the hour I'd play those old radio dramas; I owned (and still do) a huge collection of audio cassette tapes that I'd been given by a retired radio host back in Victoria. Anyway, long story, I had a bunch of media that was tailor made to putting out this portion of the show. I have episodes of *Suspense*, *Inner Sanctum*, *Dragnet*, and *Escape! X Minus One!* And so on. Buncha one offs. I think there's a *Thin Man* or two in there. Big collection, lotsa variety.

From one o'clock on, the show would feature me reading a longer piece of weird fiction and over the three or four years I did the show we covered a lot of authors. There was Lovecraft, of course, and Bloch and Clark Ashton Smith, and the others of the Lovecraft Circle. But then I also worked in a lot of New Wave writers; I read Moorcock and Ramsey Campbell and once or twice a couple things from King's short fiction collections. The Bachman books? Maybe. I read Barker's *The Hellbound Heart*. "In the Hills, the Cities." Round Valentine's Day things would get a bit racy and I'd read some gruesome erotica. I raised money for the station during their annual fundraiser. You know the type. Do crazy things for money on air. I suppose this is all ancient history. I mean, fuck it, I'm fifty years old, I know this is seriously prehistoric stuff. It's another life to me entirely, and the person who crawled out the other end of that working only bears a passing resemblance to the human thing I am now. I dare not claim beinghood here, I'm a cthulhusattva through and through, as are you in the act of reading. And to think, this prehistoric stuff was obsessed with even more ancient stuff, real culturally relevant old media there, boy. Ah, but it got you through, didn't it, this stupid spoken word radio programme, from before the days even of proper internet. Remember that time the station got robbed while you were on the air? Dumb kids rifling through the offices while you blathered on in the studio because the last host, the guy who did the punk show, had forgotten to lock the door to the street. But then you *hear* them and chase them out and instead of going back in you run after them and of course they have an accomplice waiting out there in the bleak Saskatchewan November night and this kid tackles you from behind in a parking lot. Breathless, bruised, you return to the studio where you relay your recent adventure to your listeners. Darcy came and picked you up that night. We miss Darcy.

Yes, Weird Tales. I called it that because fuck copyright and besides, I didn't even know the magazine was still publishing while doing the show. And who would have noticed, or cared, even? Rinky-dink little radio station in the middle of nowhere, in what they call the Paris of the Prairies. It's because of all the bridges over the Saskatchewan River. Pretty town in the summer. Bleak as literal fuck the rest of the time. I lost my wife there, and my religion. Almost lost my life.

Weird Tales was a placenta that I built and maintained myself.

A magical incubator, a what do you call it, alchemically. A *crucible*. The host character that I played, the mask of the Landotter; based on indigenous myth systems of the west coast I had left, the landotter creature is the spirit of a drowned person taken physical form. They have all-black eyes and they sharpen their teeth. Shape shifters. I felt myself to be one of these things, then. And still. Still, perhaps. Fun game for the scholars: track the figure of the landotter through my fiction. In the case of Weird Tales the radio show, The Landotter was like The Whistler, a mysterious figure who dwelled in the Subterranean Caverns below the station, as mentioned above. The Landotter would hijack the feed, you see. Come in from the Other Side. Those worlds opening one to the other, see? I'd open the show a few moments before midnight and after the commercial break with "Flee!", the twelfth track from the seminal compilation album by The Darkest of the Hillside Thickets, *Great Old Ones*. Start as we intend to continue and summon Cthulhu right off the top of the hour. Pain, madness, death. I gotta tell you, the goth kids ate it up.

It wasn't long before the show became autofictional. I began to detail the trials and tribulations of exiting a high-control cult like the Jehovah's Witnesses in these little segments I'd do just after the intro. Called it *The Landotter's Mystical Journey Journal* and it soon became a highlight. I started getting listeners. I started getting invited to host goth dance nights at local clubs. I was asked to be a guest NPC in folx role playing games. Shit. What had I become? But then things in chrysalis are often mainly goo-based until they take on their proper form. I'm not ashamed. I'm not. Like the kids say today, it is what it is. Or was.

I met some of my greatest friends through that show. The Brothers Knisely, Mic and Che. Heidi. Darcy. Christian. I celebrated my first birthday with Kate and Christian; they brought me a little chocolate cake with a frosting pentagram on it. I cried. I'm not ashamed. Do you smell ozone?

THAT WAS MY FAVOURITE SHIRT

So you know that scene in *Naked Lunch* when Peter Weller's Burroughs is talking to his wife, played by Judy Davis, and he says, he says *I thought you were done with all the weird shit* and she exhales this huge cloud of smoke and replies *I thought I was too but I guess I'm not.*" All laconical like, I fail to mention, which I regret. It really is a great scene.

"I'm Burroughs, then," says my wife.

"Yeah, I'm back on the curse train with Raymond."

"Jesus fuck, Scott, why. I thought when you didn't use the rat it was a good sign, a sign that you were done."

"Yeah, well, see above. Guess I'm not."

"What's the point even anymore."

We're sitting out on the porch. The air is warm and fragrant. Hummingbirds fight over the feeders. Everybody Hungry.

"I think the point is balance. I saw him the other day, you know. He was driving past me on Fernwood, I yelled abuse at him but he didn't notice. He doesn't get to not notice. He doesn't get to drive around town with a smile on his sharp, uneven face. He doesn't get to forget me, or my sister. And I did use the rat, after a fashion."

"You said you wouldn't. I watched you carry it to the garbage."

"You didn't want to bury it in the hügelkultur. But anyway,

166

never mind, the point is I've used it but I've done so in the novel, which is just as good and maybe even better, the way I'm conceiving of things."

"I just do not understand you anymore. Don't put me in your novel."

"Oh, too late for that. I don't name you, if that helps at all."

"And don't do anything that's gonna bring the cops here either. Can you imagine what that would do to Sean and Meri?"

"This work necessarily skirts the borders of illegality," I say, "else how effective would it really be?" I stand by this. If you are not willing to physically assault and harm the person you are cursing then you should not be entering into the work in the first place. That is the level of effectiveness of a proper piece of sorcery.

She swears again. A squirrel chitters from the walnut tree. What a glorious day. I take a long drag off a joint and cue up some *Handsome Boy Modeling School* on the little remote speaker I keep next to the porch altar. Have I told you about the porch altar yet? Give me a moment to check.

Good lord, this is a *book*. Ecclesiastes eleven verse eleven, kids. Wearisome to the flesh, but then, there's nothing better for transmitting thought across spacetime. Somewhere I imagine that there exists a kind of infinite book, a tome without a middle page. Could only exist in a terrible realm, imagine the library that could hold such a book. It shakes the mind to its foundations. Feed me chapstick, let me puff on that mary.

The porch altar. The backsplash, you'll immediately notice, is a large plaster cast of the classic Mayan doomsday calendar. You know the one, with the serpents and jaguars and pretty glyphs all in a row along the various circumferences ringing the thing like a bell. 2012 rolled around like any other year, they say, but nowadays I'm less sure and more convinced that we exist in some transitional bardo just next door to the physical world and all the societal and cultural weirdness is humanity attempting to crack that old cosmic egg, you hear what I'm saying? Anyway, I've concealed the light source that highlights this fearsome clock at night by placing it in a small plant pot. Next, the candles, all red, all burning down. Three Cthulhus and a ceramic horror toad. Pine cones. Little piles of burned down incense. It's a shit altar, I know.

DRILL is a heat sink, I tell my wife. Something that can process the heaps and heaps of existential shit this curse is generating. Can't you see it. It's in the white space around the letters, I swear it. See it writhing there. See it.

Later that night I smoke too much on top of some beers and end up puking all over the porch. Soaked the nice expensive Glerups slippers she got me for my fiftieth. The Cthulhus watch cryptically while the toad laughs.

REAL DRILLERS IN THE HOUSE

We descend from this reality into a denser one, a kind of subterranean universe that underlies the rational daylight universe. Sappers, understand. We go beneath. We tunnel and we excavate and we burrow through the Ground of Being, which is to say the Body of God. We are the Activity of the Drill. The Sapper's Union is strong.

I tell this to the postman on his route, waylaying him again in the charming little Fernwood town square. We talk in the shade of the gazebo, like old-timey lovebirds. He requires so much proof, so much convincing talk with this one. I tell him about the dimensional shadow wall and though the revelation does not surprise him, nevertheless he distracts and dissembles with a reminiscence of something similar read in a Castaneda book at one point on the spacetime supersphere. He babbles away. I find it irritating but press on. Our numbers this month are substandard. That's what I had to say to my team that morning. Rookie numbers. We gotta get em back up, I said. We need a big score, find us some massive piece of ordnance, something to really soften up the godbod. Someone like Scott himself, or his father. Or even JHVH1. Now wouldn't that be something? To what extent does a Gnostic bastard monster godthing like Jehovah correspond to the actual, pristine God, whose guts we are currently in the work of drilling through and rendering into a thick, nutritious slurry for the Things that travel behind the Drill, eh? Everybody Hungry. There's a one-to-one spark in everyone, how many yotto-jules of energy do you reckon we could pull out of a thunder god? These are the things that set my sapper's mind to thinking.

In the end I plan on showing him the method itself, a live demonstration if you will. We talk some more, about hypermatter, ordnance models, the Bulk. He asks what the pay is and I have to remind him that being a sapper means you get rich incidentally. The movie rights alone. Finally, I tire of discourse and pull Jones outside the Drill and outwith the time stream. Only a moment or two, enough to feel the density of the air in his lungs shift, enough to feel his brain quiver in its sheath of bone and fluid at the sheer effrontery of it. He weathers it with a sorcerer's aplomb, discreetly puking into a convenient hedge upon his return to consensus reality.

"It really is an underground space, isn't it? Somehow, we're all already buried." Horror slowly dawns on his face. "We're dead and buried already. It's like a containment dome. God, I mean. We need to get out!"

I tell him that is what we are in the business of doing. This was never a war, it's always been a rescue mission. We free minds, souls, what have you. There's a little packet of energy you carry with you, distributed through your body mind as a discrete and unreproducible algorithm, allowing for animation. Alan Watts says that the power of a human being is not so much in his particular individual identity as in a certain kind of emptiness through which something can flow. We are talking about a source of energy that is as close to getting to First Causal things as is possible, so far as we can tell from our researches, our excavations. Tremendous power, to keep an animatronic mass of grease and hair and organs moving through Time. These are timesuits we wear, as other, wiser pop cultural gurus have mentioned, and Time is a ferocious environment. So ferocious that our suits begin to break down after around thirty years.

"Sappers detonate souls," he says and I'm almost proud of how he's handling it.

None of those three words mean what we think they do, I tell him. I'm the closest thing to an angel there is and if that doesn't make you sad to the bone, Jones, there's nothing that can. No, we don't detonate souls, but yes, something is extracted, harnessed, released and upon release there is a corresponding state change in the Body of God. And this allows the Drill, which is to say reality, to dig deeper into the stuff. We're making progress.

"I thought the work was infinite because the Body of God was infinite."

"Well, what's an infinitude, at the end of the day. Just a moment. We live in small eternities, son, whirling around us like eddies in the stream. We can't point to Time and know it truly for what it is, what makes you think you could grok the infinite. Yes, the godbod is infinite and there is nothing but solid rock beyond the walls of the simulation, but that rock demands a Drill, Jones, my boy. Demands one. This is what the archons know and affirm, believe me when I say they've cracked the code. We're fine with this; we didn't come from money. It's why they build their Drills, or grow them. However a reality is made, anyway. When a Drill is set to drilling, life and species evolve on it until enough of them become sappers. There are Drills and sappers every possible where at all possible times. I've met sappers from other Drills, even, mostly at conventions but sometimes I'll run into one out in the field and even when you're prepared it can be a bit of a shock. But we're all dedicated to the Excavation, all brothers and sisters in the Union, we're all here for the

Drill and the drilling. And one of us, one of these days…"

I pause, let the moment grow heavy. Jones improves in silence, I'm finding, like a fine whine.

"One of these days we'll pierce the heart or brain," he finally breathes.

"Or whatever organ corresponds to those in the Body of God. The effect will be ruinous, I assure you."

AGAINST THE POWERS AND PRINCIPALITIES AND POSTCARD 2

They have this concept, the Jehovah's Witnesses, or should I say the Governing Body of the Jehovah's Witnesses have this concept, that of spiritual warfare. This is something they take totally seriously, so far as I've been able to tell. I try not to watch their videos too much; it can colour the curse working in a positive way toward them, to the target, which you as the worker of the curse do not want, you don't want this shit coming back to you. In this I'm backed up by generations of sorcerers before me. There are ways, natch, to block recriminations but the work remains, *remains*, dangerous. I cannot stress that enough. Let's see, the scripture, ah yes. Ephesians chapter six verse twelve. Kids! It's a fun one. Let's use the English Standard Bible for the sake of clarity and one other thing which you'll note immediately if you're a fan of yours truly. The English Standard version's got it like this, friends.

"For we do not wrestle against flesh and blood, but against the rulers, against the authorities, against the cosmic powers over this present darkness, against the spiritual forces of evil in the heavenly places."

Fuck me sidewise how was I supposed to not smack down a plump stack of existential dinero for a sales pitch like that! I sold timeshares in my soul for a piece of that action. "Cosmic powers of this present darkness"! Holy shit. I signed up for the Archons and went to the academy within days. Psst! Don't tell Greg M. as I'd hate to be around when he learns I'm like a double agent. Ha! Naw, I kid, I kid. You know what it was? Flashes of another life, probably temporal lobe epilepsy the way my luck is holding. Never mind me, I'll just reincarnate as everything. All the white space, spilling out of the void. Good Times in Bad Lands, is what the mailman's often saying but he never hears himself, isn't that a funny thing? Poor servant of Hermes, the ease and speed with which he compartmentalizes himself is almost uncanny. But *we're* here now, and talking bout that spiritual warfare.

Well, they believe it, the Governing Body of the Witchtower Bubble and Cracked Society of Pedophilia, or do so cynically in order to better seduce the rank and file with their apocalyptic ravings. Certainly the rank and file go in for it with a notable gusto, there is a reciprocity to the relationship. God knows the fuckers make money off their real estate dealings and investments but they're not pulling it in hand over fist like other television preachers do by fleecing their flock wholesale, so what's the deal, what's the attraction and friends, say it with me now, it's Control rearing its centipede head again to clack mandibles at us. I'm ready to throw down with the ugly fucker, I'll just say it out in the open like that, too. C'mon you many limbed freak, I'll clean your chitinous clock.

So, they believe it. And their lackeys, like my father, Raymond Francis Jones of the community of View Royal, Victoria, British Columbia, Canada, well they believe it. In spiritual warfare. Christian soldiers, onward, with the full set of spiritual armour girded round yo loins, for you are in battle against the wicked spirit forces of the heavenly kingdoms. Ooh! Let's check what the New World Translation, the Jehovah's Witness bible, renders the scripture. I'm suddenly curious.

"Because we have a wrestling, not against blood and flesh, but against the governments, against the authorities, against the world rulers of this darkness, against the wicked spirit forces in the heavenly places."

Yawn. Well, aside from the side-eye worthy political slant they put on it, it's not that exciting a version. My apologies. I went and looked it up in my actual copy, doncha know. All kinds of traumatic. The things I do for you, for this. For Ray. He has no idea the way this helps him, but I'm going to make him famous. Everyone's gonna know about the shitty cultist in Victoria who shuns his kids for religious reasons spread by a publishing company. I'm not saying I don't deserve to be shunned, at this point in my career as a sorcerer I've done some truly awful things. I've ruined lives, probably.

All right, but then who better to bring the warfare to them, say I, than I? It is I who will do it, am doing it, continue to do it.

The postcard featured a sigil on one side, in black and red, and in the corners the letters J H V H arranged in a clockwise fashion with the J at the top left corner. A clever little conceit, yes. Orienting the viewer. On the other side, along with his address for the postman to consult and hand deliver, ahh that most bespoke of information wrangling activities, some days I *do* enjoy my job, it's true and I'm man enough to admit it. Today, for instance, was a glorious day on the route, a real spring miracle with the birdies and the girls in skirts on bikes. You'll believe me when I tell you I saw some things today that warmed the cockles of me degenerate heart and no mistake. On the other side of the card, these words, in black Sharpie:

YOU DON'T GET TO FORGET ME, RAY.

I'm going to make him famous. I wonder who will play him in the miniseries? Fuck that. In the movie. Callers, we're heading through the night on the subject of grown ass men who curse their half-insane fathers, let's roll a clip.

WOKE UP AND CHOSE VEHEMENCE

Start with the saddest thing you know, or can. So goes a piece of writing advice I picked up somewhere. Probably from a comic book, knowing my taste in philosophic literature. Start with the saddest thing and the work flows out from there. Well, I'm not starting *DRILL* with that but it's here, anyway, isn't it. Embedded like a tick in the flesh of the thing, somewhere halfway along its length, this novel, this worm of text, this working. Welcome. Here's some tissue.

It's my birthday as I write this. I've taken the day off as one should for your own personal holiday. I even went so far as to poll the folx on Twittah about whether I should go into work and the results came back unanimously in favour of *not* doing that and so here I sit, nine thirty in the morning, worrying about what some relief postie is gonna end up doing to my route in an hour or so and writing or starting to write about the saddest fucking thing I know. I'm fifty-one now. Hits as hard as fifty did, maybe harder, as I am no longer as fit as I was a year ago, this largely due to changes in the diet and longish spells of depression. Too much Coca-Cola and philosophy, basically. High protein and carbs, very few vegetables, I'm getting soft in the middle now.

All things I'd say to my mother if she were alive to be making her birthday call to me. She'd call, see, early in the morning round six thirty or seven, which was the time of day I arrived in the simulation proper, she'd call and ask me to congratulate her on however many years of excellent parenting it had been. This was her little work around, understand. As a practicing Jehovah's Witness and the wife of a Jehovah's Witness elder, she couldn't in good conscience wish her son a happy birthday, just come right out and say it, but she *could* reverse-engineer the wish. My mother's sorcery was strong. Not strong enough to keep her alive or anything, but up there. My mom was up there and I loved her. So much. She'd call, see. Early.

I'd say mom I'm fifty-one now, congratulations on fifty-one years of being my mom. Your grandchildren are eleven and nine, your daughter-in-law is forty-four. I'll list off number after number. I make twenty-nine dollars an hour and walk eighteen kilometres a day for work and in my spare time I am writing an autofictional Gnostic novel called *DRILL* and also I'm cursing your husband, Raymond. And she will be shocked and upset to hear it and I will have a time explaining things but any time on the phone with my mom is precious so I am grateful for the opportunity to explain and so delay the eventual end of the call, my birthday phone call from my mother.

I'd have to explain things. How Raymond destroyed her family after she died, first shunning me and then years later doing the same (with far fewer tears) to my kid sister and her husband. That in order to have my revenge on dear old dad, I've become a willing tool of the Devil. It's a real Mephistopheles deal, mom, I'll say. That Faustian bargain kinda thing, you feel me? She will nod and murmur. Now we can see each other because of course I'm fifty-one and the year is not 1997 but 2023 and this is clearly a video call over Zoom or whatever the fuck the kids are using these days. That's how I can tell she's nodding, understand.

But it's necessary, mom, I'll continue, and needed, the Universe being what it is, which is Empty and Awake. There is literally no justice for a thing like this, what he's done. It's a violence being done to me and mine, a subtle violence, an intergenerational thing that comes for me in the night when I'm weakest at like three in the morning. I have demons, mom, I'll say, and she'll say oh honey no and I'll have to explain, again, but even I don't know what I'm saying anymore. My brain stem feels infected, like I'm being piloted and made to say and do and be this way in the world, which I'm increasingly of the conviction, mother, is a simulated one. It's my birthday and I might go buy into the grift later and eat a nice sandwich. She'll laugh, and you know she had a lovely one.

DRILL WRITING SOUNDTRACK FEATURING TANGERINE DREAM

T hing is, and I mean the truth of it, is that I'd kill him if I didn't think I'd be the first fucking suspect. That's where I'm at. For who he is, at his heart, and for what he did to my mother's family, *his family*, and for what reasons, what sickening, stupid, ugly reasons, in service of what kind of god? He passed his children through the fire in sacrifice to JHVH1. It's a curse, and it carries with it all my malice toward him, all my love-transmuted-to-hate toward him. I cannot feed your compliments to all my children. The only time I show up is when I'm insincere and I goddamn keep what I kill. That's the vibe with this curse, that's how it's going down. I would. I'd do it. If there was some way to do it and not get convicted, by Dagon I'd give it a go. God help me if I ever see him outside again. Let me tell you of the time when just such a thing happened and my courage failed me. Really the curse against Raymond Francis Jones began that morning in the industrial suburb of Victoria known as Rock Bay where I briefly held Walk 329 out of the Glanford depot, as a relief postie. I may have decided to perform the curse that weekend, after three joints on a Saturday morning as detailed elsewhere in this narrative, but the curse itself, the proper event, occurred then.

I passed him in the street, first. I was focused on my mail but some outer fibre of my luminous egg vibrated against his and I caught him, to my left, just out of the corner of my eye, at the last second. A wash of agitation passed over me, leaving me in a green room of sudden cognisance. Had it really been him? Like a brush with royalty, or some celebrity or anyway mythic thing. I felt like I'd seen the ghost of sasquatch or something. It took a dozen more steps to the corner of Bridge and Hillside for me to stop in my tracks, suddenly absolutely sure that yes, that had been my dad, Raymond, passing me in the street all unawares. I turned then, just in time to see the back of his hawkish head duck into the Mile Zero coffee shop.

I must have waited there on the corner five, ten minutes. I hemmed and hawed and I paced and paced. Considered finding a washroom and taking a nice long cleansing shit. Caught myself obsessively flipping through my bundles of mail as if to ground or hypnotize myself. Driven to madness, basically, of an instant. Finally, I turned and walked back down Bridge, each step a decade, it seemed to me. Longest fucking walk I'd done that day, those few backtracking steps. I went off route, I performed what posties call a deadwalk, namely, a portion of the route where no mail is delivered due to diversion or detour. By the time I entered the coffee shop I felt like a phantom. I had been reduced in those few steps, stripped down to raw rage and every nerve firing but uselessly, uselessly, I was useless in the face of him but look! Look how frail and old he seems, see the receding hairline and all of it shot through with the grey. The spots on his hands. He's thin, *vegan* thin because of course like many Jehovah's Witnesses, he and the wife have gone in for the supposed diet that all good JWs will be eating in the New System on a Paradise New Earth. Nuts and berries and plenty of the dark veggies and of course *LEGUMES* feature prominently.

Paradise will be gassy, who knew? But he looks thin and weak, in a blue cardigan not unlike one I wear myself around the house, actually, so funny, that. When you think about it a bit. He's wearing a tie with a nice shirt and a blue cardigan over all. For a moment it is like looking in a mirror but only for a moment.

I stood there in the door with the sunny spring day shining in behind me for a little eternity. There he sat, calmly sipping coffee with someone I immediately pegged as another Jehovah's Witness elder. What, like you can't spot em in the wild? Don't be so down on yourself, you know you can do it if you really try. I've got that faith in you, kid. The whole scene screamed informal elder's meeting. Something was going down in the local JW noetic space and these two fine brothers were holding a small conclave to jaw about it, perhaps bow their heads in public prayer for that extra sheen of impious religiosity. Whitewashed graves, like the scripture says. Five will get you ten that they were deciding the fate of some poor, struggling Witness mother or some defenseless, horny teen who went a little too far with her boyfriend. The iron grip these fiends have over the sex lives of their congregants would make a fine and interesting paper for someone to write. A sordid history. I stood there, staring. Just taking it all in and finding as I did so that I couldn't walk further into the shop.

Which would have been the thing to do. There was a chair right next to him. I could have walked right on up and plunked my ass down. Somehow, I knew it would be better to block the exit. I glanced to the counter; there were two employees there and maybe half a dozen customers scattered through the shop. Ray and his compatriot were seated at a corner table. I could have done it. But then, what would have happened? He would have got up and left, is what would have happened. Oh, I'm sure of it. No, though I paint it as cowardice here, I think perhaps there was a germ of wisdom in standing there, backlit in my postie blue-and-yellow uniform; I felt the egregore of the Post rear up behind me, even, the vast might of the mothercorp and behind her, naturally, Hermes, god of messengers himself and was I not there to deliver a message, in any case?

I stood there, still staring and finally Raymond, my father, finally he looks up and sees me standing there, vibrating with rage. A curious look passes over his features and his friend turns also to stare. Ray's confused. He doesn't know who I am, he doesn't fucking *recognize* me. I take off my postie cap. Still, nothing, but now his eyes are riveted on me in interest since I can feel the knives pouring from a space just between my eyes. Surely one might burst his little bubble, pierce the heart or brain. I would kill him, remember, if it weren't for the obvious fact that I'd be suspect number one and rightly so. He's just shunned my littlest sister, too, understand. I've only just learned of it the week before and my anger is very near the surface. I take off my sunglasses now and finally recognition dawns on his evil old face and a dour expression replaces the confusion. Ray half turns to his elder buddy.

"It's my son," he says.

It is my son. Something breaks in me with that. On the face of it, a perfectly normal way to indicate that the atomic mailman at the door is related to you. But that *IT* really did it for me, pushed me into another realm entirely. I could feel the message pour out of me.

"Do you have *any* idea how hated you are, Ray? How much I hate you?"

"I'm sorry to hear that from you, son."

"You're sorry...sorry? I've read your precious Shepherd book, by the way." It's all I can think of to say in the moment. "You should be ashamed." The elder buddy visibly bristles, you can see the hackles come up right through the suit jacket.

The book entitled *Shepherd the Flock of God* is the secret Witchtower elder's manual and boy howdy is it a *read*, friends! You only get this book when you become an elder and no one else is allowed to read it or even have access to it. Not your wife or a ministerial servant or even another elder. Women never see this book; it's printed and shipped only by qualified male staff at Bethel. Imagine a book that devotes a single paragraph to murder, assault, and robbery, or namely the spiritual punishment to be meted out by the elders in case of these crimes but dedicates *twenty-one whole pages* to sexual indiscretions. They love to get you on the sex, basically. Most disfellowshipping events are as the result of this crack-brained prosecution of normal human sexual behaviour. If you're a dedicated and baptized Jehovah's Witness and you aren't in a heterosexual marriage, look out, I mean for god's sake be careful how you sleep around, don't let them catch you at it or even suspect you of immorality because WHAM! down comes the shun hammer and that's it! You've lost everything, your friends, your family, your social groups, in many cases your means of living (many JWs work for other JWs, natch) and all for what? Because you like a little cock or pussy every now and again. Because you watched some porn or went down on your husband. It's always a sex thing with these low-grade perverts.

But Ray knows I know this, if I've read the *Shepherd* book. Which, as stated, I certainly have. He knows what's in there, he knows whereof the focus of his so-called ministry lies. A little red comes up in his cheeks as the bristling friend continues to bristle and clutch at his muffin.

"How did you get a copy…"

"I got a PDF off the fucking internet because your little cult is like a sieve, Ray. You got leaks and leakers everywhere." You, reader, can download one right now if you like, they are easy to find. He blanches and the elder buddy makes a large *har-rumphing* groan. I've got them, yelling at them from the door of the coffee shop, I've *got them* and they can't leave without it turning into more of a scene and Ray is vibrating now too and now everyone is watching, the customers, staff. I can feel people behind me on the sidewalk, gathering, and something else, too, in behind the forebrain, wrapped around the lizard stem, and as it rises I recognize it as my daimon, here and in the daylight and in public, a great black hiss from below, in the place where I do my living best.

The torrent of glossolalia when it comes is fearsome in the extreme. A fractured, howling blast of ragged and ripped syllables, shredded consonants, mutated and mutilated vowels. Double-esses and triple-yous. Pure sigil, uncut curse translated and run through the gears of my language engine with the meaning governor disengaged and the whole thing spinning, spinning and throwing off sparks. There are shocked cries from the customers. And there it is, finally, in my father's face, an answer to my rage in his own, there it is there it is I can *see* it, like looking in a mirror. There it is, my father's true face, the face he wore before he was born. What he came into the world with. I do love a moment of unbridled honesty.

The glossolaliac firehose subsides and I slump against the doorframe, little phonemes of inchoate hate dribbling from my lips. Ray is frozen in his chair, his eyes desperately searching the ceiling of the coffee shop. The elder friend is glaring at me, half-turned in his chair as if to rush me should I start it up again. Is it enough. It's enough. It must be. I drag myself away, back into the street, suddenly aware of what I've been doing, how it must have *looked*. Suddenly I'm worried about my *job*. Surely customers will complain about the loud postman. I stagger away,

putting my glasses and cap back on, out into the anonymous in-
dustrialized streets. I feel like I need to puke but nothing comes.
The mail pulls me back into its rhythm and I try to fight the
pace, my mind blazing with the thought of returning right then
and putting my hands around his throat.

Later on in the day, I return to the coffee shop to apologize
to the owner, try to explain. He gives me a donut and a listening ear. I was, apparently, not as loud as I'd thought, and much
of the distress I thought was being expressed in the shop at my
actions was hallucinated. I am delusional, I am delusional. I am
an empty vessel and awake and it is the most horrible thing, I
think. At the end of the day.

"You shouldn't serve that guy or any of his cronies, when they
come in," I stammer out around mouthfuls of cruller. "They're
a cult, and a dangerous one."

"You don't say."

"I do say. I do say that. They murder their members and destroy families."

"Murder? No way."

"Absolutely. They force people not to take blood transfusions
for life saving medical procedures, I don't know what else to call
it. Seems like murder to me."

"That's fucked up."

"The thin one was my dad."

HEINOUS HYMNS OF
ABOMINATION

In what way does the hate I hold for my father colour the love I show or don't show my son. I like to think we're reasonable with him but sometimes. Sometimes when he falls into these I dunno they're something like a mini-rage and he can't see past the immediate moment and we tell him, his mum and I, we tell him *ten minutes, Sean* when he's got ten minutes left on the video games and then five minutes after that we give him the five-minute verbal warning, I mean does this sound unreasonable to you, fellow parents? Do I even need you to sound off in the comments or such like? No, I do not, I *am* being reasonable, I think with a ten-minute and then a five-minute warning any reasonable gamer should be able to bring whatever quest or mission or level they're on to an end and or simply *save and quit*. I fucking *know* that's a feature in most if not all games, I hardly think it's such a goddamn hardship to hit exit when your time's up but you would think it's the literal end of the world and this happens every goddamn day. I feel so hollowed out from yelling at him when he just won't listen. And how much of this is Ray? How much of this is Ray.

I try to remember what he was like with *me*, how he treated *me* and I just come back with nothing. It's like there's nothing there of the man, in my memory, any especially heartbreaking punishment or enraging discipline I suffered at his hands and I've got nothing, nothing. It's as if he saved up all his horrible behaviour for my adult life instead. So how much of him is me and I don't know it? Did he ever tell me to shut up when I couldn't stop talking. Did he criticize and openly speculate about possible punishments for unwanted behaviour? Because I've done these things. Just today, even.

The dead are terrible to behold. The dead make terrible fathers. Probably I have already said the damaging thing that will lodge like a shard of radioactive material in the luminous egg of my beautiful, sweet, and much beloved son. What kind of father is made from a father like mine? He will grow and it will remain lodged there and I will probably never know what it was, the thing said that wounded forever. I told him today, I said son, I fear that one day this relationship, of you, your mum and I, this little antagonistic triad will one day produce a bad moment, you know like a real opening of the abyss at the core of all Being kinda thing, and one or two or even all three of us will say something we'll regret for the rest of our goddamn lives and he teared up. He teared up, my lovely, kind, compassionate boy why am I not more patient with him? How much of this is me, how much Ray, how much a demon or a god. I feel atomic powered, fueled by conflicting synchronicities smashing together at the core of me, I want to irradiate the inside of my skull and burn it all to ashes in there, every reference, every influence, every bad idea and worse action. Inferno. Drill it out.

I don't even have any good Dad Jokes fer fucks sake.

By exorcising the JHVH entity from my father, will I also burn those parts of him from myself that are still resident and evil within me? Will I know my daimon in a pure way and not this sideshow freak of a phenomena. Will I ever forgive him.

Will I ever forgive him. I can't see a path to it. I can't. On weak days I want to, I do, I want to call or show up at his door and apologize for all this, to take it all back and make it as if it could never have been but that. won't. happen. Will it? It will not. Will I ever no never.

How could I? I've gone too far and said the unnameable thing, I have uttered the true speech and cursed my father, Raymond Francis Jones. For this I am likely dammed, after a fashion. To have such an ugly thing on my conscience, and for what? For fucking what? Stupid beyond belief, this rudimentary campaign of milquetoast harassment directed against a stupid old man and I'm a stupid old man for doing it but it's done, isn't it, or at the very least on its way to being done. The Cult of Done.

I'll get none of this energy back. Won't matter how many people read *DRILL*. Won't matter if Willem Dafoe plays Ray in the movie. Won't matter if the curse works and the ritual is enacted properly and Jehovah is killed in cold ectoplasm there in the basement of some decommissioned church. None of it will be on its way back to me, that energy is lost forever. I am lost forever. The dead are terrible. It's the sunk cost fallacy that's killing my dad and whaddaya know, it's killing me, too. What a round up. Can't stop, won't stop. Not until it's truly over.

Greg M. has a plan, he tells me. The details of the plan itself he has not been forthcoming with, but there is one. "And it's a good one, Jones," he says and claps a hand like a slab of beef on my good shoulder. "But we'll need things from you. Certain forms must be maintained for the kind of operation I've in mind."

For one, he wants me to get off the weed. Not forever, just for now, just until arrangements can be made. And I need to harvest bore worms from the source, a task which I am assured I will have the assistance of Greg and his entire team. It's one thing to hit the small ones in the hügelkultur with the koan-thrower every other weekend and quite another to slip the shadow wall and enter the precipitous Bore Hole on the other side of the Drill where the real monster worms dwell and multiply in their fictional millions. There'll be no riding, nerds, Usul will not be calling a big one, but there is a method to attract them and turn them into the bore worm leather straps we will need to bind the Jehovianic energies in that room. That's what we need them for, their narrative hides. Nothing holds down a godform like bore worm leather worked into a plaited rope. We're talking about some kinky stuff now.

Oh son. Oh my Sean. Your dad is insane. I can feel it in the back of my head like there are ants back there chewing, chewing. Centipedes. What I should do, friends, readers, is leave. I should leave this place and go to some other place. There are so many reasons I'm not a good dad for you, boy, and I'm realizing I don't even know half of them, I am blind, I am *occluded*, my boy my darling boy. Your father labours in the dark of his own mind and finds the work lacking in honour. Better to pierce my eardrum and let the blood drip on blank pages then sit here *masturbating* into a Word document and you! You! Reader! Sitting there letting it happen. Where is *your* decency? Where is *your* good taste that you would stay and let this degeneracy flow forth into you, I mean, my god. Jesus heavenly Christ.

I've gone mad. Greg and the sappers prove it. I've seen things, am seeing them now. There's a Tillinghast Resonator in my attic, wouldn't that be a thing? Yes.

I'm mad. Gone mad.

THAT SPECIAL GLOW IN THE CUT

I t's a hyperstitional beastie we're hunting," says Greg M. one morning. "A proper fictional entity what's gone and done made itself real, through the usual channels." The team nods in agreement, to a person. Wee Frederick grunts.

JHVH1: A memetic organism gone bloated and sick on feeding from eight million fractured and malfunctioning souls that comprise the membership of the Jehovah's Witness cult. The earth is being killed, they say, and the people who are doing it have names and addresses. Well, what is being killed in the here and now, in this empty awakeness, where all is one and one in all, as the Necronomicon does relate and affirm vis-à-vis Yog-Sothoth, the Dweller at the Threshold. This, friends, this unabashedly Lovecraftian turn is, I am afraid to have to say it, entirely appropriate to the Jehovah entity, or as I've already termed it elsewhere, the JHVH1 memetic organism. It forced itself into being through a combination of cult antagonism in the Fertile Crescent and the lucky pickup by a millenarian Baptist in the late nineteenth century. It tore a portal into the noösphere, a thing of No Thought broke through into the place where our species does its Thinking, our Collective Mind, as Alhazred knew and affirmed. The thing speaks through hallucinations, burning bushes and fiery wheeled angels full of eyes and so on.

It's a former storm god so it delights in flooding, in destruction and disassemblage, of institutions, of people and families, of social bonds and biological bonds. Lightning and death are its meat, it delights in decomposing the links between things in electrical fire, severing at the molecular level. That's a storm god. That's JHVH1.

And that's who Greg M. and Wee Frederick and Lazy Susan and the rest of the team, the twins whose names I can never get right, Greg's handpicked sapper crew, are going after. I'm going with them, naturally. There's no way they could do this op without me: I am the Key and the Gate in this instance and there'll be no real manifestation of the Jehovah entity without me being there to facilitate the interchange.

Greg M. says that my talent lies in locking the entity down into its constituent narrative strands. It can't *not* be itself around me. The fact is that I have long-dormant copy of the JHVH1 memetic viral material in my own bodymind; the fucking *shape* of a Jehovah's Witness is still there imprinted in my luminous egg and in behind the blue of my eyes, which I'm told are rather nice if you'll allow a moment of pride in my appearance, I mean, fuck it, I'm fifty-one now, and a couple of weeks. I'm proud of my body, weak in places though it may be. My legs are strong and my feet sure, with Hermes' blessing. How long is this fucking novel going to take although let's be honest, we can all feel it, we're getting down to the short and curlies now, ain't we. Oh yes. The attraction for the very dominant print of JHVH1 in Raymond will be undeniable and we'll be able to lock the entity down in the interstitial space between father and son vis-à-vis the bore worm cable, which, have I described? I have not. I have mentioned the process, but not described it. Well, here goes…

Bore worm cable. First, secure bore worms, the larger the better. You want Type 3 or greater, anything smaller that that just throw em back into the BoG. Body of God. Where I am assured they will set to munching like good bore worms should, yessir. Take a simple knife and insert it between the fourth and fifth cervical vertebrae, severing the narrative thread. Pay no attention to the worm's pleadings at this point, it will wax poetic and that stuff gets everywhere, simply insert and press; the narrative thread in a Type 3 bore worm is huge, unmissable, and even a nick is enough for the whole thing to bleed out. The story will die and the worm's carcass will be ready for harvesting but this must occur *immediately*, do you understand? Not a second must be wasted because the bore worm skin will begin to dry out and go to a very unworkable leather if you do not first cut and strip the hide from the worm and begin to plait it into a three or five cord cable, as the situation demands. A threefold cable is fine for lesser angels and demons; for something of this tier, jumped up as He is, you'll want fivefold cable. And you don't have to be fancy with it, there's no points for craftsmanship, just whip the strips of hide together as quickly as you're able. That's it, like that. Not bad, you've got a fine form. A natural. Once you have enough cable you'll be able to lock down and truss up even the most potent of godforms.

So Greg M. assures me and Wee Frederick grunts. We make arrangements to go bore worm hunting in the hügelkultur out in the back forty at Stonefish House. Greg M. scoffs about the name, again.

"So, what's the plan for when you die, Jones?" he asks out of the blue like someone who knows about such things.

"It's on a sliding scale of legality and tastefulness. It depends on what my survivors will be able to put up with. Top tier disposal looks like this: a green burial for my headless corpse, and my skull preserved and placed in a ceremonial box of exquisite craftsmanship. Another option is to have my headless body cremated and turned into life gems—artificial jewels formed from harvested carbon—which could be used to adorn the skull or otherwise decorate the box. My family and loved ones down through the ages will cherish Scott's skull as a precious heirloom. Dare I hope for a panoply of occult effects in the box's surroundings? I dare, friends."

"I like to think that we are friends, now," Greg says. "All things considered."

"What with what we're trying to do heah, he means," Wee Frederick puts in.

"Yeah, thanks. I am aware."

"Good. Then also be aware of this. The operation could kill your dad. It could kill you. Certainly a very large amount of energy is going to be released, and we'll do our best as sappers to shape and direct that energy, but goddamn. The twins keep coming back to me with readings that make my eyes blanch. It is exactly as if it knows we are coming."

Well, I wouldn't put it past it. I do go on.

"Second tier disposal would be a basic burial. Please make it a cheap pine box like my mother was buried in, out at Hatley Park Memorial in the community of Colwood, just outside of Victoria proper. Where I grew up, Colwood, basically the sticks at the time. No sidewalks and little lakes spotted everywhere below the low rolling Sooke Hills where once I panned for gold in the streams and rivers. Blessings on thee, little man, barefoot boy with checks of tan. Put me in an unworked box of yellow wood like my mom and lower me.

"God-tier level disposal, though. Somehow drop my corpse in the cold Pacific at the coordinates tattooed on my upper chest in a gentle arc beneath the shoulders. This will require some travel on my widow's part and probably not some small expense, either, for the place where I wish to be dropped is far from any shipping lane and will require some custom routing."

Greg M. coughs in a significant way.

"If you wanted to be really difficult, Jones," he says. "You could insist that she learn how to open a conduit from any Pacific coastal waters to R'lyeh, the whole being of the same medium, after all, that thing that links us all psychically in the simulation, ever present and roughly eternal. Water itself, I mean. All the universe's water, every drop, it's all a lubricating coolant for the Drill, without which the mechanism would seize and destroy itself. But you've done the ritual, if I'm not mistaken; there's traces of it still in the fibres of yer luminous egg there."

"I didn't think it would show."

"Everything shows, bucko," Wee Frederick puts in.

"She could open a conduit here and dump your ashes there without ever leaving the comfort of Victoria. Remember, she'll be old."

"How do you know."

"Well, *older* let's say. You've years left ahead of you if all our readings are right and whether that works out as a blessing or a curse will be up to you. Lookit me, I sound like a motivational poster over here!"

"Not the ashes, though. The entire thing, my corpse. Or, if unable to do that, ashes, fine. But it must be all of me burned down. The complete essential saltes. A clean cremation in a pre-cleaned, fresh oven so that no particle of any other dead slob gets mixed up with mine. For there is naught but liveliest awfulness in that which is called up from imperfect saltes," I quote.

"Nerd," says Greg M.

OBITUARY DRILL 002

The route on which I'd met my father at the coffee shop with his Jehovah's Witness elder buddy, the episode in which I dropped a pallet's worth of glossolalia on the floor in front of them, to my horror and sometimes shame, it was on that route, known as Walk 329, that I found the dead man.

329 is in an area called Rock Bay and it is a rough zone, largely mixed industrial and some apartments and halfway houses. It was in front of one such halfway house that I found them, lying on a discarded chesterfield on the sidewalk, legs akimbo. Immediately, I clocked to their extreme state; if they were not all the way dead then they were certainly close. The eyes had that non-look look to them, the opposite of seeing. I shook the person by the shoulder, shouted, pinched through the material of his jeans to grab a hank of leg and twist it. Nothing. It was at this point that I called 911.

The paramedics, when they arrived a few minutes later, were able to get maybe three breaths out of the body before calling time of death. I stayed through the whole thing, answered questions, and witnessed, witnessed. I had found them and so I figured it was only right and moral to stay through the end. I offered up a half-formed prayer to their gods, whoever they might be. Then I spoke to their spirit itself, if it was still hanging around. The cast of the sunlight in the air, the mingled speech of the caregivers and surrounding onlookers, the flight of crows overhead, all these weighted the moment in such a way that I suspected their spirit, *ka*, or whatever, that animating principle was still present, and so I spoke.

David, I said, for I'd learned from distraught residents of the house that their name was David, David I said, you've died of an overdose on a side street in a bad part of town David, you've died in the middle of the morning while looking up through the branches of a tree which I dunno, it sounds nice to me, I hope your passing was at least halfway pleasant by way of the drugs, and David, if as I suspect there were evil men and women in your past, then let not your ghost rest easy at least for a little while. Instead, come with me David and gain a little power in the world, attach yourself to a fetish on my person and I can transport you to a place where you can learn so many things, if you're willing. A place where demons and wood sprites and all manner of ghosts and unalive things wreak their wonders on a terrible old man.

By other omens I discerned that the offer had been accepted, so that night, after a pleasant rest of the day off from work for reasons of emotional distress—I had after all discovered a dead body, I milked that for two days off, paid, and you know it—I prepared the fetish and delivered it to my father's house.

"Godspeed, David," I said as I integrated the fetish into the curse as it was then. New elements necessarily reconfigure the parameters. What would David bring to the mix? I was excited to see.

I'll never see. There is nothing to see here, nothing to suggest that anything is happening with this curse at all. Publish or perish, I suppose. Same as it ever was. For the sake of my children and possibly also for the sake of whatever literary legacy I may have in the future, *DRILL* must see publication. For the sake of the correct way this curse is to work itself out, *DRILL* has to be a book and readable by the world. Else the world unfair. Else this madness unredeemable. This madness has to be redeemable in some way. Cash rules everything around me, dollah dollah bills yo.

It's what David would have wanted!

A GENEROUS WORLD SUGGESTS GENEROUS LIVING

Around Stonefish House this evening lays an effulgent glow of warm spring and warm feelings. Happy wasps sup at the hummingbird feeders and a crow has appeared to caw and burble at me from the porch railing. My children are happy and safe, my wife is satisfied after an evening working in the hügelkultur. She reports no bore worms. There's a light breeze; has been all day, cutting into the warmth of the sun. I know my curse works in this magic hour as I bask in my blessings. I have had doubts recently, misgivings aplenty, but I am past all that now and feeling good about things. Feeling right.

The simulation is creamy. That's something I've been known to say. The simulation is creamy this morning or *mmm creamy* when for instance the feed is *very* strong and there's a vanishingly small amount of dropped signal and I just feel *invested* and infested in the moment, in the totality of the program. Good job, Archons, you'd never know it wasn't actually a thing. We imagine, with our ape brains made of salt and fat, that we somehow are able to discern the nature of the NATURE in which we are embedded BUT as products of the simulation how much real trust can you put in that, anyway. And worse, what if the simulation is broken, as I sometimes suspect in a very strong way. Now listen, hear that? Ice cream truck. You seen some of these crazy new-fangled frozen treats they're selling the kids these days? Why, I saw a SpongeBob ice cream thing that looked like a soul spent too long in the Styx, mah boy. Cream. Cash rules and you know the rest.

It's a money kind of feeling, this knowledge that the curse is working. Yes, the best revenge may well be living well but how much better to also know your target is living worse. Now that, my friend, is a toothsome dish and I long to sup. And so, an accounting of the blessings of Stonefish House, as a counter to Raymond's now haunted cardboard condominium domain. See the blessings of Hermes, and of other, stranger gods...

Garlic and rhubarb and onions and roses and fig trees and grape vines and a couple of palm trees, a plum tree and three yucca plants and a holly tree where the hummingbirds live. The wife has herbs growing everywhere. Walnuts in season. And there shall he dwell, each under his own vine and fig tree, like the psalmist says. A sizeable garden plot, once we put a simple wall of boards and cinder blocks around the hügelkultur. A working, paid for, dependable vehicle. A no-longer functioning hot tub, sadly, *but* everything in place to hook up a new one once the money starts rolling in from my various projects and we can afford to plunk down several thousand. I'm sure there'll be big savings on installation when the time comes and lemme tell ya my old poetic bod is looking forward to *that*. Yessir. Speaking of the day job, look, we all know it's a good job but a tough gig and it will either kill me or keep me alive an unnaturally long time, even for a Jones—we are notoriously lengthy in our spans, my great gramma lived to one hundred and three and didn't really start losing her mind until she got that letter from the Queen at her one hundredth birthday, though she'd lost both her legs to the gangrene—but I'm grateful for it because fuck it, Canaduh Post keeps food in my kids' mouths and clothes on their backs and I think that counts for a lot these days, all things considered, sure I may not be dad of the year or anything, I may smoke too much and not discipline enough but I'm doing my bit, as a father, as a citizen, a sorcerer. Soon, a sapper. As a postman. It's got to count for something, right? It's a thread in the great tapestry of existence, it *must*, must make a difference somewhere down the line. I don't even care that I'll never see it, I just would like to know, *need* to know what's coming down the pike. I think we'd all like that.

A sorcerer. Where the blessings in that aspect of my being. Many and multiform are the dim horrors of earth, or so they say. What can I see with my wizard eyes, friendos? The very existence of my wizard eyes begs the question! Such things! Such things have I seen, and such like beings as would boil your brains in your skull. I can see your luminous eggshell upon which you build your perceptual apparatus and I can affect it with my own. If I wanted to, I could shift your assemblage point right now and cause you to view the shadow wall to the left of all sentient things and I could teach you how to plunge in that impossible direction to plumb the very pit of negation and horror. To draw forth what gems, what treasure?

For all the treasures of heaven there are corresponding riches in the lowest depths of hell, great wonders there to be unearthed, great spoils for the enterprising sorcerer, so the Desert Fathers knew and affirmed.

I want Ray to see me, to truly see his son. The way you see and can *only* see a sleep paralysis demon when they appear, that single-pointed vision, that cyclopean focus. And so I curse him. As honestly and robustly and dependably as I can, as a first-born son should when it's everything that matters to me at the end of the day. It is. He spits on me with each day he continues to shun me, he spits on this glorious spring evening he could be spending here, in the expansive and pleasant back yard of his first-born son, servant of the Crown and published author, and attended to by loving grandkids who are just really super kids, I'm not saying that as their dad, I'm being objective they're quite delightful, he misses out on all that, all of it. That's punishment enough! cry the wags in the audience but you don't understand. It's not enough that he *merely* misses out. Don't you see. He's *happy* to be doing so, he's making his god Jehovah happy by shunning his children, his eldest and his youngest. No, it's because he's also spitting on me. He spits on my marriage. He spits on my job, my writing. He spits and spits and it's a firehose of derision from my father, this constant stream of each day's spittle from his pallid old man lips and so no, the curse works, and is successful, because with each postcard delivered, each reminder placed strategically at his door, each fetish tied to the posts of his house, each voicemail left on his answering machine heard or not, he will be forced to face head on the *enormity* of the crime he continues to commit against his own family, against my human rights and against the human rights of my sister and our family. Our family, Raymond, you tore it apart and for what for what. Why, why would you ever think it would be a good idea to do this, to shun your own children? Raymond, Raymond, we are coming for you and your little god too. I'm going to tear it out of your still-beating heart.

LIVELIEST AWFULNESS

There had been an argument, after ▓▓▓▓▓▓▓▓ died. It seems most of the people surrounding my mom in her last year had been living in a kind of denial and there had been no preparations or discussions among family members about ultimate disposal. The day arrived—December 17, 2001, for those keeping track—and suddenly there's the mad rush to figure out what they were going to do with the body. Raymond seemed to think ▓▓▓▓▓▓▓▓ would have preferred cremation but Roger, mom's brother and patriarch of the Robertson side of the family, insisted, and pay attention now to this bit, *insisted* that she be buried, in a plot, at a specific location on the earth, so that and *get this*, so that Jehovah would know where to find her and bring her back to life. Right out there at Hatley Park Ceremonial Gardens out on the little two-lane highway going out to Sooke, that's where the Holy Spirit of JHVH1 will reach down, into the ground of my mother's fucking grave and pull her bodily back to some form of tangible life. For some reason, Jehovah requires an address and a scrap of genetic material to perform his wonders. And so the argument went on for hours until finally another aunt volunteered to pay for the box and so my father relented.

My mother's body was placed in a cheaply made box of unfinished pine boards and two-by-fours and we gathered a day or two later, or maybe even three, time behaved very strangely then, as it perhaps does still. It's almost like I'm back there now. It would only take the slightest effort to project myself outwith the Drill and land some when and where else on the illimitable screw. I could be there this evening and I am, and you with me, reader.

Ray is in tears as the box is lowered, as am I. But then he remembers something, some documentary television programme surfaces in his head like some imp of the perverse and his grief-addled mind seizes on it in the moment and he cries out and he yells WAIT and STOP because you see there's a factoid from this program that's blazing white hot and that factoid, this intrusive thought is…what if she's not in there. What if they've got the wrong body in there? He'd seen it on the tee vee, that time in that place when they buried the wrong person, they get mixed up all the time, it happens more than we know, it could be happening *now* and there it is, the insistence that they raise up the box and open the lid. Open the lid. Open it.

So we all get to see her one more time in crepuscular west coast December afternoon sunlight, which is not the best, may I just call out the lighting director for December in Victoria, you're doing a crap job, bud. Jehovah's Witness funerals are never open casket, the body is not even in the building, they outsource the process almost entirely to the funerary services and the memorial service for the deceased that they *do* take care of is largely a recruitment drive talk hooked to a brief ten-minute recap of the dead person's life. Yes, she's dead, but she had the hope of the Resurrection, which she got here, in this very Kingdom Hall, line up to be implanted with the JHVH1 memetic organism today, like ███████████ did. Mom was much beloved at her workplace, see, she was part of the typing pool at the Ministry of

Health and Welfare just down on Blanshard and she had friends, work friends, who came to her funeral. It was toward these un-lucky people that the majority of my mother's funeral service was directed. ████████████ was wise, ████████████ knew what was up, in a cosmic way, she knew which god was deserving of wor-ship and if *she* knew this, this lovely, compassionate, worry-wart of a woman who everyone loved, well then friends, don't you want to know how she knew this, and why she believed? Never mind the apocalypse, never mind the fact that we murder thou-sands each year by denying them medical treatment using blood or blood products, never mind our baked-in racism, misogyny, homophobia, and straight up fascist leanings, ████████████ took strength and comfort from these beliefs. Why can't you?

REEFER MADNESS

G reg M. is right. I have to get off the weed. I've become a caricature of a stoner. All the assumptions and suspicions there are to be had about stoners, I fulfill them. That's me. I wear a baggy rainbow coloured-surfer hoodie every goddamn day and socks with sandals in the cooler months. I smoke too much. I smoke to my detriment. I smoke until I'm sick. I smoke and I listen to jam bands, real stoner classic shit like King Gizza and the Lizza Wizza and WEEN and shit like that. "Gila Monster" on repeat. I smoke and I drink and I write and I occasionally do a kind of furious yard work and I fucking *own* that eighteen kilometre a day mail route because Praise Hermes, I do! Fuck yeah.

But Greg M. is right, I have to get off the weed. His words, chummy and inelegant. He's right, though, as mentioned, because what we are about doing will require a laser focus on my part, as I will be both the conduit and the trap and the bait for the JHVH1 entity at some as-yet-undisclosed future time. The Key and the Gate and the Threshold. Greg M. and, in fact, his entire team, are being necessarily cagey about specifics. I can't get much out of them. Much depends on the tides and the placement of certain stars in certain parts of the sky, apparently. Greg M. has confirmed my sorcerous intuition, that there are Ley

Lines everywhere and the enterprising and in-tune with their luminous eggshell fibres will readily discern that which they may
need in the environment, there to be harvested to their will.
He and the team are location scouting across Victoria and the
bedroom communities like Sooke and Colwood. Maybe in the
woods, I think the woods might be nice, but then when I bring
this up Greg M. will likely have some reason why the woods
aren't the best. What do you think? I think it's likely. Like, he'll
say "Too much ambient spiritual energy in the forest and remember, it's a storm god, it can feed off those natural energies."
Actually, that makes sense, now that I say it out loud. I have to
get off the weed.

Marijuana is the dream killer, to be sure. My dreaming body
needs to be strong for the task ahead; I have to be able to feel the
chill from the shadow wall to my left at all times, ready at any
moment to step in that impossible direction and end up outwith
the Drill. There is music out there. I realize, only just now, even,
that I've never mentioned the music, or, more properly, the Music. It's that kind of sound, on the Outside of the All. The Music
of the Spheres, as gone on about by philosophers and compos-
ers alike. Dreaming. My dreaming bod must be as fit as it can,
though, and therefore I must quit smoking the weed, so as to
get back into dreaming shape. The ritual will take place across
several planes at once; I must be prepared for any eventuality.

I hope it will be at night. I'd feel most comfortable in the dark,
doing this. I don't like broad daylight workings, all that Apol-
lonian energy pouring down from a literal star disrupts the lunar
mood I need to get into for a decent piece of sorcery. Cover of
darkness, like the evil thing Raymond imagines me to be. And
perhaps, I am. Perhaps I am. So, not the woods, probably, and
preferably at night. I don't know. I'm afraid.

I can admit it. I'm a mediocre writer, a so-so husband, an

OK dad, and a milquetoast sorcerer. Fuck, of course I'm fucking afraid. I am going along with this with a big fucking smile
slapped over my face but I am terrified, *terrified* of what is happening to me. I can write it out, *am* writing it out and I worry
terribly that I've gone and broken some essential part of the cre-
ative machinery of my soul and am spewing only drivel. I write
and I write and can't tell the difference between genius and shit.

I have to get off the weed. There is a book, in my personal
library, that I hold in high value, not for the content but for the
object lesson it provides me. A kind of *memento mori* in textual
form. It was written by a long-ago friend, one Frankie D., who
was the stoner boyfriend to Kate M., my Australian roommate
in the second-story cold-water walkup in Saskatoon. Frankie
was prone to disassembling garbage and building garbage in the
shape of ray guns with the pieces. Frankie was up all hours.
Frankie was very loud when he fucked Kate. And Frankie, years
later, in fact long after that whole friend group broke apart and
moved across the world, Frankie D. wrote a *book* and went
ahead and self-published that book. And I can't give you the
title because that would be unpleasant and mean and no doubt
result in increased sales for it which in turn would have Frankie
D. wondering about his good fortune and finding out I'd said
awful things about it in my own book, so! No title. But I will
make one up for this, *DRILL* version of the book. The book that
Frankie D. wrote.

The Mystic from Another World.

And there's a clearly photoshopped spaceman on the front of
it, in a gold lamé suit. A spaceman with a beard and there's cannabis smoke swirling around this dude and do I have to open
it? No, for I have glimpsed the contents, once, and it's a sight
I regret to this day. It's a book written while high, I fear, much
like *DRILL*. Random chapters on various thorny subjects strung

together over a loose psychedelic skeleton like slabs of reeking meat and set to rambling over the moors, howling, howling. There's a through line of sorts, a narrative cable that pumps and writhes and buckles in places. That's what *The Mystic from Another World* was, and is, and so, ah I fear it, I fear it. I shall need to make a note for Greg M. so we can add it to the list. We are listing my fears and I need to get off the weed.

But listen, listen. It's not as bad as all that, not really. See, listen, *The Mystic from Another World* is like my canary in the coal mine, you unnerstan? It's simple, whenever I think I'm getting too high to write, I need only think of Frankie's book, or, in more extreme cases, go to the bookcase where I keep it and take it out, flip through some pages. There's a kind of divine chaos there; I have dabbled with the idea of using *The Mystic from Another World* in bibliomantic research.

I'm making myself sound mean. What a pill, right? Ragging on some poor stoner's psychedelic peace love and unity gonzo scifi story because I'm afraid my own dreck will be worse. I loved Frankie, I thought he was a righteous dude, even if I did cut my foot on a disassembled ray gun on the kitchen floor that one night. Rambling shit, like that. Dear reader.

I need to get off the weed. I suspect I may be an AI, that's how bad it's got. I don't know about you, friends, but I feel piloted most days. It's not an unenjoyable experience. Merely plunking down these sentences at a good steady rate hovering around the 75 wpm mark is a bit of a puppeteering type thrill; I can feel a thing working itself out through me and building, building. Feels like an origin story.

If I do, though, if I manage to cut my consumption like that, real cold turkey, what's going to happen to *DRILL*. Will it get worse, or better, or you know, like really bad. Much, much worse. Not for the first time, I feel like I'm going mad here, that essential pieces of some grand cosmic puzzle are being withheld from me, my paranoia is world-class and I am punching way above my weight. Never mind. Never mind. It has to be done. I have to get off the weed. Greg M. says and by god, I agree now, it is *well* past time. When it's over I can smoke up again and won't that be an excellent moment, that first inhale after this is all done. A consummation devoutly to be wished. I'll have earned it by then, won't I? I'll have earned it and my reward will be sweet indeed, surely, that sweet sweet leaf.

THROUGH THE SHADOW WALL

We're like explosions that leave you feeling good. Greg M. has shown me the techniques necessary to seeing and then entering the shadow wall to the left of All Things. You have to enter it at speed and with noble intentions. Faster than the speed of wall. There is a deep, unsettling vertigo with the action, there is an ache in the pelvic region, an existential cramping, and a sound, not unlike the roaring of great benthic behemoths and a cold, a temperature more like that of the hadal zone than anything here on land under Apollo's daily flight. He shows all this to me on a fine, sun-drenched day in late May and the difference, the essential affront to reality, is clear. I am in the presence of demigods, these sappers. Working class psychopomps and excavators. You need work boots with steel toes and a grim disposition to even begin to think about traversing the shadow wall but once done, it's done, and thoroughly so. All things move toward their end and there is something to this action that precipitates, antici-pates that cessation. All things being eventual.

Inside the Body of God there are great caverns, massive and unthinkable carven spaces in all that illimitable Flesh. Cosmic cathedrals that hold the remains of stars, the titan corpses of entire galaxies exist there as dust motes. There is a dome, and a kind of light that is not light: the Essence of What Is shines with its own inner effulgence. The size of the Drill, too, becomes relative once you are Outside it. I have seen our entire reality reduced to a small, spinning speck. Not unlike the five-dimensional models Wee Frederick produces with his special equipment, the printers and higher-order algorithms. Have you ever bled from your eyes and anus simultaneously? I have, for there are things you can never unsee, real horrorshows a mere tweak of your perceptions away and behind you. Sorcerers like non-Euclidean shapes bent out of true, barely human and more geometry than anything else. It's always behind you, the Drill, the Body of God. We are entrapped. Here's a spoon, dig your way out, only that's not possible and never will be, not on your own. You, dear reader, and I and everyone, well, we need the sappers. Without their rough ministrations, we would be left to clot and seize in some impossible mass of divine tissue. We would be locked in, forever, embedded in this eldritch simulation called life. The way out is forward, always.

There is a beauty to it, as well. I would be remiss if I didn't mention the sublimity of the experience. I have walked my route in the daylight and in the negative light of the Godbod simultaneously, delivering mail to what creatures, what minds. I know now what waits behind each painted door; we imagine that every resident of every house is human, like us, but I am here to tell you truly today that this is simply not the case. Each mailbox a portal to another life, another mode of being. Little slips of paper, sometimes plain, sometimes laminated, all printed with scraps of information. Where does it all go and why? We, that is to say postmen, keep the world going around. There should be solidarity, I figure, between the Sapper's Union and posties. The suggestion box at the Glanford depot is stuffed with my entreaties to get the two groups to sit down, talk, hammer out some mutually beneficial arrangement. The Canadian Union of Postal Workers has yet to reply. I don't mind so much; they've got a lot on their collective bargaining plate and don't need my sorcerous hooey gumming up the works.

But the hooey remains, thick and pungent. Greg M. has asked that I also eliminate pork products from my diet and increase the amount of potassium I take in each day. Bananas, mostly. I crawl out of the vacant lot of my history but the helping hands have all been burned. I don't mind so much, the lack of bacon in my life now, or the lack of weed. The wife is particularly happy at the removal of a meat product from our family diet. It's a savings at a time when the grocery budget is tight, so there's that. There's a clarity to my thought now and my mood is light and sweet, expansive and gracious. Wee Frederick has advised me to listen to marching band music, particularly the Band of the Royal Corps of Engineers out of the UK, in order to feel that sapper bonhomie which will sustain us through the operation, keep us warm on the other side of the shadow wall. It's the opposite of stoner music, a cheery, martial din that I'm told the JHVH1 entity will particularly detest. We'll get Him off balance, see. Jehovah will be wrong-footed from the moment it sees us coming, and believe me when I say, it does. It sees us coming. There is an ontological pressure bearing down on me from the future, from that event where we will kill a god. Greg says the phenomena is common in the weeks and days before a working of this magnitude.

How, I ask, will Greg M. and his team acquire Raymond for the working. It's not a concern *per se*, at least not for me, but I am fascinated by the logistics of it. I hope they will employ the sapper's roughness in the acquiring of my father.

"We'll be extracting his astral body from a point in the future. The Protocols will be enacted," Greg M. explains, "and the core parts of your father, that which animates and vivifies him, will be brought across the shadow wall and to a spot of our choosing. Remember, there are Ley Lines everywhere and we have the map. Transportation is simple, but it takes some doing. His assemblage point will shift and we will be there to carry and direct the load."

Will it be easy, or hard.

"Oh, a piece of cake, at the end of the day. Somewhere within that astral form we will be able to locate the entity's entry point into this world and draw it out. It won't be able to resist you, my boy, for any number of reasons."

Jehovah will recognize the remnants of itself within my own bodymind and be eager for a taste, eager to reinvent itself within a former slave, eager to trigger that spiritual latency within me. Fucking terrifying but oh, so worth doing. I lick my lips in anticipation of meeting it again, doing to it what I've been dreaming of doing for so long. Through all the long nights and brutal years of being shunned by my family, I've longed for it. A consummation devoutly to be wished, as the man says. I've lived my life like a canary in a coal mine but now it is time to exit that subterranean space and breathe the clear light of the actual.

Recall with me the summer of the year 2001. It is August, my mother's death is mere months away. They are doing what they can to fight the cancer. The chemo. The radiation. Her hair defies them and remains, still, waving locks of silver blond. My mother is more beautiful to me now than at any other time, of this I am certain. I am visiting from Calgary and we spend a pleasant day driving up to the Cowichan Valley to visit a farmer's market. It's the last pleasant day I will spend with ▓▓▓▓▓▓▓ and on some level I think we both know this. Despite the sun and the cool breezes off the Pacific, the air is fraught with something between us. There is a darkness to the day, the shadow wall presses close like a cold bank of fog. She asks me much of my life. How I'm living now, and why, and whether or not I am happy. I am, at the time. The relationship I am in, with the brunette Heidi, is going well though it will sour shortly, and I am feeling positive about things. There is ice cream and funnel cake. We return home with our shopping, to the house on Kelly Road which Ray moved the family into after I left home at seventeen. We sit in the kitchen, which is small, smaller than she deserves, really, but there are trees with feeders outside the window and she loves to watch her birds. We drink coffee.

Soon, she begins to weep.

I am not well prepared for this. Who is, for a weeping mother, soon to die. I try to help, asking questions. Stupid ones, mostly, about mortality and how she's approaching it but these are not her concerns, I learn quickly. It's the religion that's bothering her. Her Jehovah's Witness faith is splintering, coming apart in the face of death. As it should, to my mind, but the pain is still very real. She wants to know if she's been a good mother.

"You've raised us all and we're happy, mostly," I reply. "As happy as is possible, given circumstances." Time and unforeseen occurrence befall us all, as the scripture says. She laughs through her tears. I remind her that all her children are successful, each in their own way. Capable adults moving confidently forward into their lives and what more, really, could a parent ask for. Her weeping continues. There is something she is trying to say but I am not asking the right questions, I am failing as an interlocutor, failing as a son.

Is the problem spiritual in nature, I finally ask. Yes. Have you considered seeing a counsellor. No. Jehovah's Witnesses are trained to view psychological health care in a negative light; the Witchtower knows that under examination, their own influence and dire ministrations will be brought to the surface and correctly identified as the primary source of the mental unbalance. I ask if she's spoken to the elders about her fears and she scoffs. For a moment the tears cease and her face turns angry and skeptical, she huffs and gives out a derisive laugh. After a lifetime under the Jehovah's Witness grift, she knows how useless the elders are, how unfit to be doling out spiritual guidance, or any guidance really. These window washers and janitors, these glorified stock boys and yes men for the Witchtower, her husband included. Has she spoken to any of her family, her brother Roger, or Ray, I ask. Have you spoken with Dad. Your husband. God no, comes the answer. God No.

"It would be a betrayal," she says. My mind seethes with possibilities, each one eradicated in turn as I consider how ridiculous the scenarios are. An affair? I think. Impossible, knowing her loyalty and kindliness. She is a gracious soul, ▨▨▨▨▨▨▨▨▨, and a worry wart of the first water, always concerned for others. An affair would not be like her. No, it's the cult. She has left the cult; in her mind and heart she is already gone. Betrayal. Months later, in that bleak December as she lays dying in hospice care, she will refuse to reminisce about her days as a JW missionary in Zaire with Ray, she will express distaste for the sickly sweet recordings of cult music. *Kingdom Melodies*, my ass. All the bright idiots of her life surround her, then. Aunt Jackie and the insufferably cloying Aunt Barbara. My fiercely dedicated to the cult sister, Melissa, and the sullen face of Cameron, my younger brother. She will drift away on clouds of morphine and speak instead of nature. She will watch her birds as she dies and remember a dog, Caesar, she had and loved as a girl. She will refuse the cult ministrations of both Ray and the elders. All this I learn later, after her passing, the details of which I have elaborated on elsewhere.

I am incapable. I am stumped. I can go no further to aid her here, as I don't know what to say. There is no comfort from her eldest son, not at this time, this place. I am available, only, to listen and be silent. This obituary drill. Hopefully it is enough to be there, to listen and be confused with her. I hold her hands. I reach up to her cheeks to wipe away tears. I am destroyed and it is right to be so. I am destroyed.

Perhaps the curse against my father began that day. His narcissistic hand at work, keeping his wife, my mother, from a fuller expression of her soul. For was it not Ray that kept the family locked into the cult mindset. Is it not Raymond that today still holds two of my siblings in his iron cult grip, with the promise that they will see their mother, see ▓▓▓▓▓▓▓▓ again in the Paradise New Earth his grifter bosses have promised? We will never see ▓▓▓▓▓▓▓▓ again, she is gone and one day when we have all also passed, she will be forgotten, utterly. All things move toward their end, but JHVH1 promises something else, something wrong and evil and against nature.

I cannot wait to kill the thing. I look forward to it with excitement and a species of effervescent glee. Alive with the murderous fire, stoked and burnished, brought to a high shine and polish by the anticipation. Glorious truths reveal themselves to me on the daily. Come along and see.

WELCOME TO FLAVOUR TOWN

We've harvested all the bore worms from the hügelkultur that we can and the harvest has been good. The Type 3s and larger have already been stripped of their hides and fashioned into the cords which we'll use to bind the godform of Jahweh.

Now for the ichor, which Greg M. tells me will be a key part of the working. And it is, certainly, an ichor in the technical sense, which is to say the blood of the deity, the watery discharge, sometimes golden, often foul smelling and toxic, that the bore worms carry with them from out the Body of God. Let us not forget that bore worms are made of the same stuff they feast upon. Where the Body of God gets gristly, veined with higher-dimensional fat and cartilage, that's where the bore worms form, by some process yet to be understood by the sappers, or hell, by anyone. The ichor is their blood, and they borrow it from the stuff they eat, which is the High Mighty Chungus Flesh. Is it gross? Yes indeed. Should you get it on your clothes? Probably not. The stuff stains more than just fabric, it can leave a permanent taint on your luminous egg.

Harvesting ichor from a bore worm is simple enough. They must be ground up, for one thing, their flesh reduced to a rough and mealy paste. The paste must be passed through a filter. Wee

Frederick employs one of the twins' machines for this. It is not good to watch the process but you have to keep a weather eye on nonetheless. Safety first in this business as with all business, really.

"What are we going to do with this stuff?" I ask Wee Frederick. He fans a dial to the left, checks the feed from the grinder machine. The ichor, a deep blue colour in this case, is flowing smoothly from a spigot at one end of the machine.

"It needs fermentation, first. We brew a kind of beer from it."

"No shit."

"None at all."

"Do you get drunk on it?"

"Impossible. You get sober on it. Utterly, completely sober. All time and space periscopes down to a single point and you see the all-in-one reduced to a mere flip statement. You laugh incidentally. It makes your vision clear, decalcifies the pineal gland, promotes a healthy gut microbiome, puts a flush to the skin and a brightness in the eyeballs. Your shit flows out pure and firm but not too firm and smells like freshly baked bread. Your mind will race but not so fast you can't keep up."

"Jesus."

"Had ichor flowing through his veins. Like Prometheus and Talos and every god and demigod before him. When the Roman soldier put the spear in his side, ichor flowed out. Blood and water, my diminutive ass. It was ichor, which made the spear so valuable and legendary. Anyway, we're almost done here."

It takes a mere three days for this celestial, sobering beer to ferment. Like Christ, three days buried in the ground in special jars, I'm told, and then the resurrection. Cheers.

THE RED DOOR

On the day it finally happens, I wake early and go downstairs. Make some coffee in the French press and drink it. Then I wander back upstairs to the writing nook at Stonefish House and start back up on *DRILL*. We are nearing the climax, friends and gentlepersons, and the words flow in a great torrent these days, for which I am grateful. It's a pleasure to sit down at the terminal and pound something out in the early dawn hours, before the house wakes up. I sip more coffee, and write, and in the pauses I glance across the nook to my brag shelf and for once I don't feel like throwing up. For a moment, just a moment mind you, I'm proud or at least somewhere adjacent to pride. It feels good.

Greg M. has told me to be ready at any time. I've been off the marijuana for over a month now and even the Fleshlight™ is gathering dust in the linen closet. I figure as long as I'm purifying myself for my encounter with JIIVH1 I may as well go whole hog. Pork's out, and simulated porking (bye for now, Stoya ORclone!), and smoking, and drinking as well. I'm as sober as I've been in a long time. Sober and up at four thirty in the morning, writing. Greg M. and his team have changed me. With their training, and their rough friendship, and their myriad marvels.

On the day it happens, I wake from a strange and expansive

dream in which I am moving through a kind of infinite fun-house maze slash cabinet of curiosities. Since quitting the weed my dreams have been amazing, epic in scale and bursting with life. Everywhere I turn within this seemingly higher dimensional space is crammed, floor to ceiling, with wonders beyond belief, comprehension, or description. I am reminded of the inner lining of Greg M.'s coat, of some of the things I've been shown by Wee Frederick. L'il Dougie, too. How am I so lucky to have these entities in my little life, let alone my beautiful wife and amazing children. I shed a few tears in the dream for my good fortune.

The day itself, once the sun rises, is unseasonably warm. The air is still even in the morning and progresses into a deeper stillness as time passes, until by the early afternoon the skies are utterly windless and the sun locks down the air around me, molecule by molecule. The heat is oppressive as I walk the route and I cannot seem to drink enough water to hold back the worst effects. I sweat like the proverbial pig. Wildfire smoke from the mainland dirties the colour of the sky and I walk beneath a brazen bowl.

Walks at Canaduh Post are divided into three sections, which are colour coded. You have your orange day, followed by your pink day, and day three is blue. Then it repeats. They do this so you don't have to deliver all your flyers on one day, you can split it up between the three days, and the colour coding helps them track when the flyers are going out, when they're supposed to be finished. Orange, pink, blue. Why those colours and not others I'll never know. Probably they only had access to paper of those colours back in the day and the system stuck. Orange covers the first third of a route, pink the second, blue the final third.

The decommissioned church on the corner of Fernwood and Balmoral is one of the last points of call in my blue section. Thankfully my mail is light, and I have no blue flyers this day. Later, after it's all over, I will ask Greg M. how they came to decide on this address as the location for the final working and he will say he read of it in *DRILL*, which surprises me as I've made sure not to give them access to the files. He laughs and says they've been looking over my shoulder the whole time. I believe it.

When I arrive there, I note that despite the ringing stillness in the heated air the shitty driftwood art pieces that hang from the trees in the churchyard are spinning, spinning almost quickly enough to become rainbow blurs in my vision, spinning in the still, quiet air. Some of the bigger pieces seem to generate a low hum as they twirl, and the ropes that suspend them from their branches bunch and contort with the action so that the chunks of wood, with their shards of embedded mirror and junk shop gewgaws flashing in the bronze light, rise and fall as they spin. The water in the shitty cement birdbaths, at least those with pumps that move the water, flows backwards and there is a terrible whine from the pumping machinery. The denuded mini-groves of stripped sticks stuck in their beds of cement vibrate slightly as I approach. I am immediately alarmed.

The Red Door to the basement has been painted, also. Finally. It is now a red door. Deep red, like bull's blood, almost black in the heat. It's a shock to my system. My guts turn to water when I see it, and then the red door opens and Greg M. steps out into the bottom of the stairwell. He fills the space entirely. He looks up at me.

"Thought I heard you coming, postman," he says and he smiles, showing broad, flat teeth through his beard. "You ready for this? You'd best be."

"Why here?" I ask, appalled. "People live here. It's the middle of the day." My mouth is dry and tastes of old milk for some reason, sour and thick. My tongue swells against the back of my teeth. In answer he waves me down the stairs. My feet are hesitant and I have the shakes.

"Why not the, I dunno, Springridge Common or fuck, the abandoned mansion on the 1800 block of Chambers, I mean, c'mon."

"Springridge Common," Greg M. says, "regularly hosts the local daycares. That mansion is a firetrap. This, though? This is a decommissioned church and right smack on a ley line node to boot. You knew we'd pick it, come on. Why write about it if you didn't? It's the only place you cared enough to go on about, after all. Not the mansion, or the Common."

"I suppose you are right there."

"Care to guess what we found behind this door when we arrived, Scott?" he asks. "Storage closet. Barely big enough to hold me, let alone the team, our equipment, least of all you and your dad. But all that changed when I read the Protocols over the place and now we've a swinging little pad in here, a carven space from out of the stuff of this world. The residents of the place won't even notice, and besides, they are a nice gay couple and that's gonna irritate your Jehovah more than anything. Lazy Susan went ahead and repainted the door properly while we were about moving in the gear. She shares your tastes."

"Does she. That's nice."

"We deal in ideals, son. The Red Door simply could not stand as it was, not with what we're about this fine, cooking afternoon. Fuck, it's hot, though." He stands in the doorway, darkness spilling out around his massive shoulders, and I can feel a coolness from behind him. "You coming in or what."

I am unmanned in the moment. My mind so chaotic that it feels like one, buzzing thing, that one-pointed awareness despite or perhaps because of the noise.

"I have to go in there. Like this?" I gesture to my postie gear, my red-and-blue satchel stuffed with mail, my ridiculous hi-viz yellow shirt and bright shoes. My sweat-stained ball cap and workman's blue cargo shorts. Greg M. laughs. I hear a clatter from inside, beyond him. Someone swears.

"If you want this thing finished, yes. Yes, you do." He steps out from the door and closes it behind him. In three steps he is up the stairs and by my side. One hand comes to rest like a plank of wood on my shoulder.

"You're fine. These are a labourer's clothes. You, sir, are a man of the people, purpose-built for a job like this, and a servant of great Hermes besides. How many kilometres you walk in a day anyway, postman? Ten? Twelve?"

"Eighteen."

"Eighteen. Daily. Be proud of that. Your old man never walked eighteen clicks a day in his born life. I can tell. And what's more, you do it for those darling spawn of yours, and to give yourself time to think, to plan. How is this route not part of your writing process? And so, all things that happen on your route are part of that process. Well, this is a thing that is happening on your route. Walk it. Walk it with purpose. Walk it with courage. Come on inside and let's get this done."

A fine motivational speech and it unlocks something in my hips, my legs, and I am moving forward, past Greg M. and toward the stairs. The Red Door, now merely a red door, pleasing in its simplicity, finally, stands at the bottom of the stairwell. I put my hand to its surface and find it almost too cold to touch.

"Beyond," says Greg M. behind me, "a work floor, if you will. I asked you to be ready, remember. Step inside."

"Raymond's in there," I say. It's not a question.

"The parts of him that matter are. Why not see for yourself? We've got everything set up. Wee Frederick is particularly eager to begin…"

STONEFISH JONES AND THE THING
IN THE BASEMENT

There is a kind of foyer beyond the door, occupied by the ghost of the storage closet that is still there, somehow. I pass like a thought through shelves of tools and paint and old rags. The coolness seems to emanate from their phantom presence, the real world reduced to a suggestion of itself. I don't even remember crossing the shadow wall, something of what they've accomplished here included that movement. It feels deeper, richer. The skin on my arms and bare legs goes to goose pimples immediately and then flushes with heat as I step across the threshold. As I do, I can hear the tenants of the house, for that is what the place is, now, not a church at all but a house for the Quebecois folk artist and his husband, I can hear them moving around up there. They have a dog, a small one, a Bichon-Frise or something, more hair than beast, which is currently going mad by the sound of it. Greg M. walks behind me, chuckling.

"All that yapping will make a fine, torturous soundscape for our work here. The entity won't like that at all." He shoulders past me, into the space on the other side of the ghostly storage closet. "Isn't that right, Wee Frederick?"

"Guaranteed, boss. I can barely stand it myself."

The hypogeum space they've carved out with their anomalous

machines is roughly circular and either fifty metres across at its widest or fifty miles. A dome, impossibly high, extends upward and I can see the artist moving about like a sketch through the air on the phantom floor above. The walls are of some kind of porous, semi-tangible stone or stone-like material, and they drip with a sweet-smelling, dark blue fluid that shines in the light of the arc lamps set around the perimeter of the space. More ichor? Hard to say, it seems a natural part of the respiration of the stone. Wee Frederick and the twins are hauling the anomalous machines out of the way, dressed in white haz-mat suits. Lazy Susan is seated in a folding camp chair against the wall, typing into something that looks less like a laptop and more like some species of mollusk. The twins are hard to see despite their white clothing, fading in and out of perception. I've never met them properly and at this point I'm glad of that. I hope to never meet them, now. Wee Frederick gives me a terse wave as I enter.

"That's your old man in the chair, there," he says, waving toward the center of the space.

I can't look. I feel a great refusal rising up in my chest, and keep my shaking eyes as focussed as I can on the walls, the sky-high domed ceiling, on Frederick. Sorcery, we must recall, is a millstone around the neck, and the body often resists its pull, the gruesome gravity of it. There is a revulsion, some of the time, and I feel it now. Greg M. circles back behind me and I hear his voice in my ear, he is at my neck, speaking, speaking…

"We pulled him from a spot in his future. Not far, a month, or two. This is hardly ever exact, this thing we do. He sleeps, when-ever he is, we know that."

"Why can't I look at him."

"He's hard to look at, for one thing. You're a sorcerer, so you tell me: how many parts make up a man? And more, what parts are essential to that man? Where his soul, where his memory, where the tasty bits? We are, given everything, all about the tasty bits with this operation, the parts that a creature such as JHVH1 would find toothsome. And so he doesn't look like much, our Raymond. But there he is, nonetheless. Like I said, the parts that matter are here. The luminous egg. The memory lattice. Most of the hyperchakras, along with a few of the regular chakras. The root and throat, mostly. Those we'll need. The others? Not so much. His third eye is almost entirely calcified so he's not picking up on a lot of the more let's say spiritual aspects of our operation here."

"Does he know what's happening?" I ask. Slowly, I am becoming acclimatized to the space, which they have indeed carved out somehow. Bored out and excavated from out the lower dimensions of the simulation. A cavern or cistern of some kind. I notice there are odd-shaped drains in the floor. Some of the blue liquid from the walls is making its way in lazy rivulets down to the drains. All part of the show. Slowly, I begin to turn my head to the center of the space, to the chair that's bolted to the floor there.

"He does. Sorta. For him, all this registers as a kind of dream. He's a host, after all, and the activity of his passenger is barely to be comprehended. So, a dream. But a very real one. If he wakes up—"

"When he wakes up."

"*If* he wakes up, he'll think he's awakened from an all-time champion nightmare. We are about to extract a god from his person and that's gonna sting some."

"We live in hope." I am beginning to get excited now. Less than an hour ago I expected nothing more from my day than a work-weary exhaustion, an evening meal, time with my spawn, and finally sleep. Now here I am, inhabiting some infradimensional room manufactured by the sappers, in the basement of an old church on my walk. I can feel my daimon getting excited and it mirrors my own. This is sorcerer's work, and I am starting to feel gratitude, gratitude for Greg M. and his team.

"We do indeed. Else what's the world for, son," he says. "Can you bring yourself to look at him, Scott. Your father. He's right there."

I look, finally.

The chair is simple, the barest Platonic suggestion of a chair. A seat and arms upon which to rest and a provisional back, four legs. I don't really notice the chair; it's not there to be noticed, only to hold the bits of Raymond. And Raymond, such as he is, is also a suggestion, a kind of sketch, like the people rummaging around their house upstairs, but a more detailed one. Imagine an x-ray painting by Alex Grey if that great artist had eschewed psychedelics for, say, meth and ketamine. He is naked and old and transparent. His thin, frail bones shine in the light of the arc lamps, catching photons and painting themselves in the glow. His eyes are limpid pools of watery blue floating in the air of his face and his teeth, suspended in the milky atmosphere that surrounds his seated form, chatter constantly against each other like castanets. His hands are nearly solid, as are his guts and his genitals where they rest on the seat of the chair. The connectome of his brain fires sporadically, little currents of biochemical lightning coursing through the fat and water beneath the vague hairline. His ears twitch and his knees knock together randomly. The skin is translucent in most places, like the shed skin of a snake, clinging, and I can see the rush and plosh of his blood and organs functioning in the depths of him. The fibres of the luminous eggshell that contain him are dull most everywhere except the areas around the hindbrain and the base of his spine, which shine with a distinct malevolence, like liquid gold corrupted by some foreign light. At the same time, the figure in the chair is simply

Raymond, my father, sleeping fitfully in his bed some weeks or months in the future. A tear escapes my left eye and I wipe at it quickly. I cannot show weakness, not at this late stage.

There are cables, I can see now, cables tying Raymond to the chair. These are the bore worm hides we've harvested and crafted into ropes and I am surprised at the looseness of the knots, the seemingly provisional tightness. I worry aloud that the JHVH1 entity will get away, slip these simple bonds.

"There's usually a swelling," says Wee Frederick. Lazy Susan types furiously into her mollusc. "They'll tighten up once we have the thing properly here."

Raymond stirs. His hips, ancient and brittle, jerk and rise. The eyelids, like tissue paper, barely there to begin with, flutter open and the clear blue of the eyes shines forth with more strength with the exposure.

"Can I speak with him?"

Greg M. laughs and Lazy Susan starts typing again, a sound like keys being depressed into flesh. The dog upstairs is going properly insane now, trying to scratch through the floor to get to us, but there's no way it can. We are outwith the spacetime supersphere by a few degrees. We are through the shadow wall. This is eternally outside, this inner room.

"Of course you can. In fact, why not introduce yourself. Remember, he takes a while to recognize you now. The coffee shop? Your beard and tattoos confuse him. Your costume, too. He doesn't see you as a labourer, can't imagine you doing anything good for the world or yourself."

He's right, I know. The long minutes he took to recognize me in that coffee shop impress themselves upon me afresh, each a terrible finger around my throat. I crouch down before the ghostly figure in the chair, my thighs burning with the strain. I'm a walker, not a kneeler.

"Raymond. Ray. Look up. Look at me."

He does. His pupils swim in seas of white. His voice when it comes is layered in static, a cross-dimensional fuzz tone. Reader, you're about to hear him for the first time. Imagine that. His few words in the coffee shop on Walk 329 don't count, or his few letters and notes as detailed elsewhere in *DRILL*. No, this is his voice, speaking in your head for the first time. Sorry it's so ultimately disappointing, but then, what did you expect from him, embedded in this situation as he is. You'd say the same thing. Raymond speaks.

"What's going...on?"

"You've never known the answer to that one, Raymond, so why ask now. Something awful," I say. "And you're in the middle of it."

"What have you done with me? I want...to go home. I don't want...to be here."

"I feel you there, old man," I reply. "But here we are, nonetheless. We've got some work to do, you and I."

Raymond strains against the bore worm cables. "Let me out of here. Who are you?" He begins to come into focus. The areas of flesh around the throat and brain take on a fuller solidity, and there is a red, angry region in his abdomen. "I know you."

I can't help but laugh but even I recognize the sorrow in the sound. Greg M. shuffles his massive feet as he hears it. Awkward.

"You sure do, Ray. And if you didn't before, you will when we're done here. I'm your son, Raymond Francis Jones. I'm Scott, your first born, who you betrayed. Who you've shunned for these many years."

"Scott?" The neck cranes, the head wobbles on the top of the spine like a sunflower heavy with seeds. "My son." He says it with a great sigh and we can all see the light going out in him as he does so...

"Disappointment."

The word drops from his lips like a speck of shit. I stand and turn to Greg M.

"Let's get this over with. What's the next step."

"Simple. Let's get the god out of there. Ready?"

I nod. I have never been more ready for anything.

Greg M. signals to Wee Frederick and the twins, who had largely faded into the walls. They now reappear, clad in their white protective gear. The twins don some kind of full head covering, visors and mirrored faceplates, like you'd see in the movies when the environment is toxic. Fumes and what not. I wonder briefly whether I need such gear and then think better of it. Theirs is a support role and probably the headgear is necessary for their work and safety. I note that the others go bare from the neck up, though. So will I, then.

Wee Frederick is carrying a tray with six small glasses on it. Inside the glasses, a blue liquid. Bore worm ichor beer. He passes the tray around and we all take a glass. Nothing for Raymond, though.

"Best advice?" says Greg M. "Knock it back in one."

We do. The flavour is unexpectedly like that of cherries, to begin, an intense cherry-on-cherry-on-cherry taste, and then, as the liquid courses down my throat a heat like chilies spreads instantly throughout my body. There is an almost unbearable tingling in the extremities and a feeling like coming instantly awake from a bad dream, a kind of existential relief. I feel, in the next moments, as if I'd been asleep for aeons and have finally opened my eyes. The feeling passes quickly but the clarity remains. I am awake now and utterly sober. I don't recommend it. Raymond's eyes track me as I begin to pace up and down.

"See the brighter areas on his luminous egg, Scott," Greg M. says. "That's where the god lives, or rather, where it accesses your father from the place where it lives, which is the place where humanity thinks. That's the place from which it gets its food."

"How to extract it."

"Prayer, basically. Call out to it."

I shudder at the thought but see the utility of it. Of course it would be prayer. I try to remember how I used to do it, and then begin.

"Oh heavenly Father Jehovah, your servant calls out to you," I say. I am praying in my room as a little boy, as a teenager, as a young man whose heart is filled with doubt and a new thing, a nascent anger that heats me from within. I am praying that Jehovah bless my baptism even though I half-emptied the pool with my clumsiness. I am praying that Jehovah heal my first marriage. I am praying that Jehovah quiet my doubts. I am praying that Jehovah prove himself in some way, anything, a sign, an omen. I pray that Jehovah save my mother. I am praying to Jehovah to let me die. "Hear my prayer this day, Oh Jehovah, and grant—"

That's as far as I get. The god shows itself before I can get another word past my lips. My tongue freezes in my mouth. The room, that vast, domed space outwith space and time, contracts and the walls seethe. The air becomes both frozen and electric at the same time. I hear Lazy Suzan behind me gasp and begin to type faster and I can only imagine what data she is transcribing into her machine.

Raymond's ethereal form buckles and jerks in the chair. His muscles flex and clench. The gums pull back from the teeth and the teeth themselves begin to bristle, multiply, and grow long. His tongue darts from between dry, encrusted lips. The eyes take on an unhealthy sheen, a crepuscular glow, sick lightning yellow piercing the blue. His hair, already far in recession, disappears entirely and is replaced by I don't know what, some kind of bony structure that erupts from the skin, all ridges and unnatural curves. Ray is becoming what feeds upon him. Gorge rises in my throat.

"Keep it down," I hear Greg M. say. He is right behind me, like a solid wall of living rock. "You may want to shit yourself. Or puke. Don't. Don't give it anything it can shame you with."

Raymond's body swells, as Wee Frederick predicted. The knees and elbows buckle and spikes of obscene bone protrude. The hips flare and expand, pressing against the bore worm cable, tightening the knots. A deep violet light begins to pulse from the cords. Raymond's shoulder blades erupt from the skin. The threads of his luminous egg are now vibrating in time with each pulse, cycling through impossible colours and spiky, unnatural shapes. The head begins to jerk back and forth and side to side, at incredible speed, a terrible torsion animating it. Look and see, dear reader, with me. A dragon. See it moving. See it moving within him and about him, this god-thing, this creature of pure idea and hate. For that is what comes off the spectral figure of my father, my transformed dad, a pure, almost gleeful hatred flowing like liquid smoke into the air, up against the ceiling. The bore worm cables stretch and cut deep into the thing's spectral flesh and something like blood shines in the cuts. Electrical fire courses through the musculature and the brain is bright with it as well. Alex Grey from the Reverse of the Tree, something qlipphotic and dire. Sparks jump between the shining bones. Storms begin to brew in the air above it. I look up through the dome and planets—Jupiter, Mars, mighty Yuggoth—loom close through reeling coils of smoke and mist, leering, eager to witness this manifestation.

JHVH1.

"Hello there, old god," I manage to whisper. "Hello and welcome."

"Fuck you, too, my son. My most beloved."

The thing is sick and bloated where it sits, the form of my dear old dad imprisoned within it. The worst nightmare of his born life, Greg M. had said and I believe it. Reader, believe it with me. JHVH1 is a glutton and its gluttony shows in every aspect of its being as it sits there, straining against its bonds. It's like a moral failing made flesh, an abomination.

"I love you, my son," it says, the words falling from its maw like gobbets of sour meat. "I love you the way you love a good meal." Imagine it, right now, as an old man who is more bone and cartilage than muscle and fat, a terrible, walking, nine-foot-high skeleton of a beast. The elongated head. Flaring nostrils black with blood. The veins standing out on the jaw and temples, writhing beneath the crepe paper skin. The multiple eyes popping in and out of a variety of sockets, and not all of them on the face. The clawed hands an almost pleasing pink, the staining a result of millennia washing in the blood of the innocent. The fucking halo, a defensive weapon, arcing with lightning behind the hideous head and spinning, spinning, impossibly bright.

"I feel bad for you, son," JHVH1 says, voice like a buzzsaw in flesh. "Three years and his wife hasn't touched him in all that time." It's not even trying to disguise itself now, not even trying for the Old Man in the Sky routine. The awful head inclines toward Greg M. and the team behind me, conspiratorial and monstrous. "Did you know that, sappers? You've practically brought me a virgin." An ichor, not like that of the Body of God, but a counterfeit liquid, oozes from suddenly forming and bursting pustules on the abdomen and upper back. The thing grins, a mouth of fangs in the front and great grinding flat surfaces behind, eager for flesh. Did I not promise horror. Did I not say there'd be a fucking payoff. Look at this pale, inhuman thing that my sorcery and the efforts of the sappers have brought to screaming life in the world, inside your head.

"You worshipped me once," it hisses. The tongue, purple and splitting with the effort of speech, lashes about the lips. "Do so again." For a moment Ray shines forth out of the thing's vicious countenance, but only a moment, just long enough to quote fucking scripture at me. "Psalms 57 three," he gasps. And then the thing is back, flexing against reality. "Let me out of here." Summons titanic energies. I don't know how my father's form can bear it. Somewhere within the roiling mass of god-thing before us, Ray must be in incredible pain and yet the manifestation persists. He has hidden strengths.

"See me," the god-thing commands. Pleads. "Psalms 90 two."

"I see you. I see you."

I begin to feel myself mirroring the thing in the chair before me. I can feel my own teeth lengthen in response to its presence, feel my muscles ache with its own strain. My teeth gnash together as my jaws clench and there is a howling, from deep in the back of me, the way back back forty, where the daimon lives and in the moment I know, certainly in that way you know things in a dream, that my daimon is my response to JHVH1, an antibody. Part of my defense system against this apocalyptic divine incursion. It shares so much noetic DNA with Jehovah I am both relieved and appalled at the same time.

"Reveal yourself to it," I hear Greg M. say. "Make the darkness visible. Since we're all in such a sharing mood."

And like that, the darkness pours forth from me. From us. You and me, friend, together again for the first time, host and guest, here in this white nova space of the page and in that basement closet and in that dome, the Body of God Itself sloughing away out of reality in an ecstasy of fulfillment around us. We are the Drill and the Activity of the Drill.

"Remember," says Greg M. behind me. He must be at my shoulder, his voice comes in a fierce whisper that somehow sneaks beneath the clamour and noise from the thing, the dog overhead. "Remember, a day is like a thousand years to this thing. Keep it here while we sever its connection to the noösphere!"

The Ray-thing within the god-thing howls. "Second Peter three eight!"

Greg M. laughs, a sane sound in the chaos like a clear bell in the night. "Yes!" he yells. "Good answer, Raymond. What a good little JW you are!"

The abyss yawns wide and we yawn back. Bored. Done with it all. My father can only speak in scripture, there is no person left within him in any kind of real way; he is a shell of a program that was implanted in him at a young age by my grandfather and the virus has eaten him alive from the inside, over the long decades of his life, as it must. First Law of the Universe: Everybody Hungry. Second Law? Probably: Drill, Baby, Drill but what do I know about anything. I feel a species of pity.

Bore worms fastbreed down out of the cracks in reality as the daimon and the god lock teeth into each other.

I once asked or wondered aloud. Whether or not there'd be blood. And there is, I see it now. There was always blood. There was never anything but this blood between us, black and thundering in the cataracts of our veins. Blood in extraordinary quantities, flowing out of the wounds we make in each other. It is the blood that runs in rivers toward the drains in the floor, blood to the bridles of the horses. This is Armageddon. This the End of Days. A thousand years are as a day. Call forth the corvid armies, let us bathe in the stark radiations of the cosmos. Let all flesh burn in judgement.

Around me I can hear the team screaming at the sight before them. JHVH1 regenerates parts of itself as quickly as I rip them off or chew them away with my teeth. Greg M. is shouting into the maelstrom, something foreign and incomprehensible. Language breaks down in the presence of JHVH1 and everyone is glossolaliac. Electricity crackles between all our joints, joining us in a perfect storm of blue fire. Phonemes pour from my monstrous mouth, blackening my lips and teeth as I tear at JHVH1. My daimon howls in ecstasy. It's pure curse, unfettered and joyful. My claws near the heart of the thing.

Die, you fucking monster, I think. *Die. You killed my family, tore it limb from limb. Die.*

The entity is fully revealed, pouring out of the glowing geriatric in the chair. Gaze upon it with me now and see as it shifts and reforms, becoming a vast unbroken field of hate-filled faces, each flowing into and around each other as the thing screams. Thunder gushes from its many mouths, claws of lightning tear at the walls. The planets have all fled. There is nothing but solid rock stretching away from us to infinity. An endlessness that blasts the mind and withers the soul. This is what it means to be incarnate, to feel the hand of death upon your every molecule.

From a far distance comes the sound of Lazy Susan's fingers travelling at light speed across her instrument and it sounds like the yapping of the little dog in the sky above. Wee Frederick is saying something to the twins, and there is a cough, as of an engine under great stress, starting up, being coaxed to life.

There is only so much a being can take.

I look up from my terrible feasting and gouging to fix Greg M.'s eyes with mine.

"We're locked on it now, Jones," he says. "Hold on now."

"Please," is all I can say. In my hands I hold the thing's still-beating heart. "Please."

THE DRILL

To see it in its entirety is to know Death. The death of God. The death of all. It is the heat death of the universe, entropy made machine. It is beautiful. It is appalling. It's where you live.

Greg M. reaches out to my gnashing mouth and places an impossibly broad forefinger against the lips. I am quieted in the moment and find that I am wrapped around the ghost of my father, hugging it tightly as it dwindles to vapour and ash. The threads of his luminous egg cling to mine. There is a humming, and an activity. I see the JHVH1 entity compress in the air above us, white hot and inchoate with rage, before spiraling inward and outward to the void point at the tip of the Drill. At the same time, I see Wee Frederick cross the fingers of both hands in anticipation. My vision is three hundred and sixty degrees in all directions and the suffering I see manifests as a mandala, startling in its complexity. Suffering is what drives the Drill forward. Suffering is all that I see, all that ever was.

There is a pop somewhere, hardly noticeable in the vastness.

"Well," says Greg M. "I was hoping for more."

As were we all, friend Greg. As were we all. What to expect, though, of a thing built out of air and thought. It could only correspond to itself.

"My turn now," I hear something like my self say. It's the voice I hear when I'm reading, perhaps not unlike the voice you're hearing now, after all. At the end of all things.

"Your turn indeed, son," says Greg M. "I've hopes for you, boy."

I feel. There is a thump on my back from behind. Greg M. has hit me, low and near the spine, with the flat of his massive palm. I feel something pull from my body, ungluing itself from a space within myself that I could not point to, not even on my best day. Not as a sorcerer, or a father. I am delivered. Not even as a son. The deed is done and it was ever thus. I am delivered. The mailman, delivered. Hermes is a column of light to my right, the ghost of my mother a warm current of darkness on my left. I am sober through it all, dispassionate, unmanned literally. There is only momentum, the universal imperative. The echo of my feet on the route, slapping down their idiot metronomic rhythm.

I soar forth, my speed increasing with each turn of the Drill. The blades beneath and around me chew heartily at the Body of God, digging deep, the gristle flying from their Scythian edges and I fly. I fly. Bore worms forming a halo around my crackling skull. I am coming apart. Magma and ichor pour from my eyes. Speed. Red shift to blue in an instant. Momentum on momentum, a great rushing upon rushing and I am turning, turning ever inward and upward, stretched thin, every molecule of my being mapped and sorted and brought to bear on the corresponding flesh in the High Mighty Chungus ahead. I see the Plateau of Leng. I hear the song of eternity and it is coming from my own lips. I rain puke on the stars. My lungs puncture and flap useless in their ring of bones. Heart a spinning void. The point of the Drill. I am every one and every zero. My hips split and intestines unfurl in a great peristaltic coil. Cum pours from my penis and falls upward, a rain of glistening pearls cast before the ultimate swine. My balls shrink and grow dry and fall away. My feet are dusty bone in their skeins of flesh, streaming away into nothing. I am a ribbon across the sky. I am her son. I am his.

It's the sapper's dream, to pierce the heart or brain.

I am a bomb.

AN EPILOGUE OF SORTS

There's a story among sappers, about the Drill. The story goes that it didn't always exist. I contend that the Drill is eternal, at least as far as that goes. A once-was-and-always sort of arrangement, like the inframatter it cores. At least as far as it concerns us. Sappers. I don't know how God feels about it. I expect it smarts a bit.

When it's over, I gather my team and perform the closing rituals, sealing over the dead space we made in the storage closet. Paint and cans and tools and tarps return to being just that. Lazy Susan folds up her terminal while the twins disassemble the machinery and load the trucks. Wee Frederick lights up a joint, weeping silently beneath a spinning piece of rainbow driftwood.

Jones is waiting for us outside, on the sidewalk. He is jumpy, moving his weight from the ball of one foot to the other. The mail lies undisturbed in his satchel. Time has gone all funny, the way it does after you set off some ordnance. I am disappointed but sanguine about the results. The heat of the day has broken and there is a breeze, the suggestion of rain.

"Well if this isn't nice, I don't know what is," I say. Jones looks at me strangely.

"If I didn't know better..." he starts but then seems to trip over himself. There's a blankness in behind his eyes now and it makes me a little sad.

"You'll be fine," I say.

The French-Canadian and his boyfriend appear at the back porch to the house. Now a house proper, with ghosts and everything, I figure. Resale value in Victoria goes up when there's a haunting, Jones has told me, but they can't know that, not yet.

"Ey you guys! What are you doing here?"

Routine maintenance, I want to say. I'm a sapper. Same as my dad. I excavate and I core. I create, mold, and plant explosives. I make the tunnels and the warrens and the great carved cavern spaces within the Body of God.

"Mail delivery," Scott pipes up. "Sorry about my friends. They were just on their way to a job, caught me in the middle of my work day. You know how it is. Is that your dog? What a handsome little beast."

He vaults up the step to the homeowners, two at a time, hands off a few pieces of mail, reaches down to pet the twitching animal. The twins signal that they're leaving. We'll meet up later. Lazy Susan is long gone. Wee Frederick joins us as Jones comes down the steps.

"Jones, it was good working with you." I reach out my hand and he takes it in his. If there's a difference to him, I can't tell you.

"You, likewise." Wee Frederick hands him the last of the joint and he gratefully takes a drag.

"Stay strong, brother," I say.

"Will do."

Rain finally breaks from the orange sky.

"There's a type of moment I like best," I say. "After the rain, when if you catch the street at just the right angle, the whole thing lights up like the on-ramp to heaven."

"No shit? I'll keep an eye out for that."

He shuffles his feet, the little angel. For is that not the meaning of the word. A messenger. A divine postman.

"Safe travels, postie," I say. "I hope the book turns out all right."

"It all turns out one way or the other." He shrugs and puts out his hand again. I take it. "Thanks, Greg."

"Anytime. Can we call on you, in the future."

"Sure. Why not? Bring my union card next time."

And before it can get any more awkward, he turns from me and heads off along his route. Somewhere in the future, his father dies, a little man, alone and broken, and then, a bit further on, so does Jones. His children and his followers will revere his skull for a time, maybe read a book or two of his, and then they'll die. They all go spinning off into the void.

I labour on. I'm a sapper. I excavate and I core and I sift the world for ordnance in our eternal work. Someday, we'll pierce the heart or brain and then the whole of it will die, sublimate into the next thing, maybe. Yes, I'm the closest thing to an angel you're likely to meet, on this side of the Drill, and if that doesn't make you sad to the core, I don't know what will.

Pray you never meet me in the flesh.

THE END

Scott R. Jones is a Canadian writer living in Victoria BC with his wife and two frighteningly intelligent spawn. He was once kicked out of England for some very good reasons.

Printed in the USA
CPSIA information can be obtained
at www.ICGtesting.com
CBHW020749050824
12657CB00027B/289